STOLEN

Ron Chudley

VICTORIA ◆ VANCOUVER ◆ CALGARY

TouchWood Editions
#108 – 17665 66A Avenue
Surrey, BC V3S 2A7
www.touchwoodeditions.com

TouchWood Editions
PO Box 468
Custer, WA
98240-0468

Library and Archives Canada Cataloguing in Publication
Chudley, Ron, 1937–
    Stolen/Ron Chudley. — 1st ed.

ISBN 978-1-894898-59-1

    I. Title.
PS8555.H83S76 2007   C813'.54   C2007-904915-X

Library of Congress Control Number: 2007931911

Edited by Marlyn Horsdal
Proofread by Marial Shea
Book design by R-House Design
Cover design by Jacqui Thomas
Front-cover photo by Tara Flake/iStockphoto

Printed in Canada

TouchWood Editions acknowledges the financial support for its publishing program from the Government of Canada through the Book Publishing Industry Development Program (BPIDP), Canada Council for the Arts, and the province of British Columbia through the British Columbia Arts Council and the Book Publishing Tax Credit.

The Canada Council | Le Conseil des Arts
for the Arts | du Canada

BRITISH COLUMBIA
ARTS COUNCIL
Supported by the Province of British Columbia

for my son, Aaron,
who cared about it first

PART ONE

ONE

The instant John opened his eyes he remembered it was the big day, and exhilaration and shock hit him, both at once, sending his insides into a tailspin even before he was fully conscious. But he pushed away the emotions and sat up, a determined grin on his face, even though there was no one to grin at. He was doing it: going away at last with Nate. That was the only thing that mattered.

He got up quickly, threw some instant coffee into a mug, shaved and showered. As he dressed, foregoing his usual stylish attire for Levis and loafers, he couldn't help glancing through the window. Crammed into the front drive of his townhouse, squatting like a brute beside his elegant little MG, was the camper he'd rented.

God, just don't let Val screw me up again.

Those words kept drumming in his head as he put his toilet articles into a flight bag. Everything else he needed for the weekend was already packed and stowed in the camper. One thing only remained to be gathered up, and John went through to the living room to get it.

The package was lying on the couch where he'd tossed it when he came in last night, but before he could get it, his cell phone rang. He decided to ignore it, then realized it might be Val. If his ex-wife had changed her mind about letting their son go on the trip, it would be just like her to wait till the last moment to tell him. So he picked up the phone. "Hello?"

"Hi there, John. Great news!"

It wasn't Val but his agent, Artie Klein. "Hi, Artie," John said, trepidation replaced by impatience. "What news?"

"I tried to get you last night, but you were out." Artie never answered a question directly.

"What news? Look, Artie—I'm just on my way out the door."

"Okay, okay—so listen. You snagged the Laxol account."

This news was not "great" as Artie had claimed, but certainly welcome. John's acting career in Vancouver had been going fine for a number of years, with a lot of good stage parts, a lead in an American-produced TV series and several fat film roles. Were it not for the fact that he was doing so well in this beautiful town—plus the unalterable reality of his son being here—he would seriously have considered the big move to Los Angeles. His career was certainly ready for it. But right now he'd been going through a brief dry spell, so doing the voice-overs for Laxol TV commercials would mean a considerable amount of welcome cash.

"That is great!" John said sincerely.

But Artie's next words turned the whole thing around. "They want you to come in and tape the first half-dozen tracks on Monday."

"*This* Monday?"

"Sure!"

"Artie," John said heavily. "I won't be in town Monday. You know that."

Artie sounded astonished, the way he always did when he was bullshitting. "Are you working? I'd forgotten. Where?"

"Not working, Artie. I'm taking my son on a holiday. It's very important. I *told* you."

Now Artie sounded really annoyed. "The agency decided on the Monday session, not me. Put off your holiday, buddy. They need you."

"Not as much as I need this time with my kid."

"Can't you postpone it?"

"I already told you that too. My ex-wife hates my guts and she's got full custody of Nate. It's been like busting rock just to get these few days with him and she only did it, I know, because she wants some time alone with her new husband. If I louse things up for her now, I'll never get the chance to have the boy again. Do you understand what I'm saying, Artie?"

"Sure. But what I don't understand, sport, is why it's so damn important."

John gritted his teeth. But Artie's bewilderment was reasonable enough. After all, John himself scarcely understood the compulsion that had grown lately to develop relations with his growing son. But it was there and it would not be denied.

"It is important, Artie. Let's just leave it at that. I'll be away till next weekend. If Laxol want me, they'll just have to wait."

"I don't know if they will."

"Of course they will, Artie. Don't mess with me."

"And if they won't?"

"So be it. I'll be out a small bundle, and you 15 percent of same. I don't reckon it'll kill either of us."

"Speak for yourself!" Artie said. Then, in a more conciliatory tone, "Yeah—well, I'd better get on to them."

"You do that, Artie. And don't sweat it. They'll come around."

"Yeah? You're not all that big a star, you know."

John laughed. "So find me some parts to make me one. Come on, Artie, this is Laxol, not Hollywood. Cut me some slack, eh? It's important."

"Yeah, yeah!" Artie said ungracefully. "I'll let you know how it goes."

"Sure. Leave a message on the machine."

"You can't even answer your cell?"

"I'm not *taking* it. This is a holiday, man. For a week I'm out of the loop."

"Out to lunch, more likely!" Artie said, and hung up.

John shook his head ruefully. Even for an established actor, turning down work is never easy. But he refused to think of it further. In fact, he'd already pushed the interruption out of his mind as he finally unwrapped the package that he'd bought yesterday: Teddy Ruxpin, a cute talking bear that had been all the rage when John himself was a child.

Along with a million others, he'd loved that bear. When he'd thought about getting something special for Nate, Teddy had come to mind and, surprisingly, he'd found a modern version still on sale. Examining it now, he was delighted: the fat, bug-eyed little guy was smaller than he remembered, but it talked and moved in much the same way. "Come on, you cute little bastard," he said. "You and I have work to do."

Clutching the stuffed animal like a talisman, John headed downstairs for the camper.

TWO

Bud hated cities with a passion.

That had started years ago, when he was an independent trucker driving his own rig. The open road was fine, where the hours drifted by and good money could be made, but cities were clogged and dangerous, eternally frustrating to anyone whose income was a constant battle with the clock. Even with his own trucking business centred in Calgary, Bud managed to avoid that city most of the time. The freight and yard bosses handled the routine stuff while he kept away, managing his other enterprises from the isolation of his ranch.

At 7:00 AM the big motorhome, travelling on the interstate, reached Olympia, Washington. From there I5 headed for Seattle and, finally, Canada, which for 20 years Bud had called home. He didn't mind driving through Seattle on the freeway, but he had no intention of stopping there.

Saturday morning traffic was light. By 8:00, with the cruise-control on 55 MPH, he could see the sharp outline of Seattle's Space Needle in the near distance. Bud sat comfortably in the wide driving seat of the vehicle. At 55 he was in good shape. Strenuous activities such as hunting and trekking in the Rocky Mountain wilderness had helped preserve his physique. He had good wind, fine circulation and a solidly healthy heart. Had it not been for his silvery white hair, he might have been a fit man of 40.

Doubly ironic then that he was almost at the end of his tether.

By 8:30 the motorhome was well north of the city. A few minutes later, just south of the town of Arlington, he saw the sign for a highway rest area. At the same time his stomach began to grumble. Bud hit the flasher and glided into the exit lane with the effortless ease of the long-time trucker. At the same time he got his first big surprise of the day.

A hand fell on his shoulder.

He gave a start. His hands paused momentarily in their swing of the wheel, making the motorhome lurch a little. He recovered quickly—only then looking around at his wife, Mimi.

The long journey they'd undertaken was supposed to have been a healing holiday. Departing Alberta three weeks previously, they had driven into Montana, then down through Wyoming, Utah and Nevada, finally into California, continuing the huge circle by heading up the Pacific Coast toward home. But during the entire trip, regardless of such scenic wonders as the Rockies, the Grand Canyon and California's Big Sur coastline, Mimi had done little more than sit listlessly. Then at night, she would take a pill, which knocked her out till around noon next day. Bud didn't blame her for that: despite the distraction of the trip, the only time she seemed able to find relief from her endless sorrow was in unconsciousness. During the long mornings he'd grown used to thinking of himself as alone, a trucker once more, tooling the endless highways. So when she just appeared like that, without warning, he got quite a shock.

His second surprise came right on the heels of the first. Mimi laughed. It was the old throaty chuckle he'd loved since the day they'd met. But so long was it since he had heard it that instead of pleasure he felt apprehension. He pulled into the parking area and hurriedly applied the brake.

"I'm sorry, sweetie," Mimi said. "I didn't mean to startle you."

He turned in the seat and looked at her, receiving yet another surprise. She was fully dressed.

Mimi Wetherall, at 42, had the same petite figure she'd possessed as a young woman. Her dark hair, worn long and now pulled back in an old-fashioned ponytail, had only the slightest edging of gray. Her pale features were still girl-smooth, with barely a wrinkle. Only her great, black eyes were old. Centuries of grief, of boundless, awful torment looked out of Mimi's eyes. It was as if all of the sadness that they both had endured was gathered there, a synthesis of their agony and failure. On the occasions Bud dreamed of his wife, that was all he ever saw these days, those two dark pools of pain.

Except this morning they weren't sad at all. Incredibly, they actually succeeded in joining the rest of her face in a real smile.

After an astonished moment he said, "Are you okay, doll?"

"Yes, dear, of course. Don't I look it?"

Bud couldn't stop staring. "Yeah, you look great. I mean ... "

She laughed. "What you *mean*, sweet man, is that you can't understand what on earth your wife is doing up and dressed at nine in the morning and not looking like a zombie. Is that about it?"

His heart quivered. She sounded so unbelievably happy—so *well*! He didn't know whether to feel delirious or scared shitless. "That's about the size of it."

"And I don't blame you. I've been awful, I know. Just terrible. Here you've been spoiling your Mimi rotten, spending a hundred thousand dollars on a motorhome to give her the trip of a lifetime. And all I've been doing is sleeping and mooning about you-know-who. What an awful companion for you. But all of that is going to change. Bud, sweetie—I've decided."

Inevitably, Bud found himself thinking about the incident that had caused his wife's original breakdown: the tragic death 18 months ago of their only child. Ever since then she'd been numb, impenetrable, sinking ever deeper into depression. Did he dare believe she'd reached some kind of turning point, that she'd finally found some will to get better?

Well, what the hell? Stranger things had happened, he supposed. Whatever this might mean—a real start on the road to recovery or simply a momentary relief—at least it was a change. And things could hardly be any worse. So, making his voice sound as confident as he could, he said, "Well, that's just terrific, doll."

"You're not surprised?"

"Damn, I'm amazed. But who cares? It's terrific."

"You think I can keep it up?"

He spoke very sincerely. "Listen, doll—you can do anything you want, and I'm happy as a bug! You hear me now?"

She came across the cabin and kissed him. The kiss was different too, because for the first time in memory she was putting some heart in it. Abruptly Bud was hit by a bolt of happiness, so clean and hard that it forced tears to his eyes.

Mimi went to the stove and calmly began to put on breakfast. Bud switched to the passenger seat, swiveled it and watched his wife preparing her very first meal in their travelling mansion. After a while she said, almost casually, "Bud—know what? Last night Gabriel came back to me."

His heart lurched. The name of their dead child had scarcely been spoken since the day of the horror. Carefully, he said, "What do you mean?"

She laughed. "Oh, I don't mean back back. His body wasn't there, of course. This was a sort of vision, perhaps caused by those new pills. Or maybe it was even a real spirit."

Bud stared. "You don't say!"

"Bud, don't look so worried." Mimi tossed her ponytail back happily. "It doesn't matter what it was. The only important thing is that Gabriel finally found a way to talk to me."

"Really?"

"Really! Do you want to know what he said?"

"Er—sure."

Mimi flipped some bacon, her expression rapturous. Bud had to admit she looked radiant. Twenty-five again. "Gabriel told me we're very near the end."

"Of what?"

"Why, darling—of all of our troubles."

THREE

They were free.

Though John could hardly believe it, they'd actually done it. From the Vancouver suburb of Richmond—leaving behind the faceless split-level where he'd picked up Nate—they hit Highway 99 south, then took the Dease Tunnel into Delta. As they emerged he was feeling so good that he started to sing.

"I'd like to be—down by the sea—in an octopus's garden in the shade ... "

The ancient Beatles number was Nate's favourite, and the boy sang along lustily in his piping three-year-old soprano. Glancing across from time to time, John couldn't help thinking how beautiful the little kid looked; round face, black hair trimmed in a rough page-boy, dark eyes saved from postcard perfection by healthy lines of mischief. When the song was finished Nate wanted it again, and the delights of the octopus's playground kept them going until the turnoff onto Highway 10.

John had no idea where they were going on their holiday. In fact, he didn't care. The likelihood of his actually getting Nate pried free had seemed so remote that he hadn't dared plan beyond that. The only stipulation he'd made was that this was to be Nate's special time. Although he loved his son dearly, he had little idea what would turn a three-year-old on. It wasn't much use asking Nate, since his imagination was limited to living forever at McDonald's, and a vague idea of visiting "space," which he believed was the dwelling place of "Transformers." One of these—a plastic robot that changed by simple manipulation into a space ship—he now clutched tightly in his hand. The new bear was safely stowed in back, as yet unrevealed. John had been in show business long enough to know the value of always keeping something in reserve.

As to where they were going, John's options were limited mainly by geography. North beyond Vancouver were the mountains, west the sea. To the south was the border with the US—and Val had flatly refused to allow Nate to be taken out of the country. That left east.

East was the Fraser Valley, the 150-kilometre trough between the Cascades and the Coast mountains. John had a vague memory of some Disney-like attractions near Hope, at the valley's eastern end, so he took Highway 10 east to where it joined the Trans-Canada Highway.

Just before the freeway he stopped at a PetroCan station. He checked the oil, and Nate wanted to be hoisted so he could see in the engine. John topped up the tank, unsurprised to discover that the big Chevy was a real fuel hog. His MG got three times the distance out of a litre of gas; unfortunately a little sports car was no good for a camping holiday.

Nate wanted to help with the pump. When John explained that it wasn't practical the little boy began to snivel. "I want to do it, Daddy."

John smiled patiently. "When you're older, kiddo. You're just not big enough now, okay?"

"I *am* big enough," Nate wailed. "Other Daddy says I'm big enough. *He* lets me."

John felt a rush of peevishness, either at Nate's unreason or the comparison with his rival in fatherhood. He said brusquely, "Well, you're with me right now. And I say you're not quite big enough."

"But Daddy ... "

"No!"

Nate turned away, pouting. John finished the fueling, realizing that he was feeling ridiculously grim. He shook his head. Good grief, this was just a little kid. If he started right off getting mad because the boy acted like the child that he was, they might as well turn around and go home. Okay, this is where it would stop. He dearly wanted this holiday with his son. So, for heaven's sake, no more anger. Let grimness cease forthwith!

John went into the gas station, paid with his Visa card and added the price of a candy bar to the bill. When they were both buckled up he produced the candy like a magician. But instead of grabbing it with delight, Nate just looked at it.

"Well—go ahead!" John said. "It's for you—because I got mad at you just now when I didn't mean to. Go on, Nate! Show Dad how quickly you can make it vanish."

Nate didn't make it vanish. He didn't even take it. "Mum says I can't have candy."

John felt his anger rekindle. That was all he needed, to have damn Val haunting them for a week. "Why?"

"Because," Nate quoted parrot-like, "when you eat it, it eats your teeth."

This cute axiom on the childish lips sounded so smug that John could have screamed "Oh, come on," he snapped, "that's only if you scarf candy all the time. This is a holiday. So take the candy. Go ahead."

The little boy just shook his head.

"Why not? I said it's okay. Do you believe me?"

"I guess so."

"Then why don't you want it?"

"'Cause Mum says I can't."

"But you're with *me* now, and I say it's okay." He had a sudden thought. "Or maybe you don't like candy. *That* it?"

"No—I love it!"

"Then cool, take it!"

But Nate shook his head, looking so stubborn that John again felt himself getting unreasonably angry again. Goddamn Val. He stuffed the candy bar in his pocket.

They had just got comfortably on the Trans-Canada Highway when Nate said, "I got to go pee!"

In all the time they had been stopped at the gas station Nate had not once mentioned the bathroom. Neither had John thought to remind him, but that didn't stop the anger welling up again. "Christ, Nate—why didn't you go back at the gas station?"

"I didn't have to then."

"But now suddenly you do?"

"Yes!"

"Well, you can just wait," John muttered, glowering through the windshield, continuing to drive. Five minutes later, beginning to feel pretty mean, he glanced out of the corner of his eye at his son. Nate was just sitting there, expression unchanged except for the eyes, which were squeezed closed. Down either cheek was a thin wet line.

"Oh, man!"

Hurriedly John pulled off the road. He leaned across, undid Nate's seat belt and opened his door. Beyond the hard shoulder and grass verge some bushes led into a stand of Douglas firs.

"Okay—off you go. Go have your pee."

Without a word Nate climbed down from the camper, trotted across the verge and disappeared into the bushes.

John sat, cursing himself silently. This was just stupid. He loved his son, hadn't come on this trip to fight with him. When the little boy came back he'd apologize and they'd be on their way. And no more of this petty nonsense.

He was still thinking this when he began to realize that Nate had been gone rather a long time.

"Nate!" he called, though the open door. But there was no reply, nor any sign of the child returning.

John got out of the camper and walked across to where his son had moved out of sight. Beyond the line of bushes the firs had crowded out all other growth. Underneath, the needle-covered ground was open and quite empty.

Nate had vanished.

FOUR

The Customs officer was a pleasant-looking older man. He came across to the window and said cheerfully, "Good afternoon, sir. Are you both Canadian citizens?"

Bud grinned at the fellow, taking note of his cool, sharp eyes. American born, he still felt a trifle odd answering to another nationality, even after all these years. Not that he wasn't happy about it. Although Canada might never feel completely like home, it was certainly a gentler place to spend one's later years, while being rich territory for the tough operator who still dwelt beneath his genial skin. "Yes sir, we are," Bud replied.

The officer glanced along the ponderous bulk of the motorhome. "How long have you been out of the country?"

"Three weeks," Mimi offered, with a brightness that Bud was still finding astonishing. "My husband bought this great big elephant especially for this trip. Now I feel guilty I couldn't appreciate it more."

The man looked at Mimi more closely. "You had troubles?"

"Not at all," Bud said quickly. "My wife hasn't been feeling well, is all."

"But I'm much better now," Mimi offered.

"Glad to hear it," the official said pleasantly. Then, to Bud, "Any more passengers in back?"

"No, sir."

"Any major purchases in the States?"

"No!"

"Any liquor or tobacco?"

"Neither of us smokes. But we've got a bar—some beer, a few bottles of liquor. But most of that I brought from home."

It was all routine. The officer looked as though he were about to end the interview. He made to step away, then suddenly looked back at Bud and said quietly, "Are you carrying any firearms, sir?"

Bud was mildly surprised. Once, this would have been a question reserved for Americans. But since 9/11, everyone was so paranoid that even innocent-looking retirees were likely to get the third degree. He understood this but wasn't about to let it get in his way. The truth was that he did have a gun, a Colt .38 Standard Automatic in a clip directly under the driver's seat. He'd carried such protection all his years of pushing rigs and never once had he had to haul it out. Installing a gun in the motorhome had been little more than a reflex, a formality. But, probably because of his American background, he also believed that carrying it was his right—and no one else's business. He was fully aware of the unlikelihood of this rig ever being searched, so when the question came, he looked the guy straight in the eye and shook his head. "No way!"

"Okay, then. Welcome home, folks," the Customs officer said with a nod of dismissal.

"Thanks," Bud smiled, and drove away. A moment later he felt an urge to do something totally uncharacteristic. He reached under the seat, checking the gun, finger tips lightly brushing the outline of cool steel. But instead of feeling reassured, to his surprise the touch of the weapon made him oddly apprehensive.

FIVE

"Nate!"

John ran through the trees, up a slope that swiftly grew rugged and broken. This was the only way that his son could have gone without being seen from the road. Surely he couldn't be far away. Surely no farther than over the little rise up ahead.

"Nate—where are you?"

And then, coming over the rise, he saw him. In the middle of an open grassy patch the little boy was sitting, silently crying with big, shoulder-heaving sobs.

"Oh, man—Nate!" Feeling his gut twist, John strode to the boy and scooped him up, hugging him hard. "I'm sorry," he whispered into the boy's neck. "Dad's sorry. I didn't mean to make you sad. Honest, kiddo. From now on, any time you have to pee—or do *anything*—just say it and we'll do it. That's a promise. Okay?"

After a while Nate stopped sobbing. Pretty soon, hand in hand, they walked back to the camper. They got in and as he was being buckled up, Nate looked around and—tears still staining his cheeks—gave his father a radiant grin. The miraculous forgiveness of the very young.

Now John remembered something that would be just right for

this moment. From the back of the camper he hauled out the thing he'd been keeping as a surprise.

Nate's eyes grew round. "Teddy Ruxpin," he squawked.

"You *know* this bear?"

"'Course I know him! He's on TV. Is—is he for *me?*"

Nate's voice was barely audible, he was so thrilled. From being broken hearted a few minutes back he was in paradise. John found himself amazed; kids were capable of emotional swings that in an adult would be plain crazy. Still, with this toy, his intuition had obviously been spot on: he had once loved Teddy Ruxpin and now, apparently, so did Nate. Maybe this would finally get them going on the right track together.

They began driving again, heading up the Fraser Valley toward the mountains, where it looked like a summer storm was brewing. Then, quite suddenly, John was struck with a memory: of himself, crying much as Nate had done earlier, and in an automobile ... Then he had it. No doubt the association had come because the incident had happened on this very highway.

A few kilometres farther east, where the valley turned into the precipitous Fraser Canyon, on a route now bypassed by all but tourist traffic, there was an attraction called Hell's Gate. As a child, on the way to or from holidays, he'd longed to see it, but his father was always in too much of a hurry. Then one year, after much begging, a promise was made to stop on the way home. John still vividly remembered the thrill of anticipation as they'd started down the canyon—and the tire blow-out that had almost sent their car plunging into it. By the time his father, furious and shaking from shock, had put on the spare, an hour had been lost. Reaching Hell's Gate, oblivious to all pleas, he'd driven right by, and John had spent the rest of the journey home in a fit of seven-year-old pique. The next time the family travelled inland was years later. His father avoided the Fraser Canyon entirely, taking the newly built Coquihalla High-way. To this day, he'd never seen Hell's Gate.

Now, spurred by the memory, he glanced across at Nate. "Hey, Nate, when we get up the road a ways, there's something I think you'd really like to see."

Nate's excited expression was quite absurdly appealing. "What, Daddy? *What?*"

John smiled. Taking Nate to Hell's Gate couldn't repair the past but maybe, in the boy's reaction, he could capture for himself some of the old missed wonder. And in doing so he might even manage to draw a little closer to his son.

"Can't tell. It's a surprise," John said. "But I'll bet you're going to like it a whole lot."

SIX

"Hell's Gate," Bud said. "You know, hon, in all my years driving, I never stopped off here."

"Let's do it," Mimi said happily. "It's about time I did some real sightseeing,"

Feeling as he did right now, Bud would have taken his miraculously restored wife anywhere. Giving her a happy nod, he swung into the eastbound parking lot. Then he and Mimi crossed by a pedestrian overpass to the river on the far side.

It was years since Bud had driven this route and he'd forgotten just how impressive it was. The canyon walls swooped up, rising in places two thousand feet from the river that had chiselled them. There had been heavy rain earlier and, in the strange half-light that followed it, the rocks looked the black and red of half-dried blood. Far above, where the mountaintops vanished into the departing storm, there was a continuous slow-dance of cloud forms, reflecting on the river like giants in some huge mirror. With this scene around them, Bud and Mimi crossed over the walk and descended to the canyon edge, arriving at last at Hell's Gate itself.

Bud's first realization was how appropriate the name was. The "gate" was a chasm through which the Fraser River passed, the whole vast outflow of this slice of the continent tortured into a rift not much wider than two hundred feet. The resulting maelstrom did everything to emulate the monstrous outpourings of hell.

As they approached nearer they could see that cables had been slung across the canyon and enclosed gondolas moved slowly back and forth, affording tourists a safe journey above the boiling cauldron.

Bud turned to catch Mimi's reaction to this wonder and got another of the day's many surprises. She was looking positively ecstatic. "Are you okay, doll?" he cried above the thunder of the water.

She laughed. "Okay? Sweetie—I never felt better. This place—it's wonderful. Magic!" She caught his hand. "Bud—let's take a ride!"

They got tickets and waited. Right ahead in the line was a young guy holding a child by the hand, who in turn clutched the paw of a stuffed bear. For some reason the little one looked vaguely familiar.

His father gave them a swift glance. He was about 30, pleasant looking, with a hesitant smile. Bud grinned, indicating the gondola that was even now swooping in from the chasm to meet them. "Great lookin' ride."

"Yeah. Been wanting to come on it since I was a kid."

"Looks like your own kiddy won't have to wait so long."

The guy looked pleased about that. "Right."

"Well, enjoy it, Mac."

"Thanks. You too!"

"Yeah!" Bud realized that he'd been chattering like a regular tourist. If anyone had told him 24 hours ago what things would be like today, he wouldn't have believed it. Glancing at Mimi, he saw that she also was aware of the son of the guy he'd been talking to, the child with the bear. Bud was freshly amazed. Mimi had been hardly able to look at children, especially little boys, since the loss of their own. To see her eyeing this stranger's offspring with such equilibrium was the best evidence yet that his wife was on the mend. Not wanting her to catch him spying, Bud turned away and examined the little cable car as, with a solid clash of metal, it arrived at the cliff side. The gate opened and the occupants emerged, looking awed. As the gondola refilled, Bud and Mimi were the last to find spaces. Right beside them were the young guy and his boy with the bear. As they sat down, Bud heard the child say, "Where's the seatbelt, Daddy?"

Bud laughed—he felt very good. And he saw the dad was chuckling too.

Mimi also had a smile on her face. She was not looking at the little boy anymore. Just sort of staring into space, looking quietly happy.

Mimi, happy! It was like some kind of miracle. *Jesus,* Bud thought, *whatever's happened here, don't let it go away.*

Beside him the gate swung shut. The gondola began to move out across the abyss.

SEVEN

Mimi was oblivious to everything around her—everything except the child.

As the gondola lurched forward, beginning its journey across the raging chasm of Hell's Gate, one word alone sang in her head.

Gabriel!

The moment she had laid eyes on the boy with the bear—the child so like the one who'd been taken that it was astonishing Bud hadn't recognized him too—she had begun to understand the real significance of her vision. In it Gabriel had talked of an end to their troubles. Did it begin here, with this look-alike infant? If so, she had no idea how that might be. It was a real puzzle. But just being near the little one made her so happy that, for the moment, she was content to drink it in.

Downward into the canyon on a gentle curve the gondola swooped. Somewhere there was the amplified voice of a guide, listing endless details about the chasm. Far off could be heard tourist chatter and the growing roar of the river but she paid attention to none of this. It was as though an invisible cone surrounded her and the little boy. If only they could be here together like this forever, she thought. If only everyone else could simply disappear and leave them, like a real mother and son, lost in their own private universe; that would be better than anything else she could ever imagine. Of course, that could never be. But just thinking about it made her glow inside. And though she still had no idea what the vision of Gabriel had been trying to communicate, merely being in the presence of his little look-alike made it seem that somehow anything was possible.

The gondola had reached the other side and started back before Mimi's good feeling began to go sour. Soon this machine would disgorge them where they'd started. And then the child— the echo-of-Gabriel—would be borne away by his stranger father. And what would become of her lovely new feeling then? If this short time of happiness was all that Gabriel's visit had meant, it was too much to bear.

The gondola came to rest. The door opened and they all emerged into sunshine. Directly above, a gap had opened in the shifting cloud-pattern. The asphalt was steaming. The golden light that bathed the gondola and the tourists and even the seething pot of Hell's Gate was like a sign from heaven.

But a sign of *what*? Mimi knew she had to do something now, but she had not the smallest idea what it might be. She fell into step beside the father and child, saying loudly, "My! Wasn't that exciting? I think I was just about scared to death."

The man looked at her amiably enough. "It's a lot safer than it looks, probably."

Mimi gave a little laugh. She still had no ideas, but instinct told her not to show any further interest in the child. "Yes, I suppose it would be. It doesn't seem so bad now the sun's shining."

"I guess you're right."

They had reached the ramp back to the eastbound parking lot. The man and child took the ramp. As they moved away Gabriel's twin said loudly, "Daddy, I'm hungry."

"Okay, kiddo," the man replied. "We'll find you something as soon as we get back to the camper."

Mimi took Bud's arm and they followed the others across the ramp. She appeared to pay no attention, but in fact never let them out of her sight. And the desperation that had been growing was receding again.

So they had a camper. And they were moving east.

EIGHT

As soon as they left Hell's Gate the clouds socked in again. Not long after that a light rain began and John realized he'd better start looking for a place to stop for the night. Unfortunately, in the Fraser Canyon there were few flat spots for campgrounds. After driving 30 kilometres he was still looking. Then, about to give up hope, he saw a cluster of trailers, RVs and tents, down by the river. Some of the RVs even had lights in their windows, and through the drizzle the place looked quite cosy.

They checked in at the office and were given a site at the far end of the campground, close to the river. John drove down, passing a long line of RVs and—eagerly noted by Nate—a little children's playground: this place seemed to have everything.

Finally he reached his spot and parked. As he was getting out, a huge motorhome slid neatly into the space next door. Together they had got the last two places. The inside lights of the motorhome came on and a man got out, tossing them a casual wave. Then after a closer look he wandered across. "Hi there! We must have followed you all the way up the canyon."

John recognized the man who had shared their trip across Hell's Gate. "Oh—hello, again." He usually felt it difficult to make casual talk with strangers, but this guy from the enormous motorhome seemed very casual and easy, and John felt his usual reticence melting. "Looks like we were pretty lucky to find this place. I was beginning to think I was going to have to drive clear to Cache Creek."

"Me too," the other grinned. "In fact, if my wife hadn't noticed your turn signal, we might have missed it." He held out his hand. "Howdy. The name's Bud Wetherall."

"John Quarry," John said. "And this is my son, Nate."

"Hi, Nate," Bud said, holding his hand out to the boy with a grave smile.

Nate took the hand, large-eyed but fascinated by this unusual adult civility. "Hello."

"And hello to you both," another voice said cheerfully, and John saw Bud's companion from Hell's Gate approaching. Bud Wetherall introduced her as his wife, Mimi. Soon they were all talking easily. Then a small voice interrupted. "Daddy, I'm thirsty!"

"Now there's a young fella who knows where it's at," Bud laughed, ruffling Nate's hair. "As a matter of a fact I was just thinking the very same thing. Hows about we all troop inside for a sundowner?"

"Well, I don't know … " John began, but already Mimi had gone to Nate.

She smiled at him kindly. "I believe I've got some Coke in the fridge, if your daddy thinks it would be okay."

"And I've got somethin' better than that," Bud added. "Come on in!"

John smiled. The whole thing was so easy and appealing that he couldn't think of a reason to refuse. "Well, thanks—you're very kind."

"Bullshit!" Bud said. And when Mimi looked at him sharply he only laughed, then she giggled too. "It's *you* who do us the kindness. Come on!"

When John saw the inside of the motorhome he gasped. He'd never dreamed anything on wheels could be so luxurious. It appeared to be half the size of his townhouse. They entered a large living room, with sofa and easy chairs, merging into the luxurious front cab. Farther back were a dining table, bench seats and a kitchen, complete with refrigerator, stove and microwave

"God, Bud—it's fantastic."

Bud Wetherall grinned unselfconsciously. In the brighter light John saw that his face, despite the expression of good cheer, was deeply lined. "Thanks, son. In fact, you and your boy are our first guests."

Mimi gave Nate his Coke and Bud made the rest of them drinks. Then they settled down. Bud, it turned out, was a semi-retired businessman from southern Alberta, who also owned a trucking company, Bow River Freight Lines of Calgary. They had no family. And this trip was the first vacation they'd had together in 20 years of marriage.

The details of the Wetheralls' life, so freely given in the wide-open Alberta fashion, were nothing out of the ordinary, but somehow it was extremely pleasant to be with them. John was hardly aware as his glass was replenished a couple of times and when, a little later, they were both invited to supper he just said thank you, and that was that.

Nate had followed Mimi to the kitchen area and she sat him at the dining table with his Coke, his bear, paper and pencils. While making supper and listening to the men's chat, Mimi also was having her own private little conversation with Nate, while helping him with his drawing. She did it all seemingly effortlessly.

John couldn't help marvelling at the woman's energy and imagination. The way she treated Nate was so sweet and natural, it was obvious she would make a terrific mother. It was a little sad that the couple was childless. But whatever the reason, that subject never came up.

A while later—remembering John's first awed reaction—Bud insisted on showing off the motorhome from stem to stern. He'd bought it to give his wife a much-needed holiday, he said, and it was a terrific vehicle. They walked down a hall, passing a bathroom and a large closet, finally entering a bedroom that had a huge, queen-sized bed. When they were alone, Bud said, "John, I want to thank you for keeping us company tonight."

"Thanks for having us."

"No—I mean—my wife, Mimi—she hasn't been ... Look—to tell the truth we used to have a little boy. Looked quite a lot like yours. Not much older than him when he—er—passed."

"I'm sorry."

"Don't mention to Mimi I told you any of this, okay? She's taken a real shine to Nate. He's the first child she's been able even to look at since we lost our own kiddy. It's kind of a miracle, seeing her like this. So—as I said—thank you."

"But we haven't done anything."

"You have!" Bud said firmly. "Just by being here, that's what I mean. Now, let's go back before she wonders what we've been jawing about back here."

He clapped John on the shoulder with his big, hard hand and guided him in the direction of the kitchen. They arrived to find Nate and Mimi sitting side by side, a hand-drawn picture between them, talking and giggling like two kids. Mimi looked up, flashed a smile and moved back to stir something on the stove.

For a brief moment John had the odd sensation that, of all the people present, he alone was an intruder.

NINE

Dinner appeared at last, a little mobile miracle. While they talked Mimi had produced a first-class spaghetti Bolognaise. They had it with salad and a good Similkameen red wine. Afterwards there was fruit and ice cream. For Nate this was the high point of the meal. He looked so cute sitting at the table wolfing it down that Mimi laughed and said she just had to have a picture. She produced an old-fashioned Polaroid camera and took a couple of shots, then took one of John and Nate, finally asking John to take one of herself with the little boy. Despite the archaic technology, the pictures were clear and charming. But when everyone had finished examining them, they discovered that Nate had quietly fallen asleep at the table. For him it had been a very long day.

"Always one drunk at the party," John smiled. "I guess I'd better get him to bed."

He rose from the table, feeling surprisingly unsteady himself. Wow, surely he hadn't had all that much to drink? But the slight dizziness passed quickly. He put it down to the good food, and a mood of relaxation that he hadn't felt in a long time.

He slung the sleeping form gently on his shoulder and, refusing the invitation to return for a nightcap, walked the few yards to his own camper. Inside, on the lower bed that converted from the dining nook, he laid out the little boy's sleeping bag. John himself would sleep in the high double bunk in the slot above the cab.

John put his son into the sleeping bag, removing only his pants and shoes. Still clutched in the boy's left hand, creased and crumpled, was one of the drawings he'd been making before dinner. John did not attempt to pry it free.

The little boy stirred and muttered, turning on his side into a ball, in a position that looked oddly like self-protection. The shirt rode up and, as John went to cover his son, he noticed something that made him pause. He pulled the shirt higher, exposing Nate's torso. Below the shoulder blades were some very odd-looking bruises, a dark area covering almost half of the upper back.

John frowned in concern. What he was looking at didn't look random; it was almost like the result of a beating. But who could be responsible? His first thought was Nate's new stepfather, but that didn't feel right. Then, remembering Nate's reaction to the candy bar, he had a worse thought: what if the child's mother was laying into him? If so, no wonder the poor kid was afraid of disobeying her.

But he didn't know that. In fact, as far as Nate's bringing-up was concerned, he had to admit he knew almost nothing. What he had to do was start being a real dad. To hell with not having custody, it was still his job to protect Nate, to make sure that the little boy was being properly treated.

John leaned down and kissed his son's cheek, tucking him securely in the sleeping bag. "Goodnight, Nate!" John said gently. "Sweet dreams. I'm going to do better by you, kiddo, I promise."

Leaving a lamp on and the back door ajar, John got down from the back of the camper. Deciding that he needed a little fresh air, he strolled around to the front of the camper.

He stopped. Something new had caught his attention; then he

realized it was the sound of the river. What at Hell's Gate had been a giant's roar was here merely a throaty whisper. But it had a quality that, in the darkness, was strangely hypnotic. John moved toward the sound. When he was away from the light his eyes, making an adjustment from the inside brightness, produced the nocturnal scene as if by magic.

John drew in a breath. The panorama before him was dreamy, magical; the essence of water, and of night. Also it had a quality of death. *The River Styx*, John thought, then winced at the macabre nature of the notion.

Directly in front of him, beyond a low rock shelf, the bank sloped to the water's edge, no more than 30 feet away. Overhead, a pale moon, its light made fitful by the banners of the earlier storm, imparted a faint sheen to the river, defining the limits of the deep. The movement on the surface was subtle but, when watched closely, it could be seen that this gigantic water creature was sweeping along at great speed. Today's storm, and many others in the late season, had added half an ocean to be drained through the great canyon. The black hulk of a log swept by, moving so fast that, imagining himself in its place, John's stomach gave a momentary lurch. He thought, *If someone fell in here they'd be in the ocean by morning.*

He pushed the unpleasant image aside and went to join his son in slumber.

TEN

In the cab of the motorhome, in the darkest hours of the morning, Mimi kept vigil.

The moon had long ago set in the west but the sky was now clear, and the glimmer of starlight divided moving water from the void beyond. The night was so still that she could hear clearly the powerful slither of the river. As a background, from the bedroom, the soft chuckle of Bud's snores wove a contented counterpoint in the gloom.

No notion had she yet of what she was going to do.

She had been very clever all evening, done everything right. She had fed them, been sweet and charming without anyone getting wind of the truth. All night her body had ached to pick up the child, to hug him to her. But she'd resolutely resisted the impulse, instead talking to him quietly, telling him stories, drawing him little pictures.

The pictures: that, she discovered, was how she could communicate with the child best. She made a little stick figure to represent him, bigger ones for his father and the creature, Val, who'd brought the child into the world. By his reactions, Mimi was certain that he did not love her. How could he? Deep down he must know that he had a higher destiny. So she had drawn a picture of herself for the boy, making her identity clear, with her long black hair and the simple pattern on her sweater. Then she crossed out meanie Val—which made the child giggle so loud she had to shush him—and instead drew a picture of him being held by herself. He liked that, oh yes! She knew he was feeling the first stirrings of who he was: who he *really* was.

Into John's final drink of the night she'd slipped the contents of two of her new sleeping capsules. Although she yet had no definite plans, obviously the first thing was to get the father well and truly out of the picture. Mimi felt that John was both intuitive and intelligent, and he seemed quite fond of his son. So, since he could never be expected to accept the truth—something that was only now becoming fully apparent to Mimi—John would have to be the one most completely deceived. But how?

She still had no idea. But as she waited in the dark cab of the motorhome, looking across the tantalizing distance to the little boy's sleeping place—hugging his forgotten teddy bear—she had not the slightest doubt that, as Gabriel had said, their troubles were nearly over. So she just sat, legs tucked under, eyes as unblinking as a night-drowned owl, and waited.

It was not long afterward that she saw the light.

ELEVEN

Nate woke up and everything was very black. He didn't know where he was and started to cry. Then his wide-staring eyes began to see something, a pale luminous square in the dark. In the square he made out tiny twinkling lights. Stars! The square was a window through which he could see the sky and then Nate remembered what this place was. The camper that Daddy had got for their holiday.

"Daddy!"

Nate called the name loudly. There was no reply. Thinking himself alone, he began to feel frightened all over again. He was about to cry out when he became aware of another sound; one that had been there all the time.

Breathing. *Breathing not his*!

Nate was petrified, then he remembered something Daddy had shown him. By the bed, on the wall under the window, was a light switch he could turn on if he needed to. Nate threw himself over there and scrabbled around and, with wonderful luck, he found it. There was a little click and the light came on. Only a little baby light for sure, but to Nate it was like the sun. Most importantly, it showed who was doing the breathing: Daddy!

Daddy was on the big high bed. Nate's relief was filled with an urgent desire to be up there too. To be cuddling up to Daddy. Mum wouldn't let him cuddle with her but his father wouldn't mind.

Then he remembered Teddy Ruxpin. New Teddy was here. He would take Teddy Ruxpin up to Daddy's bed, and the three of them would all cuddle safe together.

He looked around on his bed but Teddy wasn't there. He wasn't anywhere in the camper. Finally Nate got out of bed. Maybe Teddy had run away. Maybe he should go look for him …

And maybe there would be monsters out there.

But if he left Teddy, the monsters might eat him. And he loved Teddy Ruxpin. He had come from Daddy and was the most wonderful bear in the world. He had to try to get him. Nate looked at the door. Then he got up and stood beside it. Maybe Teddy was just outside, waiting to get in. Maybe if he opened the door a tiny bit he would be able to see him. Maybe if he was very quick …

Nate turned the handle and slowly opened the camper door. He could see nothing. Light spilled on the outside grass. It was fresh and green—but there was no Teddy.

No monsters either.

Nate slowly opened the door wider. Walked out to the edge, stared beyond the light into the dark. Now there was another sound: a low swishing gurgle, a gentle singing whisper of water. The river.

Maybe Teddy had gone down to the river. Daddy had told *him* not to go near the river. But he hadn't told Teddy. Nate clambered down from the camper and turned in the direction from which the song of the river came.

"Teddy!" he called out. "*Teddy!*"

Something suddenly loomed up ahead. A monster had been waiting all the time.

Nate took in a breath to yell but then the thing spoke. He knew that voice. The lady from the big camper, who had given him ice cream and drawn him pictures.

"Hello, little one," she said, "what are you doing out here all by yourself?"

"Looking for Teddy Ruxpin."

"Oh—you think you dropped him out here?"

"He ran away," Nate said urgently. "Maybe he went down to the river."

"Of course." The lady sounded almost as excited as he felt. "Bears are always doing things like that, aren't they? Would you like me to help you find him?"

Her voice took on a tone that made him think of the noises his mum and new daddy made at night when he was supposed to be asleep. "Dear, shall I help you? Shall we go—just you and me—and look for Teddy at the river?"

A hand was held out: not demanding, casually inviting.

"Okay. But we better be quick."

"Don't worry, dear, we'll be *real* quick," the nice lady said.

Hand in hand they walked down to the river.

TWELVE

Pain woke John. It was throbbing at the front and sides of his head, as though his brain was in a vice hooked up to a rhythm machine. He opened his eyes, and only the rhythm stopped. The pain itself remained, constant, like a squeezing fist.

He groaned, knowing exactly where he was and what had happened. Man, he hadn't felt as bad as this ever. Last night the Wetheralls had fed him a fair bit of liquor—but had it been all *that* much? Apparently. Now he would have at least a day of punishment for his indiscretion. And since this was his precious holiday with Nate, there could be no question of spending any of that time in bed.

"Damn!"

Gingerly he sat up. Even his eyeballs hurt, as he swiveled them around to look at the boy's bed. The sleeping bag was empty.

The back door swung ajar.

No sign of Nate.

John looked at his watch: 7:05. Nate, he remembered, had always been an early riser.

"Nate?"

The call made disastrous things happen to his head, and brought no response, so John swung his legs around and slowly slid to the floor. He closed his eyes and took several deep breaths, waiting for nausea to recede. God, this was how people were supposed to feel after someone had slipped them a mickey. Finally he slitted his eyes open again.

He was still wearing yesterday's clothes. The loafers he'd thrown off before climbing into bed were where he'd left them on the floor. Carefully John slid his feet into them, then suddenly went rigid. The sound of the river, ever-present, had finally intruded on his consciousness.

If Nate was playing by himself outside, that damn river was too close for comfort. Instantly forgetting everything else, John hurried to the door, pushed it right open, stepped to the sill.

"Nate!"

No answering call.

Across the way, curtains drawn, the Wetheralls' motorhome crouched in gargantuan slumber.

"Hey, *Nate!!!*"

Still nothing.

Except an echo from across the river.

John jumped down from the camper. He stood still, frozen, denying the gulf that was opening in his heart. He started to run, circling his own RV and the Wetheralls'. Then, with frantic relief, he remembered a children's play area they'd passed on the way in last night. Nate had seen it too. Of course, that's where he'd be. A minute's fast jog brought him to the spot. There was a little slide, a sand pile, toys scattered about, empty swings ...

No Nate.

"*NAAAAAAAAATE!!!!*"

This time it was an explosion. Agony. Despair ... Knowing!

John at last forced himself to the inevitable. He threw aside the putting-off and wrenched his steps in the direction of the river.

When he got there he stopped, numbly staring. Leading from where he stood, directly to where the great continent-drain was sluicing by, clear and perfect in the sand, was a line of tiny footprints.

At the river's edge, nose submerged like a desert wanderer at an oasis, was Teddy Ruxpin.

Quite alone.

PART TWO

ONE

Missing, presumed drowned.
That was the official report, and no blame was attached to John. That is, no charges were laid, but he blamed himself bitterly anyway. Had he not been passed-out on that fatal morning, Nate would never have had the chance to walk alone into the river.

After all the official stuff was over, and he'd dealt with the media types with their sickening "tragedy for well-known actor" stories, John shut himself away. He cancelled all appointments, shut off his phone, turned on a deafening rock station, and sat: not able to weep, not daring to think, because all that came were images of self-destruction. Finally he got up and did something that he'd not permitted himself since that dreadful night by the river: he poured himself a drink.

After consuming half a bottle of Scotch he felt a stirring inside, the first cracks in the frozen wall. By the time the bottle was empty, Jericho-like, it came tumbling fast. He broke down and wept savagely, bitterly: if not a true cleansing, at least it was some small relief. After that he fell into a deep sleep and did not wake for 24 hours.

The hangover was savage, but he stifled it with several stiff belts—of vodka, since he'd finished the Scotch. Then, while the high was still running, he crammed down food, showered and dressed and got into his car; the treasured MG Midget, which today seemed as inconsequential as everything else in his life. He drove with grim concentration to Richmond.

There were lights on in the house where Val lived with her new husband: now lived with him alone. John jabbed the bell hard, several times. So consumed was he with the urgency of what he had to do that every second of waiting now felt like an age.

Steps in the hall, the door opened. Val's ice-blonde hair was immaculate as usual. But when she saw him her green eyes retracted to nervous lines of hate.

"What the hell do you want?"

John walked by her into the house. Her husband, Franklin Boyce, a fleshy man who sold real estate, appeared from the kitchen and his mouth went slack with apprehension.

"Listen," John said quickly, "I'm only going to keep you a moment. Then I'll never come here again, I promise. But just once I have to say this: I loved Nate. I'd rather have died myself than have anything happen to him. But somehow it did, and I know it's my fault. Val, I'm sorry. I'm so very sorry! I wanted you to know."

He headed back for the door. But before he could reach it his ex-wife barred his way.

"You're just *leaving*?" Val hissed. "You think you can say your little shitty piece and that makes it all right? *Is that what you think?*"

"Val!" her husband began.

"Shut up! Just can it, Frank!" Then to John, "How dare you come here with your bloody apologies?"

"But there's nothing else I can ... "

"I *know* you're guilty, you bastard. The whole goddamn world knows it. If there was any justice, you'd be in jail, being flogged with whips."

"I guess you'd like that."

"You bet I would. If I had a whip right now, buster, I'd do it myself."

Before he could stop himself, John said, "So why don't you get the one you used on Nate?"

There was a frozen silence. Val's eyes flared round, presaging a new level of fury.

"I never hurt Nate," she spat. "I loved him. I was the one who took care of him when you left. How dare you accuse me of abusing my son. You rotten asshole, how dare you!"

Right then John should have departed. Nate was dead. None of this ugliness would bring him back. And raking up Val's misdeeds—if in fact there were any—didn't make him any less culpable. He knew all this, but it wasn't any use.

"I'll tell you how," John snapped. "I saw those bruises on his back. Don't tell me he got them falling down the stairs!"

"Actually, he fell off a swing," Boyce began, but was drowned out by his wife.

"Bastard!" Val screamed. "You know *nothing*! Do you hear me? Nothing!" And delivered a bone-ringing slap across his face.

A bolt of pure fury shot through John, and his whole body quivered with the desire to belt her right back. What stopped him—only barely—was the knowledge that that action would play right into her hands: she'd love the opportunity to charge him with criminal assault. So he took a deep breath, rubbing his smarting face, and said softly, "I rest my case."

Val glared. But, guilty or not, she obviously knew she'd badly compromised her position.

Franklin Boyce, who'd been staring open-mouthed, gave an awkward cough. "Honey," he began, "whatever happened, there's nothing any of us can do now … "

"Shut up!" Val rallied. "You don't know anything either, Frank, so just shut up."

Boyce, looking sick and hugely embarrassed, turned to John. "There's no point in continuing this," he said quietly. "You really should leave now."

This time John took his exit cue. His head, already fried with the hangover and the fatal medication of more booze, was now feeling the full reaction to Val's vicious slap. He almost lost his balance as he turned away, swayed, caught himself and said quietly, "You're lucky—lucky I didn't know more—that's all. Have a good life."

Without looking again at either Val or Boyce, he made his way unsteadily to the door. When he was halfway down the walk, Val's voice erupted, "Bastard—drunken fool—I'll pay you back for lying about me!"

The door slammed.

John got into his MG, started up and headed down the main highway for town. He had been driving perhaps ten minutes when he became aware of red and blue flashing lights approaching rapidly from the rear.

Then there was a siren.

"Got a call from a lady who said you'd made trouble at her house," the officer said.

"I didn't go there to make trouble."

"Domestic dispute, not my business. But she also said you were driving drunk—and that is! Get out of the car, please, sir."

John did, knowing he didn't have a chance. After a couple of questions he was invited into the patrol car. The breathalyzer at the police station confirmed the worst. He was put in a cell. His companions were another sleeping drunk and, in the next cell, a prostitute who must have weighed 200 pounds.

John had never been in the slammer before. He lay down on the hard wooden bench, covering his eyes from the harsh single bulb, his heart slipping into black despair.

Nate dead and now this. If this wasn't the end of the line, John couldn't imagine what that might be like. After a few minutes he fell into a deep sleep.

Then he found out.

HE KNEW IT was a dream right from the start, but that did nothing to curb its reality. Or its horror.

He was on the gondola riding above the dizzying chasm of Hell's Gate. Nate was with him, as well as the people with the big motorhome, Mimi and Bud Wetherall. At the start everything was fine, except that he did notice the cables on which the gondola rode were made of spun glass. Out they rode over the abyss, which was miles across and thousands of feet deep. Looking down he realized that this must be a rift right through the skin of the world, because what was boiling past down there was a snake of fiery red lava. Now he understood that this, in fact, was a river emanating from the real hell. As they moved farther out over the chasm, John began to feel the heat frying up from below. Now the fire-river had somehow risen to within a few feet of the gondola's bottom. John realized that the sound he'd once taken for the roar of water was in fact screaming: the agony-cries of a multitude. There were people in the fire, hundreds, thousands, with hair and limbs and genitals ablaze; men and women and children, all in eternal torment. Bud Wetherall had opened the gondola gate, and now John noticed that his face was reptilian, demon-like. "All right," the demon sneered. "Who wants to go first?" "Me, me!" Nate cried, running for the gate. "No!" John screamed, but it was not he who caught Nate. It was Mimi. She was also reptilian and held the struggling child to her breast without effort. "Oh, no dear," she whispered above the screams from below.

"You're mine—all mine." Miraculously, she produced Teddy Ruxpin, which she tossed through the gate instead. Teddy hit the lava and exploded in a flash of light. An instant later the glass cables shattered. But the gondola did not fall. Instead it began to drift up, like a hot air balloon. John was marvelling at this when strong hands seized his shoulders. Demon-Bud carried him to the gate, tossed him through. As the gondola, bearing the others, drifted up and away, John plunged down, hearing Nate's voice calling over increasing distance: "Bye, Daddy. *See you!*" Then he hit the river of fire, feeling himself consumed in something that was not physical pain, but the far greater agony of loss and indescribable sorrow.

John awoke.

He was in the cold prison cell, where Val's maliciousness and his own crass stupidity had landed him; where, in humiliation and despair, he'd passed out.

But now ...

Now his quarters seemed not foul but benign, a place of burgeoning hope. Because, out of the mayhem of his dream, had emerged a shining intuition.

Nate isn't gone at all. HE'S ALIVE!

TWO

It had all worked perfectly.

After she'd seen the light go on in the little camper across the way, the plan had suddenly sprung into Mimi's mind, complete and wonderful, as if it had been there all the time. When she saw the child emerge, she left the motorhome and waited quietly in the dark.

"Teddy!" he had called. "*Teddy!*"

She had gone to him, found why he was out all by himself. He wanted his bear, and was little enough to think it might have run away by itself. Of course, she knew where it was; she'd recently been hugging it in lieu of the child himself. But she didn't tell him that.

From inside the camper she could hear the snores of the father in his drugged sleep. Now she knew why she'd given him those pills. Oh yes! Also, she had her plan. The perfect solution to all problems.

"Dear, shall I help you?" she'd said. "Shall we go—just you and me—and look for Teddy at the river?"

She held out her hand. The little boy took it, oh, so trustingly, and they had walked toward the water. When they reached the bank overlooking the beach, lit by the pale moon, the little boy gave a disappointed cry because—of course—Teddy Ruxpin wasn't there. Mimi said, "Walk down the bank to the river's edge—very carefully, mind—and see if you can see him from there."

The child obeyed. Mimi noted with satisfaction that even in this pale light his footprints were very clear. She herself walked down on a log that straddled the beach farther down.

At the water's edge, still not finding his bear, the little one had started to sob. Telling him to stay where he was, Mimi stepped from her log straight into the water. Even inches from the edge the river tugged menacingly at her ankles as she walked upstream. Not leaving the water, she plucked the child from the bank and carried him back down to the log. She sat on it, her feet still submerged, and hugged him hard for the very first time.

Then she suddenly had an idea. Maybe clever Teddy, instead of coming to the river, had hidden in the motorhome. Should they look there? Of course! Mimi picked the child up and carried him back to the RV. Inside, after carefully closing the bedroom door—even though Bud was a heavy sleeper—Mimi put on the light.

And, goodness how wonderful, there was Teddy!

The little boy was overjoyed. He hugged and scolded his wandering bear, and agreed that a cup of hot chocolate before he went back to bed would be lovely.

Mimi made the chocolate double-thick and delicious, just the way she liked it herself. One of its special ingredients was the entire contents of one of her sleeping capsules. Ten minutes later the boy was in a heavy, drugged sleep. Five minutes after that he was snug and secure in a little bed she made up for him in the bottom of the spacious closet. One of her pills, she was sure, would knock the child out for at least 24 hours.

If it didn't kill him.

But that wasn't a real worry. This plan had come from heaven, for the ultimate good of the child, whom she'd already started to think of as the new Gabriel. So how could he come to harm?

The last detail had been Teddy Ruxpin. Mimi took the bear outside, walked down the log to the water, and carefully deposited the toy on the shore at the end of the line of little footprints.

Then, with a light and joyful heart, she went to bed.

The next day everything had gone like clockwork.

Mimi, her work well done, slept like an angel. Bud had answered the frantic knock on their door. Later, after searches had been made and the police called in, what had been obvious from the outset was acknowledged: the child had gone into the river.

Having done all they could for the stricken father, Mimi made a request: this tragedy had soured her on the Fraser Canyon and she wanted badly to move on. Bud had looked at her with concern. She knew what was on his mind. He feared that the loss of the infant would trigger the return of her depression. For obvious reasons, this wasn't going to happen, but for the moment it was best that Bud not know why. It was vital that some time should pass, and they be well out of the area, before their closet's precious cargo was revealed. Bud was a marvellous man, strong and resourceful, and when he understood the full implications of new-Gabriel's return, he could be counted on to make things right. But in the interim, until they were fully committed and there was no turning back, better that she keep her life-altering secret to herself. Consulting a map, she saw that if they kept going north beyond Cache Creek, up the Cariboo Highway, they could make a long swing through the interior, on a route that would be remote and quiet enough for things to get settled.

While Bud drove—tirelessly as always—it was easy for her to monitor the child, making sure he stayed comfortable—and lightly sedated—in his little hidey-hole, until the appropriate moment. On the second evening, having left the city of Prince George, they headed south again, along the Yellowhead Highway, beside the milder headwaters of the Fraser River. They found an isolated camping spot and, while Bud took a stroll, Mimi finally lifted Gabriel from concealment. He still slept but not deeply now. Soon he would wake—and everything must be ready.

She stripped off his clothes and gave him a sponge bath, noticing some old bruises running across his back. Mimi's jaw tightened in cold rage. This was the kind of thing that happened when a child fell into the hands of the wrong parents. Now she doubly understood why it had been so necessary to get him away. But all that was over with. Mimi dressed the little boy in one of her nightgowns and put him into bed. She had almost finished when Bud returned from his walk.

When he saw their new son, her husband's reaction had been almost comical. For fully a minute he just gaped at the child, while his eyes bulged and his heavy frame remained frozen, still as death. Finally he sucked a huge breath into his lungs.

"Good God, Mimi," Bud said. "What have you done?"

She didn't try to explain, to justify. She let him think it through. Bud was a very bright man. He hadn't said, "How come the kid's not dead?" or "How did he get here?" No, only—"What have you done?" Which meant, of course, that he *knew*.

Consequently, after the correct amount of time, Mimi said softly, "Sweetie, I've given us back our life. I've found Gabriel."

He stared at her. He stared at the child, whose eyelids were beginning to flutter. Finally he said, "You called him Gabriel."

"He *is* Gabriel," she said calmly. "I told you about my vision."

"But this kid is Nate."

"*Nate is dead.* Nate's father knows that. By now, everyone does. They're all satisfied with what happened. *We have Gabriel.*"

Whereupon Bud had regarded Mimi with a new expression, something akin to awe.

Or was it fear?

Then he turned and stalked out of the motorhome.

When Gabriel finally awoke, Mimi cuddled up close and, in answer to his first question said, "Your daddy had to go away, dear. He said he loves you and he's going to make a lot of money so he can be with you always. Would you like that?"

The child smiled sleepily. "But won't Mummy come to find us?"

"Don't worry," Mimi laughed, giving him a hug. "We tricked her good."

"How?"

"Why, darling—we hid you. Now we're all going on a holiday together and your daddy will join us as soon as he can. And till he does, to keep you safe for him, we're going to pretend you're *our* little boy. And, just for fun, we'll even give you a new pretend name."

"What name?"

"Well, once upon a time I knew a very good little boy called Gabriel. He was such a sweet child and—until he had to go away— my very best friend. I thought you could use his name. What do you think?"

"Okay, but just till Daddy comes."

Mimi felt content. Gabriel couldn't be expected to know who he really was. Not yet. But this was a start.

"Thank you, Gabriel," she said sweetly. "Now I'll get you some nice hot soup. Then you can go back to sleep."

A while later Bud returned. He was still deeply shocked. She related the cover story she'd told Gabriel, described the bruises on the child's back and voiced her belief that he was probably relieved not to have to go back to his mother.

Bud listened to it all, making little comment. But again he

had given her that strange look. At last, suddenly, he rose. He had to drive, he said. He had to *think*. He started the engine and they pulled out of the spot where they had stopped by the now-gentle Fraser River.

Bud didn't head back the way they'd come; that was a good sign. For hours he drove south down the Yellowhead Highway, with the vast uprising of the nearby Rockies invisible in the darkness, while Mimi sat in the passenger seat and neither said a word. Finally they came to an intersection: their present route continued east through the Yellowhead Pass into Alberta; Highway 5 curved back south-west into BC. Here Bud turned off the road and stopped. It was dawn.

He stood up, turned to her. In his face was a new expression: not decision yet, but something very near.

"Doll, I'm going for a walk," he said. "I still have some thinking to do. I may be—some time."

"And when you come back?"

He studied her a moment, then looked back to where the child slept, as if checking that he was real. Finally his gaze returned to his wife, and for the first time ever he truly looked old.

"When I come back—I promise—I'll know."

AND NOW HE'D been out there all morning, on a rise above the river, while Mimi watched from the window; he was deciding their fate, as all men seemed to think was their right.

Soon it would be done. He would get up and come back, with his decision.

But whatever it might be, it didn't really matter. Because if he said yes, that everything was all right, that the three of them could go back to being the family they'd once been—well, that would be perfect. But if Bud couldn't do that, if he insisted on being a fool, returning the child, destroying all that she had built, that would be okay too. Because then she would know that this family had not been meant to exist on earth—but in heaven.

Her decision!

And lying in her lap, taken from its clip beneath Bud's driving seat, ready, if needed, was the instrument to implement it.

THREE

"You're lucky, Mr. Quarry," the desk sergeant said. "We've decided not to lay charges."

John was still in a state of shock. "Yeah?"

"We realized that you were that actor guy whose lad got drowned in the river ... "

But he didn't drown, a wild, capering voice gibbered in John's head. *He couldn't have—because I know he's alive.*

" ... which is a fair enough reason for getting smashed, maybe. But not for driving drunk. You understand me?"

"Yes sir!"

"But, since you only blew a bit over, and considering the circumstances, we've decided to let you off with a warning. Is that warning taken?"

"Yes *sir!*"

"Then beat it. Don't let me see you again—unless it's on the TV."

Trying not to grin like a fool, John did as he was told.

Outside the station he picked up a cab to take him to where he'd left the MG. On the way, as he started to think about it rationally, he understood that he should be feeling very afraid. To actually believe—*believe*—that his son was alive, because of a weird dream, could only mean one thing: despair had made him delusional.

Crazy!

He knew he should understand this yet somehow he couldn't make himself. By the time he reached his own car and finally started home, the euphoria from the dream was still with him, high and strong.

In fact, high was exactly what he felt, this time without benefit of booze. Also, he was ravenously hungry; he stopped at a Wendy's and consumed a huge burger in a basket with fries and onion rings, washing it down with two cups of coffee. While he was eating, he took from his wallet the Polaroid picture of himself and Nate, taken by Mimi Wetherall; since then he'd neither been able to look at it or bring himself to throw it away. His new belief made examination of the heart-rending image possible: his foolishly grinning self, Nate, his little face smeared with ice-cream and, clutched at his side, Teddy Ruxpin ...

Which brought him back to his dream.

The idea of the bear, which in the dream Mimi had tossed out of the gondola instead of Nate, that, oddly, was what excited him most. But why? That part of the dream was apparently trying to tell him something. But what ...? Then suddenly it came, what had been staring him in the face the whole time. Of course! On the fatal night—*the bear had been left in the motorhome.*

He'd meant to bring it back but hadn't. It had definitely been forgotten. He'd never gone back for a nightcap, so it had just stayed there. The Wetheralls had made no mention of it during questioning later. So how had it ended up by the river?

Someone other than Nate had put it there.

John drove back to his house. Now he realized he was starting to feel—along with the continuing exhilaration—a new sensation. *Of something about to happen.* Double crazy!

But—maybe not. He parked the MG and went inside, neither

hurrying nor holding back. Drifting. As he opened the front door, the first thing he became aware of was the pile of camping gear, dumped and abandoned in the hall after the terrible return.

It was natural now to start clearing it away. He took the suitcase first, emptied it and packed the still-clean clothes away. Then he unpacked the boxes of utensils, canned food and miscellaneous gear with which he'd stocked the camper. Finally he shook out, re-rolled and tied the sleeping bags. As he was working on the second, the one Nate had used, something fell out and rolled onto the floor. A piece of paper. Crumpled in a tight ball, it had been right at the bottom of the bag.

John bent and picked it up. The feeling of something about to happen grew so strong that he shivered.

He uncrumpled the paper, recognizing the drawing that had been clutched in Nate's hand that last night when John had put him to bed. Carefully he smoothed out the paper on the kitchen counter. People were drawn there. Stick figures, some in the unsteady hand of a child, the others simple, strong, fashioned by a grown-up.

The adult-drawn figures were easy to recognize. They were also named. John was there, and Val and Nate. Bud Wetherall was there and so was his wife. Mimi was particularly clear, because of her long black hair and elfin face. Nate was obvious because of his small size.

Then John saw that there were in fact two Nates. One was holding onto the hand of his mother. Even as a stick lady, Val had an ugly frown—and had been harshly crossed out. But from Val's Nate an arrow pointed to the second child. This Nate was chubbier, more alive-looking and happy, and his penciled grin went from ear to ear. The reason for that was obvious: he was being held lovingly by the stick lady called Mimi.

Distinctly, echoing out of his jailhouse dream, John heard the voice of his son: *"Bye, Daddy! See you!"*

FOUR

All morning Bud sat gazing at the Fraser River, which had its genesis in the vast Thompson Ice Field, in the distance off to his left. Behind him was the bulk of the Rockies, in front the equally impressive upthrust of the Cariboo Range. The trench between these stony bastions was so deep that not until nearly noon did the sun strike the place where Bud sat, not that he paid much attention to any of this.

What he did pay attention to was the fact that he was at a turning point in his life. Whatever decision he made today, things could never be the same again. The first issue he'd had to face, from the instant of the revelation of the stolen child, was that Mimi was crazy. That fact in itself had been such a shock that he'd spent a long time absorbing it.

Understanding of the second fact had come about more slowly but it amounted to this: with the child included in the equation, Mimi's condition—brought about by the death of their own child—was in effect relieved, the balance righted. With a new Gabriel in her life, Mimi acted like a perfectly normal and happy human being. For the first time since the horror, she was again the sweet, vibrant woman he had married.

Beyond all that loomed a distinctly awkward third fact: the child was not theirs.

Mimi alone was responsible for the abduction, but it would be near-impossible to make other people believe that. And even should he somehow be absolved of blame, it would still mean Mimi being charged and probably institutionalized. Kidnapping, especially of a child, was a crime to which the public reacted with particular revulsion. Even if he went free, his married life would essentially be over.

It was doubly ironic that he was innocent in this affair. The Bud of long ago—who'd grown up Bud Wittoenski on Chicago's South Side—would not have been too bothered about kidnapping, if it suited his purposes. His early years had seen a lot of brutal and even criminal activity. Only when he'd started driving rigs had he even had regular employment. That had been in the rough end of the trade, working for cut-throat outfits, rolling along the high-ways of North America with little regard for speed, regulations or the legality of his cargo. Not until chance brought him to Alberta, with the opportunity to pick up a stake in a small trucking firm, did the Bud of later years begin to take form. Even then, building Bow River Freight into a real player and finally wresting full control had involved a depth of ruthlessness that no one—at least no one still breathing—knew the half of. When he was fully established, and met and married Mimi, the final incarnation emerged—businessman, family man and solid tax-paying citizen. It was a persona he'd grown comfortable with and valued highly; being wealthy, secure and—above all—legit, had given him satisfaction and peace of mind. Now, through an entirely unforeseeable circumstance, the whole edifice was suddenly in jeopardy.

A bright light in all this was the incredible cunning of Mimi's deed: that, at least, couldn't have been cleverer if he'd planned it himself. Because of the false clues his wife had laid, Nate was presumed dead, his body carried far away. No one was looking for him. A perfect crime—in that nobody knew one had even been committed. In effect, it had never happened.

But what about Nate's real parents?

The father had seemed a nice enough young guy, but effete, and he drank too much. Indeed, he had been remiss in letting Nate wander that night, giving Mimi her perfect chance. Had things been different his son really might have gone into the river.

As for the mother, it was fairly clear that she was a harsh, possibly abusive parent. Mimi herself had discovered fair evidence of that. Sending the child back to such a person would be no favour. Whereas Mimi—restored to health by his very presence—would shower on him a lifetime of cherishing.

Bud therefore concluded that not only could this thing be done, it very well should. His final consideration then was the simplest: was this something he wanted? Already he'd lost one child. Though the tragedy hadn't scarred him as deeply as his wife, it had certainly left a hollow place. He'd grown used to thinking that there would never be an heir to his considerable fortune, never a son to bear his name. But now ...

A brand-new ball game.

By a twist of fate, everything was as it should be. Not only could this new situation save Mimi's sanity and their relationship, it could also give meaning to Bud's own existence in a way he'd never expected to know again. But one thing was also true. Once this step was taken there could be no turning back. If he made this child his own, nothing—not love, not logic nor the laws of God or man—would ever make him give him up again.

That was the stipulation.

By the time the sun, after its brief flirt with the valley, had dipped behind the western range, Bud had decided that there really was only one choice. He rose, stretched, headed back to the motorhome. It was parked all alone, a dark hulk that had somehow assumed the lines of expectation. Bud opened the door and went in.

The child, who was sitting at the table with milk and cookies, looked up at him with the cutest grin yet. His wife, still in the passenger seat from which she had watched and waited half the day, swivelled to face him. She didn't get up, and he caught no glimpse of the gun clutched beneath her cardigan.

With a brief smile at Mimi, Bud said, "Hey, Gabe, I'm so hungry I could eat a horse. How about you?"

"Yes, sir," the boy said obligingly. "We thought you were never coming back."

"Well, here I am. And while we're on the subject—never mind that 'sir' stuff. Till your real pa comes back—how about you call me Daddy-Bud?"

PART THREE

ONE

The Wild Rose Motel was a modest establishment on 16th Avenue, which doubled as Highway 1, passing through the heart of Calgary. John had purposely picked a spot on the outskirts, wishing for a chance to reorient himself to the burgeoning metropolis. The city seemed even larger and faster than when he'd seen it last. Before the towers of downtown were fully in view, he could feel the dynamic energy. The traffic flow was different too, somehow more brash and confident than on the coast. Piloting his nippy little MG amidst the swarm of trucks and fast cars, he imagined he could sense the pulse of the city: young, cheerful and extremely self-confident. Even the desk clerk at his motel, though friendly, looked as though he would have been equally at home in Las Vegas.

It was Wednesday evening. At the 80 KPH the MG averaged over the mountains, the thousand kilometres from Vancouver had taken a day and a half. Now he was here, with only the vaguest idea of what he was going to do next.

First, of course, he had to prove that Nate was alive. The dream and the drawing made by Mimi were food for intuition only. He couldn't go to the Calgary police and say, "Look, I think my boy's been abducted, do something." With the evidence available, the best he could expect would be a brush-off. At worst he'd be treated like a nut case—which he possibly was.

John was aware that his whole expedition might be the result of a pathetic fantasy. Nevertheless, the nearer he'd got to Alberta, the more sure he'd become that Nate was alive. But there was no way he could convince anyone else of this. Yet.

After the long drive over the Rockies, he was exhausted. If he closed his eyes, he could still see the image of an endlessly moving highway. After snatching a quick meal at a nearby café, all he desired was to lie down. But he couldn't do that. Until he'd at least begun to follow up on his solitary lead, he wouldn't be able to sleep.

Flipping through the phone book in his motel room, he immediately found what he wanted: Bow River Freight Lines, the company that Bud Wetherall had said he owned. There it was, right here in Calgary, as expected. John took down the address and phone number. Then he looked up Wetherall. No luck. Either they didn't live in the city, or they had an unlisted number.

In the motel office, John found a map and tracked down the location of the freight company. It was in Foothills Industrial Park, an area in the southeast corner of the city. Navigating there looked simple enough. Since Calgary was built on a grid of numbered avenues and streets, John figured that by continuing east on Highway 1, then turning south on Deerfoot Trail, he'd be there in no time.

That was the theory, anyway. The fact turned out to be rather different. To begin with, the traffic was horrendous. The highway through the centre of the city was under massive reconstruction and it took the best part of 30 minutes to crawl just 40 blocks. Also it was growing dark, making it hard to see street signs. Consequently, when John reached Deerfoot Trail, a freeway sweeping across the east side of town, he took the wrong entrance, finding himself going north instead of south. To get off the freeway, find a gas station, pick up the map he should have bought in the first place, figure out a way to get back on the Deerfoot in the correct direction, then struggle his way across the city took the best part of another hour. By the time the MG was meandering along the near-deserted streets of his destination, it was night. Foothills Industrial Park was huge, an entire suburb of factories, warehouses and miscellaneous industries. John's stamina was ebbing, his patience about gone. Nevertheless, when he got to the address he'd written down, he found immediately—and with vast relief that the journey was done—what he was looking for.

It was a large corner lot surrounded by a high, wire-mesh fence. A number of trucks were parked inside, and some unhitched trailers. To one side there was a freight warehouse. The front section of this was an office. Everything was closed and deserted but on the building was a clear sign: BOW RIVER FREIGHT LINES.

When he saw this, John's heart began to pound. Also, unexpectedly, he experienced a rush of apprehension. Next door, a lane led deeper into the block. It was dark, shielded from the well-lit yard by the freight office, which backed onto it. Without thinking, John swung into the lane and stopped. He cut the engine and doused the lights. His stomach was in a knot. His hands shook. Simple reaction, he knew, like stage fright, but somehow it didn't help.

Five minutes later, the shaking had stopped but now he was feeling like a fool. What was he doing, skulking in the dark? In fact, why had he come here tonight anyway? Even without messing up the route, he'd have arrived long after business hours. He must have known that before starting out.

But he'd had to come. Seeing the company name in the phone book was one thing; being here was quite another. Even though there was nothing to be done, arriving at the physical location of the only clue to Nate's vanishing made his belief more tangible, teased it into the light of real possibility. What had felt like fear was in fact exhilaration, balm for his battered soul.

This understanding brought a new sensation that was almost like peace. For the first time since he had started from the coast he felt relaxed. He stretched, aware of the subtle loosening of almost every muscle in his body. The industrial park was empty of life. The bright areas of light in some yards and under street lamps contrasted with the deep pools of dark in between, one of which contained the cocoon of John's little MG. Safe inside, he stretched again and yawned, hearing only the distant night-purr of the nearby freeway. He thought, *I'll just close my eyes for five minutes, then head back to the motel.*

Then the black took him.

TWO

Crash! Bang! Sickening assault on senses—horrific wrench into consciousness—blinding light—deafening voice. "Got you, asshole! Come on, out! Out!"

He was being dragged bodily from the MG by someone who was only a silhouette in harsh yellow light. Bud Wetherall had caught him: in his terror and shock, John was convinced of it. He should never have come here—certainly never lingered—and now it was too late …

Clearing vision revealed that at least one fear was unfounded. The gorilla manhandling him wasn't Bud. This guy wore a uniform and the light behind him came from what looked like a police car. The last time a scene like this had been played John had spent a night in jail. Now a paranoid part of him became sure that he must have been watched and followed ever since his arrival in Calgary.

"Okay, buster. Let's get a look at you."

Vice-like fingers pinioned his arm. A brighter light was flashed on his face. Squirming, he managed to talk. "Hey—stop—let me go!"

"Yeah, that'll happen. What's your name, dickhead?"

Pain finally produced anger, which brought him fully awake. He stopped struggling and twisted his face out of the flashlight beam.

This wasn't a policeman at all. The nearby vehicle, with its yellow roof light, was just a security company hack, his captor a rent-a-cop. This knowledge brought some reassurance and he said, "I haven't done anything. Take your hands off me. You're not a real cop."

The guard shook him. "Listen, shitface, this is private property. We've had a whole mess of break-ins, and I've caught you hiding in the dark. Believe it, I'm all the cop you need. Move it."

He dragged John across the alley in the direction of his car, opened the back door and shoved him in. The door slammed. The rear of the vehicle was screened from the front. It had no inside handles. John banged on the screen, which was solid steel mesh. "Hey, what the hell's going on?"

The guard heaved himself into the front seat, "You'll find out soon enough."

"Come on! Listen—you wanted my name? It's John Quarry, okay? I'm sorry I was trespassing. It was a mistake but I wasn't going to steal anything."

The guard didn't look around. He was consulting his watch, making notes on a pad. Over his shoulder he said, "Sure, Mac, and my ma's a goddamn virgin."

John started pounding on the screen. "Let me out of here, you creep. Look, you can't *do* this!"

Finally the guard did look around. He had a broad, fleshy face, like a wrestler, and—incongruous with the uniform—his hair emerged from his cap in a neat ponytail. "Oh, yeah, I can," he snapped. "Tell you somethin' else, buddy. If you don't can it, I can beat the shit out of you too." He sneered. "Then when the 'real' cops arrive, I can get 'em to charge you with criminal assault, as well as trespass. How about that?"

John calmed right down. "The police? But I thought you were taking me in."

"Hold...

call it in. Then ...

Now shut up while ...

Emphasizing his p...

radio mike.

Now John understood the rea...

indeed been abducted, it had been don...

must believe they were in the clear. But th... y. If

they got wind in advance that their plan was c... k, they

could panic. To get rid of the evidence, the child c... made to

disappear again, this time for real. Right now, John's only advantage

was surprise. If he got charged with a crime involving Bow River

Freight, his name could come to the attention of its owner, and Bud

would know that he'd been rumbled. For Nate's sake, John couldn't

let this happen.

But it seemed he was too late. His captor was already on the

radio, calling in the location and demanding to be relieved of his

burden. In frustration, John listened to the exchange. Apparently

something was happening elsewhere, involving a lot of police, so he

was told to wait. The guard grumbled about being held up from his

rounds but seemed resigned. He signed off, stretched, threw his cap

on the dashboard and pulled out cigarettes. Unexpectedly he said,

"Want a smoke, buddy?"

John was startled. "No. I don't smoke—er—thanks."

"Okay. Cool it and don't give me any more shit."

he tossed
to search for another.
watched his meaty hand fiddling
something else. Taped to the inside of the
door, visible only when it was opened, was a photo:
guard himself, a smiling woman and two pretty little girls. No
sooner had he taken this in than the big man, as if sensing the scrutiny, slammed the door shut.

And a desperate idea came into John's mind.

How much time did he have before the police arrived? Maybe only minutes. If he was going to do this, it would have to be good. It was not enough just to be convincing: to really make his audience care, this actor would have to give an extra-special performance and if he blew it, there'd be no second night. The guard might have some discretion in his actions, but the real cops certainly wouldn't. If John was mistaken in the intuition he'd got from the family photo, it was all useless, but he couldn't think about that. The only way to do this was to passionately believe it was possible. John took a deep breath. "Tell me one thing, would you please?"

The guard had finally got his cigarette lighted. "What?"

"Your name."

The guard looked surprised. "None of your damn business!"

John made his voice the essence of quiet reason: pleading but not whining, humble but, he hoped, dignified. "Look—I know this is a tough and thankless job, and I'm sorry I've made trouble for you. I'm not bullshitting or trying to be your buddy, but at least we can be civilized. Come on. It's not asking much. Just tell me your name. What could it hurt?"

The guard took drag from his cigarette. He muttered, "Earl. It's Earl. Okay?"

"Yeah. Hi, Earl—no hard feelings, eh?" From his wallet he

produced the Polaroid of himself and Nate in the Wetherall trailer. "But I would like to show you this ... "

THE INCIDENT THAT had detained the cops must have been serious for, after half an hour, blessedly, they still hadn't showed. By that time John's tale was almost told. "It was ridiculous coming here tonight," he concluded. "I knew the place would be closed, and that I couldn't find out anything till tomorrow. But I just had to see it, to make sure in my mind it really existed. I was so tired after driving all day, I must have fallen asleep. But here's the truth, Earl. I'm all by myself in this. No one—*no one*—believes my kid's alive but me. And, yeah, maybe I'm crazy. But I've got to know! And if I'm right, if Nate is alive, I'm terrified of giving myself away, because ... "

"Yeah, yeah!" The guard broke in, the first words he'd spoken. "Because of what they might do to the kid. I can see that. I'm not stupid."

There was a long pause in which John regarded the other man through the pall of tobacco smoke that now filled the car. "Does that mean you believe me?"

Earl, who'd been examining the picture of John and Nate, made a gesture that was both a nod and head shake, finally sliding the Polaroid back through the grille. "Tell you what I *do* think—that no low-life would have the smarts to make up a story like that."

"Yeah?"

Earl looked at him shrewdly. "You saw that photo of my family, eh?"

"Er—yes, I did."

"So you're hoping that I'd rather be made a sucker if you're lying than take the risk that you're not."

"Something like that. Well?"

Earl sucked in a breath, but before he could answer there was an interruption. Both men looked up to see red and blue flashing lights approaching fast along the avenue.

"Oh, no!" John said.

"Shit!" Earl echoed. Then, after a beat, "Down on the floor. Don't make an effing sound." He snatched up his cap, scrambled out of the car, slammed the door and lumbered out to meet the cruiser.

Unable to resist, John peered over the edge of the window to see what was happening. The cruiser came to a fast stop beside the guard. Earl was now standing curbside, cap pushed back, scratching his head, the very picture of anger and frustration.

Two officers emerged. In the flashing lights, John could see their smart black uniforms; two fit guys, both younger and shorter than the burly guard. There was an exchange that John couldn't hear. But he could see Earl shrugging and gesticulating, pointing to an alley on the other side of the road. One of the cops walked in that direction. But the other began to move toward the security car, shining his flashlight about. Pretty soon he'd either catch sight of John or notice the MG in the alley. Then Earl was in between, heading him off, guiding the man's attention elsewhere. At last both walked back to the cruiser. The other officer returned and the three men stood together. There was more talk, the sound of laughter: one of the cops shook his head and slapped Earl on the shoulder, an action both friendly and derisive. Then the policemen got back in the cruiser and drove away.

Earl, hands on hips, stood watching until the car rounded a corner and vanished. Then he slowly walked back. He opened the driver's door, but didn't get in. "I told 'em I didn't lock you in properly and you did a runner," he growled. "Made me look like a real stupid idiot."

"I'm sorry. Thanks!"

Earl reached for the handle that would unlock John's prison. "You better not be shittin' me, man."

"I'm not. I promise!"

"Yeah, yeah." He shoved the door handle down. "Okay, go."

With relief so vast it actually made him choke up, John got out of the car. "Thanks, Earl," he said quietly. "My boy's alive. I know it. When I find him I'll let you know."

The big man looked startled, began to smile, then caught himself. "Get lost!"

John nodded and started to move, but Earl's hand caught his shoulder in a bone-crushing grip. Heart-in-mouth, John stared. "What?"

"When you do find him—just don't fucking lose him again, eh?"

Bow River Freight was a hive of activity. Rigs were moving in and out of the yard, picking up trailers, loading and unloading at the big warehouse. In the bright light of day, it all looked businesslike and ordinary; hard to believe that such drama had taken place here mere hours ago.

As John mounted the steps to the office, he realized that if Bud Wetherall owned all of this he must be very rich indeed. Wealth meant power. More important, to have done what John suspected, he must also be entirely ruthless. If the man was to be apprehended without Nate's being harmed, it would have to be done very carefully.

John's one advantage—almost forfeited last night—was that if the Wetheralls did have Nate, they could have no idea anyone was on their trail. Until the boy's whereabouts were discovered and his safety assured, he dared not allow even a whisper of warning.

In the dispatch office, a clerk who looked like a trucker, smoking a cigarette, was tapping his fat fingers with incongruous dexterity on a computer. As John approached, he glanced up from the screen, but didn't stop typing. "Yeah, what?"

"I'm enquiring about Mr. Wetherall."

"He ain't here."

"I didn't expect he would be. But he *is* the owner, right?"

At last the clerk stopped work and favoured John with an appraising look. He had watery-blue eyes that looked the worse for a hangover. "Sure—what do you want with him? Hurry up, Charlie—I ain't playin' solitaire here."

John proceeded to tell the quick and careful tale he'd prepared. An old buddy of Bud's from BC, learning that John was coming to Alberta, had given him a package to be delivered. But they'd lost touch and the home address wasn't known, and John had promised to find it out from the company and deliver the package himself. "So all I need is Mr. Wetherall's address," John concluded, "and I won't have to waste any more of your time."

The dispatch clerk dragged on his cigarette. "The boss doesn't spend much time here. Doesn't even come up to town very often these days. But leave your package. We'll see he gets it."

John had anticipated that. "Thanks a lot." He grinned, feigning embarrassment. "But, I've got a sort of personal motive. I'm moving to Alberta, you see, and my friend thought, as a favour to him, Mr. Wetherall might help me get started. I'd like to deliver it personally, if possible."

The clerk looked amused. "Yeah? Well, good luck with that." He suddenly frowned. "Hey!"

"What?"

"I'm thinkin'—haven't I seen you somewhere?"

"I don't think so. I've never—"

"TV. Yeah, that's it. You look like this guy on TV."

John was startled. He wasn't a big enough star to be recognized constantly, but it did happen now and then. His last television stint had been in a series that was basically a soap, hardly the fare of trucker types, though you could never tell what guys watched when their pals weren't looking. But since the truth was at odds with his tale of wanting work, this could be awkward. Fortunately, he had a tactic that he'd used before with autograph hunters. "Oh, man!" He blurted, feigning embarrassment. "Not you too!"

"What?"

"I'm always getting that—being mistaken for some stupid actor. But I'm not that guy, believe me."

The clerk shrugged. "Sure—no offence."

"None taken. Now—you reckon you could tell me how to find Mr. Wetherall?"

"Sure. How well do you know the area?"

"Not well."

"Bud's ranch is quite a ways out. Half a day's drive if you want to know."

"That's okay."

"You'd better take a look here."

The man grabbed John's arm and steered him to a large map of southern Alberta on the wall. Nearly asphyxiating him with cigarette smoke, treating him now like one of his more stupid drivers, he pointed out where John had to go. It was all obvious and thoroughly over-explained.

But it was the trail again.

TWO HUNDRED KILOMETRES south of Calgary, a straight shoot down Highway 2, was the town of Cardston. A short distance west from there, near the US border and almost in the shadow of the Rocky Mountains, was his destination.

John entered Cardston slightly before noon. The place was bland and prosperous, filled with neat houses and shade trees, a typical Alberta foothills community, with one exception: on a rise, overlooking the town like a sentinel, there was what looked like a monstrous stone palace. Had he been in the mood to be a tourist, he would have detoured for a closer look. But urgency was growing as he neared his goal and, besides, he was starving. He stopped at a restaurant to have some lunch while he planned how to proceed.

The Wetherall place, he'd been told, was a ranch in the foothills west of Cardston, on a side road that led off Highway 5, the route to Waterton Lakes National Park. The turnoff was at a tiny hamlet called Elk Corners and a short distance south was the entrance to the ranch, which he would recognize by the name BAR STAR on an arch over the drive. Easy enough to find, apparently. What John didn't know was if the Wetheralls had come back home yet.

Or how—without warning them—he was going to find out.

"You want a menu?" Unnoticed during John's cogitations, a waitress had arrived. She was a pretty, blond thing, little more than 16, with an expression that managed to transmit both boredom and superiority.

"Oh, hey!" John said. "No menu. I'll just have a burger—a cheeseburger would be good."

The girl didn't crack a smile. She probably knew John was a stranger—hardly surprising in a town this size. "Soup, salad or fries?"

"Fries, thanks."

"Anything to drink?"

It was hot. The drive from Calgary across the summer-baked prairie had illustrated his MG's only real drawback: the English contempt for the notion of air-conditioning. So he was parched. "Yeah, I'll have a beer."

The young waitress's mouth pursed. She looked shocked. "No beer," she said crisply.

"What?"

"I said, we don't serve beer."

Her tone said more than that they didn't stock the stuff. John couldn't resist the urge to tease. "Then I guess I'll have to settle for wine. What do you have?"

The girl took half a step back, definitely not amused. "No beer *or* wine. This is a dry town, mister."

John could hardly believe his ears. "Really? I've never heard of such a thing."

"This is a *Mormon* town!" The girl's face stiff with teenage-sanctimony. "And this is Mormon country. But I suppose you never heard of Mormons either?"

Suddenly it all clicked: the scrubbed, almost prim look of the place, the stone edifice on the edge of town—not a palace but a temple. Mormon country! Well, well? Did that mean the Wetheralls were Mormons? Is that why they lived way down here in the shadow of the Rockies? He knew little about the sect, but enough to be sure that they were a tight-knit bunch. Outsiders might not always be treated with the open contempt of this child, but would surely be given short shrift if they made trouble. Not that he thought that they would openly condone kidnapping. But if the Wetheralls *were* Mormons (and being wealthy, perhaps major players) and Nate was seen as being rescued from the heathen, what kind of leeway, or protection, might not be forthcoming? Mere speculation, of course, but a factor that could not be ignored. For all he knew, he might have stumbled into a whole wasp's nest of Wetherall's allies. Until he learned otherwise, he'd have to be extra careful. All of this whizzed through John's mind at lightspeed, concluding with a wave of appreciation for his stern admonisher.

"I'm sorry," John said, trying to sound contrite. "Of course I've heard of Mormons. I didn't mean to seem disrespectful. Tell you what—I think I'll take that burger to go. A large Coke as well. And thanks for all your help."

The girl looked confused. "How did I help you?"

"It doesn't matter. It's a long story. But thanks anyway."

AFTER LEAVING CARDSTON, Highway 5 snaked west toward the
Rockies. John was struck by how different they looked from this
direction. The majesty of the largest mountain chain was mitigated
by all that had gone before, when approached from the west, through
the rumpled stone quilt that was British Columbia. But from Alberta,
with just the prairie and rolling foothills as prologue, the effect was
literally high drama. All along the southwest horizon the behemoths
stretched, a purple-gray, snaggle-toothed wall, splashed at higher elevations with dazzling white. John was put in mind of the first explor-
ers in this land who, having slogged their way across a vast continent of
hostile terrain, starved and exhausted, were finally confronted by *this*.
He could imagine their horror and awe at the sight, an almost tangible
presence that added a new urgency to his quest.

In the summer afternoon, the countryside shimmered with
heat. The land was gently rolling, but rising, broken increasingly by
shallow draws that deepened into ravines topped by lines of ragged
buttes. This was cattle country, yellow grass and sage and, at higher
elevations, packed stands of dwarf aspen. On the opposite side, away
from the mountains, the earth flowed east into the grain-covered
prairie. Dividing the two was the highway that led toward Waterton
Park and, inexorably, the end of his journey.

After about 20 kilometres, John came over the brow of a hill
to see a settlement up ahead: a house, store and gas station at the
junction of a crossroad. Elk Corners, a small sign informed him only
just in time.

As instructed, John turned left, heading south. The road,
unpaved but in good shape, curved steadily up to the crest of a small
hill, then dropped into a long, shallow valley on the other side.

About a kilometre ahead, before the road vanished around a bend, was a shallow stream bed, hosting a stand of aspen and taller cottonwood trees. As he continued, John began to catch glimpses of a house up beyond. It was large, modern, built of richly stained wood, perched above the valley. More trees surrounded it snugly in a cool nest of shade.

As the road descended, drawing nearer, the house disappeared from view but he was approaching the entrance to the ranch. In the shadow of a big cottonwood, he drew to a halt. The driveway had a wooden arch, as described, with the legend BAR STAR carved in the middle. There was a cattle guard but no gate. On a mailbox to one side was a single word: WETHERALL.

He had arrived.

But without driving right up to the house, he couldn't even see whether the motorhome had returned. So what now?

He heard a sound from behind and turned to look. A vehicle had appeared over the hill, following the route he'd just driven. It came on fast, a 4x4 with its top down, kicking up a great cloud of dust. John glimpsed the outline of a broad hat and dark glasses, as the sun-baked driver whipped his vehicle in an engine-howling approach that would send it zipping by at speed.

Hurriedly John lifted a map and lowered his head, pretending to scan it. He didn't want his real objective to be obvious even to a casual passerby. The jeep drew level. The engine roared in a double-clutch change down. There was a sharp drop in noise and, peering around his map, John saw the speed of the vehicle decreasing rapidly. It passed him and veered right, heading for the Wetherall entrance.

Over his map, John observed the jeep come to a halt with its front wheels on the cattle guard. He heard the rasping click of a handbrake. The jeep's door opened. The broad-hatted driver slid out. Riding boots scuffled on the road, then the figure appeared at his window.

"Hey, mister—you lost?"

John looked around, at first seeing only glasses and hat and a smooth, tanned jaw.

But the voice had been that of a woman.

And not Mimi Wetherall.

FOUR

John's heart had begun to beat hard, but he swallowed, forced his voice into sounding casual and took the plunge.

"No. As a matter of a fact, I'm looking for Mr. Bud Wetherall."

The woman nodded, stood back and took off her glasses. As a contrast to the tanned skin, her eyes were blue-green and piercing. Wisps of dark hair peeped from under her hat. The sleeves of her checked shirt, rolled to the elbow, revealed round but solid forearms. On her left wrist was a old-fashioned man's watch with a leather cap covering the dial. Jeans and a western belt completed her attire. She looked somewhere between 20 and ageless.

"I'm sorry, mister," she said. "I reckon you missed him."

John swallowed again, trying not to blink at those piercing eyes. "Gone into town?"

The girl grinned. It was barely more than a lift of the upper lip, but it did a considerable service for her carved-looking features. "Not into town. Bud and the missus are on holiday. Gone three weeks, likely be a heap more. Anything I can do?"

So they weren't here, might not be back for a long time. Of course John had known that was possible, but until this moment he hadn't let himself face it.

However, it was so. And the only clue as to where they might be was probably right here. John stifled his disappointment and said, "I sure hope you *can* help me, miss. Are you a friend of Mr. Wetherall's—maybe one of the family?"

The girl eyed him levelly. "Bud doesn't have family, except his wife. I run his place and look after the house when they're away. If I can help you, I will."

"Thanks," John said, deciding to keep his story as close to the truth as possible. "You see, I've come all the way from Vancouver."

The girl gave his little red car a glance that spoke volumes. "Vancouver? Today?"

"Not exactly. I started out a couple of days ago. But I had no idea where he lived, so I had to go to Calgary—to his trucking company—to find out. I guess you could say I sort of came the long way around."

She grinned. "No kidding. You look kind of like a well-dressed lizard that's been frying on a rock, if you don't mind me saying so. You best come up the house."

She turned and clicked her way back to the jeep. He got into the MG and followed her up the drive. Up close the house was even bigger than he'd thought, a foothills mansion.

They introduced themselves at the door; the girl's name was Libby McGrew. As John accompanied her into the house, the image of his son playing and growing up within these walls caught him unawares. So overwhelming was the reaction that he stopped dead, eyes closed. Man—suddenly he missed the little guy so much.

"Are you okay?"

He opened his eyes to find Libby staring at him. "Yes," he said hurriedly. "It's only the sudden cool."

With a head-beckon as brusque as a man's, Libby moved into the living room. This was large and comfortable and dim, with an enormous stone fireplace, heavy-beamed ceiling and deep pine furniture. Under a striking painting of a round-up in a Western sunset, there was a wet bar. Libby quickly found two cans of beer, tossing him one. "Here, John. That should put back some of the sweat ... What?"

Looking at the beer, John had suddenly remembered the waitress in Cardston. *This is a dry town ... Mormon country.* Now he was recalling the wine that had flowed that night in the Wetherall motorhome, something he had entirely forgotten. Since Mormons didn't drink, Bud could hardly be one of them: at least one worry was put to rest. "Oh," John said quickly, "I was just thinking what a relief it is to be—er—finally out of the car and holding a cool one. Thanks."

"You're very welcome. So ... how can I help you?"

LIBBY MCGREW, JOHN discovered, was one of the most refreshingly frank and straightforward women he'd ever met. She had what John thought of as an open, country manner, quite a contrast to the slick city girls he usually came in contact with, and he found himself liking her a lot. Were it not for the necessity of finding Nate, he would have felt guilty at the tale he felt obliged to concoct.

Back in BC—so the story went—his father owned a parcel of land by a lake in the Okanagan. Bud, on his way through, had seen the land and made his dad a handsome offer. His dad had refused and Bud had moved on. But in fact the stubborn old man was going broke, and later regretted not selling to the Albertan. He knew nothing about him, except that he owned a trucking company in Calgary. Being headed back east to Toronto anyway, John had offered to try to track down Bud on his way through ...

"And that's it," John concluded. "When I picked up the address, they couldn't tell me if he was back or not. So I came down, hoping

I'd be lucky. Now, my last chance is that maybe *you* can tell me where to find him."

She couldn't. Libby McGrew had no idea where her boss was, nor when he would be returning. And why should she lie? He'd made his story simple, and she appeared to believe it. But one of her responses gave him a surprise.

"I'm sorry you came so far, John. Especially since I can't help you. But I gotta tell you—that may be no bad thing."

"That I can't contact him?"

"Yeah. I'll be straight with you. My boss may be real rich, but he's also been having a pretty hard time."

John was surprised. "With money?"

"No sir, with his personal life. I know you're a stranger, but since you've gone to all this trouble I don't see why I shouldn't tell you the truth. You see, it took Bud and his wife, Mimi, forever to have a baby. But in the end it happened—a boy they called Gabriel. Well, 18 months ago, there was a terrible accident. Little Gabe was run over. Killed. Mrs. Wetherall has never been the same. Depressed. Mourning night and day over that lost child."

John began to feel very excited. When he'd met Mimi, she hadn't been depressed at all, but a regular life of the party. Her husband had admitted she'd been deeply affected by the death of their own child, and had been surprised at the change in her. What would be more likely to cause such a change than if she'd decided to get herself another child.

Nate, for instance?

"Buying that mobile hotel and taking a road trip was like a last-ditch stand," Libby continued. "Bud was desperate. Grasping at straws. If he told your dad he wanted to buy his land, it was probably because poor Mimi liked the smell of the air there. But I wouldn't count on that offer holding now. I'm sorry I can't tell you where Bud is but I reckon that's going to save you a heap more trouble. You want another beer?"

John did. The first one had vanished like magic and he still felt hot. As she brought it, he felt the urge to drop the pretense and confide in Libby completely, but held back. This girl not only worked for the Wetheralls, she was obviously tough minded and loyal. She might not be related, but that didn't necessarily mean she wouldn't consider herself one of the family. So the fact that he was Nate's father—even if he could prove it—didn't mean that Libby, for all her straightforwardness, would immediately become an ally. If he trusted her and she betrayed him, warning her employers, it would be too late: he'd have lost that one small advantage he possessed.

He did not confess anything to Libby. He let himself be apparently convinced by her information. But he had realized something else: even though Libby didn't know Bud's whereabouts, this house might yet hold the key. For instance, if any phone company or credit-card bills had arrived recently, they could give locations from which Bud had phoned home or where he had bought gas. Any information like that, however meagre, would be better than what he now had. A single clue might be enough to pick up the trail.

He had to find some way to stick around.

"So LONG, John," Libby McGrew said. "Sorry I couldn't help. Have a safe trip to Toronto."

"Thanks."

She again gave the MG that not exactly flattering look of appraisal. "You reckon *this* is gonna get you there in once piece?"

John grew indignant. His real father, born in England—not the mythical gent with the land for sale—had imbued him with a love for little European cars. But he was also familiar with a certain North American mindset, especially among the drivers of pickups and

SUVs, that regarded such vehicles as toys. It annoyed him but also gave him a timely idea. In response to Libby's question, he looked sheepish. "I sure hope so. She was giving a little trouble over the mountains. But I think she's okay now. Goodbye!"

He got into the car and pulled the starter, at the same time pulling the choke right out and flooring the accelerator. The car usually flooded if he did that, and he prayed it would happen this time.

It did. The engine whined over and over, and there was a smell of gas. To make sure, he pumped the pedal briskly several more times.

John gave a theatrical curse, got out, opened the hood and began his charade. He just had time to pull out the central distributor wire from the coil—thus effectively killing the ignition system—before Libby was at his shoulder.

"Trouble?" the girl said. But she was looking the car over critically, and with little surprise, he sensed she was no novice with engines. Fortunately, he'd left the disconnected lead still sticking into the coil-cover, so only the most careful inspection would reveal it.

"Carburetor," John said. "Float's sticking, I think. It's the one thing I don't like about this model."

"Well, wouldn't you know it'd kick up when it's the most trouble. Like horses and kids."

"You've got kids?"

"No!" Libby said quickly, and with surprising heat. "It was just a way of talking. You got tools?"

"Not many."

"Really? Driving around in this country in a car like that, without even … I don't know!"

Before he realized what was happening she'd gone to the nearby 4x4 and hauled out a tool box. "Okay—let's look at that damn fool carburetor."

"Er—don't you have things to do?"

"Nothing that can't wait." Libby set to work.

John stood back and watched. He felt guilty but nonetheless determined in his purpose.

SHE STRIPPED THE carburetor down to its individual parts, soaked, cleaned and checked them and put the whole thing back together again. She didn't even seem to notice the boiling heat. It took her three hours.

John stood back and watched—she brushed off any help, save for ordering him to bring more beer from the house—and wondered not only at the mechanical talent but at the single-mindedness of this unusual young woman. He realized she would make a wonderful ally. And a worse enemy.

When the carburetor was reinstalled the sun had sunk to the edge of the Rockies. While Libby took a last swig of beer, John quietly pushed the lead back into its socket in the coil. He didn't have the heart not too.

The engine started at the first turn of the key. Incredibly, it sounded better than he ever remembered. John was feeling a complicated mixture of emotions: at once grateful to Libby, admiring of her, guilty but determined not to loosen his tenuous hold on this house.

Hold on, Nate, he said to himself grimly. *Hold on, kiddo!* John stopped the engine, thanked Libby and expressed his very genuine admiration. Then he said, "Now it's my turn. I'm going to take you into town for dinner."

She looked astonished. "Oh, no, John. You don't have to do that."

"I want to. I need to." And then, as she was still reluctant, he gave her his most engaging smile and added, "I've just taken up your whole afternoon, and seen an exhibition of mechanical skill

that'd make most guys feel like idiots. You've got to let me off the
hook here."

She grinned. "Is that what *you* feel—an idiot?"

"No! I'm an actor. I'm used to working with women who're good
at their jobs. I'm no chauvinist but I do feel I owe you. Let me take
you to dinner."

She gave him a fixed stare, which turned into the pleasantest
smile he'd seen yet. "So you're an actor?"

"Yes."

"Is that why you're on your way to Toronto?"

"Yes."

"I've never met an actor before. But then, I just about never watch
movies or TV." Libby looked at the MG, then back at him. "Look,
John—we've got a lot better meat right here in the freezer than anything closer than the Beef House in Claresholm. And I sure as hell
don't feel like driving all the way there. So why don't we eat here?"

That was even better, but he heard himself saying, "How can I
repay you by also eating your food?"

"Well—how are actors in the kitchen?"

"On the whole, not too shabby!"

"Okay, you get to cook."

JOHN DID EXACTLY that.

Libby took him back inside, got them both some more beers
and showed him the kitchen. This was as huge as the rest of the
house. Beside it was a freezer, so big it was really a small room. In
it were whole sides of beef, along with shelves loaded with various
cuts of meat. Libby selected a great slab of steak, showed him the
microwave, the stove, the outside barbecue, the bin of potatoes and
the refrigerator with salad fixings.

She went off to change. He set to work.

It was all a great success. The beef, though cooked by himself, turned out to be the best he'd ever eaten. The wine she produced to go with it was excellent. They ate in a kitchen nook big enough to serve meals for a Mormon convention. And—despite the areas of his life that had to be skirted around—they had exhilarating talk.

At 10:00 he looked at his watch, realizing that he'd had a terrific evening, no small irony, considering the circumstances. A little later, Libby said, "John, this has been great but I'm on the cowhand's clock. I've got to hit the hay. C'mon, and I'll show you your room."

"Room?" By now he was feeling pretty disgusted with his charade.

"Well—I sure don't expect you to find a motel this time of night. And I reckon you're not dumb enough to figure you'd be bunking with me. So come on."

She led the way through the living room and down into the west wing of the house, to a small room with bright chintz curtains and a single bed.

"Bathroom's next door," Libby said. "You'll find everything you need. Wake any time you've a mind. But I reckon you actors don't get up with the birds, eh?"

Briskly, the tall girl with the piercing eyes turned down the bed and opened a window, striding about like a cheerful hostess, as natural with this as when she'd worked on the MG. She finished her tour and turned at the door. "Well John , I'm sorry you've had a wild-goose chase. But I'm glad you came anyway. I had a great time." She grinned. "Even enjoyed fixing your dinky little motor car. Good night."

Libby exited the room; the good feeling of her seemed to linger long after she'd departed.

John was left alone.

FIVE

John put the light out and lay fully clothed under the covers.

He hated what he was going to do. Also, he was distinctly nervous. The idea of creeping around this big house in the dark looking for clues as to the whereabouts of the Wetheralls was not only hazardous, it was rapidly coming to seem futile. But as long as there was the smallest possibility of its helping to find Nate, he knew he had to go ahead. He lay in the dark and waited.

When the light went out it had been 11:00. He decided that he'd give Libby plenty of time to get deeply asleep and not move a muscle until midnight. The glowing face of his watch now showed just after 11:30.

Bud Wetherall owned more than Bow River Freight. He had other business interests, so she'd said. John had the feeling that the ranch itself was more of a hobby, but presumably there was some kind of office here. John hadn't seen enough of the house to even guess where it might be; he'd just have to search. In fact it wasn't all that dark. The moon must be up, for a steady glow came through the curtains. He would be able to move about the house with reasonable ease.

John was thinking about that when, without any awareness of

the transition, he wasn't thinking at all. After a timeless interval, he opened his eyes. He had no idea what was happening or indeed, where he was. He sat up, peering around in the dimness of a strange room, and it all came flooding back. He must have dropped off. Anxiously, he peered at his watch. 4:15. He'd been out for nearly five hours.

John shot out of bed and stood quivering in the dark. What was the matter with him? Never mind, no time for recriminations—he had to get *going*. He moved across the room, realized he wasn't wearing shoes, decided he'd be better off without them, opened the bedroom door. The passage beyond was dim, but he could see its outlines clearly enough. His room was at the end of the wing, so there was only one way to go. Immediately he came upon the bathroom. A few yards farther on was another door. Ajar.

John stopped, listened. Nothing. He slowly pushed the door open. Peering inside, he saw immediately that this wasn't an office. There was the outline of a bed, and from it came a sigh and a creaking movement that—miraculously—was not repeated. Libby, in the bed, had turned in her sleep. And here he was standing like an openmouthed moron, less than a dozen feet away.

Heart thudding, he retreated backward, fumbled the door shut, remembered it had been ajar, corrected that, finally fled down the hall. He stopped, breathing shallowly, but also feeling relieved. At least he knew where Libby was so he could get on with his search with a little more speed.

Farther along the hall were two more rooms, each larger than the last, both of which turned out to be bedrooms. Then on the right John came to an intersecting corridor. This led off to the master suite. There were two bedrooms here, with a bathroom and dressing room in between. Bud and Mimi's private place.

There was a little more light here. John went into one bedroom, smelling soap and perfume, figuring that room had been inhabited by the dark-eyed Mimi, whom he had only known as vivacious and full of life, but who must, if what he'd heard were true, have wandered here like a lost soul. The dressing room had her things at one end, his at the other. There was a great deal of clothing—the wardrobe of folks who had everything.

Except a child.

Coming out into Bud's bedroom John saw that it was neat and bare. On the bedside table there was a single object: a picture in a standing frame. John picked it up and took it to the brighter moonlight by the window. It was a photo of a boy about three or four. He had straight brown hair, brown eyes and a beautiful little round face.

He was the image of Nate.

Understanding flooded through John, and for the first time, bitter rage. Why anger now? Because the sight of that little look-alike had at last made him completely sure. The Wetheralls had Nate all right. The picture told him so.

But being sure wasn't the same as having proof. And now he realized that what was illuminating the picture in his hands was not moonlight but the dawn.

Quickly he put the picture back and got out of the master suite. The corridor outside was now markedly lighter. He moved swiftly through a number of rooms, none anything like what he sought, coming at last into the living room. Beyond was the kitchen and beside that the big freezer, which made up the east end of the house. Then he saw there was one more possibility; on the far side of the kitchen was a short corridor.

He quickly crossed the kitchen, glimpsing hanging carcasses through the double-glass window in the freezer door. Around a corner the corridor led to an outside entrance. But beside it was yet another door. Closed.

John tried the handle. It opened readily. He found a small room with a single window. There was a desk, a computer, a couple of filing cabinets, a bookcase and shelves of papers.

Jackpot!

He started on the filing cabinets. They were not locked and he pulled open the top drawer of the nearest. Files: contracts, correspondence, survey maps. Nothing useful here. He turned his attention to the desk, considered turning on the computer. There might be e-mails, but if any gave a clue to Bud's whereabouts, surely Libby would have told him. The desk was bare except for two trays, left and right: an in-tray and out-tray, like a regular office. The in-tray held a mess of papers.

John took the tray to the window. On top was a heap of unopened mail. He riffled through it, and almost right away came up with an envelope with the neat blue symbol of Visa.

Double jackpot!

John put aside the tray, peered at the envelope. The light was now almost that of sunrise, bright enough to read. The postmark was only days old: Good—just what he needed.

CLICK.

Sharp, metallic, the sound came from right behind him. "What the hell are you up to, mister?"

He spun like a released spring.

Libby McGrew was standing in the doorway. Dawn light—the "cowhand's clock" that she'd warned would wake her—glinted on the thing she held with practised ease: a 12-gauge shotgun.

Pointed right at his gut.

SIX

"**For God's sake,** don't shoot that thing!"

Libby McGrew's face was pale with an intensity of anger that John had rarely witnessed. She raised the gun, pointing it at the widest part of his chest, and took a step forward.

"You mean, conniving bastard," she whispered. "You took advantage of me. Stole food and hospitality, and all you really wanted was to damn well get in *here*."

John had heard that hell had no fury like a woman scorned. In this case "a woman tricked" seemed more appropriate.

"All you were doing was using me to get something against my boss. Mister, I could shoot you right now—blow your head off your shoulders—and no one round here would do anything but shake my hand."

That was probably a bit extreme but he already knew Libby well enough to understand she was not one for half measures. She was so thoroughly furious that provoking her further could certainly be very dangerous. Whatever he said, he'd better make it count.

"I wasn't trying to get anything against Bud. I was just trying to find out where he might be."

That surprised her into a bitter laugh. "Do you think I'm that stupid? You don't have land to sell."

"Ah, that *was* a lie, I admit it. But in any case, I've got to find him."

"Why? You some kind of hit man? Someone in the Teamsters put a contract out on Bud?"

"Don't be ridiculous," John gasped. "Do I look like a hit man? I want to get back something. Something he stole from me."

Libby laughed again. "Stole? From *you*? Mister, Bud Wetherall is goddamn filthy rich. What could you have that he would want?"

Now there was nothing for it. John closed his eyes and took the plunge. Quietly he said, "I'm talking about my son."

HE TOLD HER the lot.

Everything, from the time he and Nate had started out on their holiday. By the time he finished, it seemed that the anger had drained out of Libby. But she hadn't moved—or shifted the aim of the shotgun.

The sun was sliding a weak beam through the office window when John finally said, "That's it. That's what I'm doing and why I'm here. I'm sorry I tricked you but you see, I had to."

There was a pause—very long. Finally John said, "Come on, at least you can see I'm not a thief. Or out to kill your boss. So would you please stop pointing that thing at me?"

She lowered the gun, took a step back, but didn't take her eyes off him. At last she said, "I reckon I believe you."

"Okay—will you help me?"

"I mean, I believe *you* believe that what you've told me is true. But is that all?"

"All?"

"You've got no proof that my boss kidnapped your boy or that he's even alive."

"I don't need any."

"You may not," she said levelly. "But I know Bud Wetherall. He'd never do a thing like you say. I'm sorry. You've obviously been through a terrible time. If I were you, I might believe some pretty strange things too."

Her words hit him like a physical blow. All this time he'd been worrying about convincing her he was on the level, but that wasn't necessary. He was genuine, oh yes—she simply thought him crazy.

Confronted with that realization, goaded by fatigue, frustration and bitter disappointment, John suddenly lost control entirely. He heard a strange sound coming from himself, a low moan, wrenched from his gut. A red haze blurred the centre of his vision, blocking out Libby's face, and he walked into that haze, his hands lifting to clutch and rend and destroy.

She backed off. He followed her out of the office and down the corridor. Then came a shattering roar. In the enclosed space the sound was so loud it felt like a physical blow. For a moment John believed that part of himself had been torn away. His vision cleared. Looking down, he discovered his body to be miraculously intact. He was now in the corridor, in the entrance to the kitchen, beside the door to the freezer.

Confronting him, one barrel smoking, stood Libby. Between them a six-inch circle of floor had been torn into splinters. A warning shot this might have been, but now the gun was once more aimed at his gut. And John had no doubt that her next action would be to spread his bloody entrails over half the house.

Their eyes met. Locked. Then Libby glanced briefly off to the side and a new determination came to her face. She moved to the huge freezer and threw the door open. Vapour from the Arctic interior drifted between them.

"Get in!"

"What?"

Libby jabbed the shotgun toward the freezer, her voice almost a scream. "*In!*"

John didn't argue. Ears still ringing from the shotgun blast, he edged sideways toward the freezer. The door swung around smartly and shoved him the rest of the way. John pitched forward onto the concrete floor. As he landed on hands and knees, there was a solid thump followed by the clang of the latch coming down.

Then no more sound at all.

John scrambled to his feet, stumbled in a blind panic to the door. Looking out the double-glass window was like peering through the porthole of a ship. Through it he could just see a part of the kitchen. Libby was standing with her back turned, facing the wall. For the life of him he could not understand what she was doing. He pounded on the freezer door. The sound didn't go through, or she ignored it, for she gave no indication of having heard.

Shock had numbed him momentarily, but now that was wearing off, as the biting cold was sinking in. He pounded harder. The heavy sheet metal was death-cold, and the pain in his knuckles gradually penetrated the fog of his mounting fear. He stopped pounding, then Libby moved and turned. He saw that she'd been talking on a wall phone. She put down the receiver and, without a glance back, walked out of the kitchen, leaving him alone like a trapped rat.

At that point, claustrophobia and fear and the raw cold clamped down on him all at once. Much worse was the realization that came as a climax to this. It was over. John was wearing no shoes. He was dressed only in a light shirt, pants and socks, imprisoned in near-dark in a frigid dungeon. And he had failed.

He knew what Libby had been doing. She'd phoned the police to say that there was a crazy man in the house. They'd think he was crazy too, so the best he could expect was to be stuffed into a straightjacket, the worst to be charged with burglary and assault and God-knows-what, while Bud Wetherall had all the warning he needed to get rid of the evidence.

John felt sick. He could feel precious body heat draining from every pore. Instinct made him sit, draw his knees up to his chest and clasp them with rapidly numbing fingers. If he was kept for long in this place, he would soon come to resemble one of the sides of beef that hung like pale corpses from the hooks above.

Then another thought came, even more chilling than the freezer air. What if that phone call had not been to the police at all? What if Libby thought him neither fool nor madman but had actually believed him. If so, that could only mean one thing: she meant to help her boss.

She might have known where Bud could be contacted all the time and the call she'd made could have been to him. What would Bud have told her to do? It was obvious. If he didn't want to be charged with abduction, if he wanted to keep Nate and avoid going to prison, there was only one thing he could have said: keep John where he was. Leave that door closed until the prisoner became a corpse, as easily disposed of as any chunk of frozen meat.

When he finally understood this, sitting in a rapidly stiffening ball on the freezer floor, he let out a low moan and at the same time became aware of something else: he was having trouble breathing. But this, he was surprised to find, didn't bother him too much. What did it matter, after all, whether asphyxiation got him or freezing? Either way, death was equally permanent. The anguish, which only a moment before had made him moan, now faded. He was filled with a strange peace that did not waver even when he understood that in itself it might very well herald the end.

In this new mood he came to a final understanding. The hunt for his son had been a fantasy, a delusion built on evidence so flimsy as to be laughable. He'd done it because he was not strong enough to face a reality that everyone else had understood from the start: Nate was dead, with a father who was nothing more or less than a blind fool. It was fatal irony that only now, when it was too late, this should become clear. But it didn't matter. He didn't care.

The shortness of breath no longer bothered him. Cold had moved through pain into a numbness that slipped into a pleasant lassitude. Everything slowed down, dark grew darker, the window that let in the glow of the outside retreated farther and farther— becoming inconsequential ...

The only thing that mattered now was Nate.

Nate—was dead—and—that was good—because soon—soon he would be joining him ...

So good—great—together ...

Together forever ...

Himself—Nateself—allself—all—all togeth ... tooooooooo ...

"JOHN—*JOHN*—JOOOOOOOOOOHN!!!!"

Light!

"John— please—please wake up!"

Pain!

"John—come on—come on, you can make it—please!"

Moving inside—something pushing stuff—inside him—hot-ness in throat—in chest—in—out—in—out—in ...

"Ahhhhhh ..."

"That's it, John—you're doing it—you're breathing. Oh—dear God—*John*!"

Sudden violence inside. He had to cough—to throw his insides outside—had to ...

"Aahhhgghh!"

Pain shot through his chest in waves. Air rushed violently in and out, refreshing and nauseating, relieving and torturing. Tingling warmth, spreading, painful yet wonderful, blending with the light, the life, the awakening, the reality of …

John opened his eyes.

He was lying somewhere—on a floor. Someone—Libby—was holding him—massaging—caressing. Her face was inches from his own. Her eyes, contracted into slits of worry, smiled as they met his clearing gaze.

"John," Libby McGrew whispered. "John, you're all right—you're going to be okay. Oh, John—I'm sorry. *I'm so sorry!*"

PART FOUR

ONE

After she had slammed the freezer door, imprisoning the deranged man, Libby felt so relieved she almost fainted. The crazy damn fool. If she hadn't had the freezer to fall back on, she might really have had to wound him. She knew she'd put up a pretty tough show but the idea of shooting someone, of bloodily wrecking a real human being with a short-range blast of buckshot, was so appalling she felt nauseated. She went to the wall phone and dialed the Cardston RCMP. At last a sleepy voice came on the line.

"RCMP."

"Hello—this is Libby McGrew at the Wetherall place."

The voice woke up. "Hi there, Libby. This is Lyall Petty. What can I do for you so early?"

That made things a bit easier. Constable Petty was an old friend, but for now she figured she'd best keep it simple. "Hi, Lyall. Reckon I've caught an intruder."

"Come again, Libby?"

"An intruder—a burglar—whatever. I've—er—got him cornered out here. And I need someone to come out and take care of him."

"Christ almighty! You okay, Lib?"

"Sure, I'm fine."

"You alone?"

She began to feel exasperated. "Except for this guy, yeah. Look Lyall, will you get someone to come help me?"

"Well, of course! You say you've got the guy cornered?"

"Yeah. I managed to—kinda shut him up."

Her old friend was beginning to sound awestruck. "I always did say you'd be a mean gal to cross."

"Look, I don't know how long I can keep him. Hurry, will you?"

"Sure, Lib, I'll get on to Waterton and get them to send someone from there."

"How long?"

"Half-hour—40 minutes tops."

"Thanks, Lyall. I'll be waiting."

"Okay. Lib?"

"What?"

"How did you manage to get the drop on him?"

"Never mind that now, Lyall," she snapped. "Will you please hurry?"

"Okay. We're on it."

Libby put the phone down, but relief did not lessen her tension. If anything, it grew. Right behind her, secure but beginning to freeze, was the young man who had insinuated himself into her life the day before.

She realized he was probably at the freezer door, peering through, perhaps pleading, though there was no way she could hear. If she turned now she would see his anguished face through the glass. If so, what would she do?

Deciding she didn't want to find out, Libby deliberately turned away, leaving the kitchen. She went quickly to her room and dressed. Half an hour, Lyall had said. Well, half an hour in the freezer wouldn't be pleasant, but John would probably be all right.

Then, catching herself thinking of him by his first name, Libby became newly angry. He wasn't just "John," a young guy who'd seemed so pleasant and kind that she'd found herself really liking him. The truth was he was either a conniving bastard or a maniac. And if he was cold and scared, locked away in the dark amongst the meat, it served him damn well right. Nonetheless, she decided to walk down and wait for the squad car by the road. That way she could ride with them right round to the kitchen entrance and save some time.

When she got to the gate no police car was yet in sight. She walked up and down, beginning to feel fretful. What on earth was she worrying about? He was all right, damn it. She heard the sound of an engine but from the wrong direction: up the valley. It turned out to be a pickup, driven by a hand she knew. He threw a wave as he passed.

She began to feel stupid, standing there like a little kid, waiting for the Mounties to rescue her when she'd already done the tough stuff. Irritated, she walked back to the house, going in the back way. This brought her past Bud's office, where she'd caught her intruder.

Libby paused, anger rising again as she recalled the way she'd found him, snooping about like a thief. That story he'd told: looking for his child? Yeah, right! She started to turn away, then her eye lighted on the computer. She hadn't checked e-mails for a couple of days. While awaiting the cavalry she might as well do something useful. She booted the computer, clicking on the Oulook Express icon. The screen came up and a bunch of mail came in, the last being from her boss.

Unaccountably, Libby's heart rate increased. That was illogical, since there was no reason why Bud shouldn't check in. But the bumping inside kept on as she clicked open the message and began to read …

THE PATROL CAR came over the hill with its lights flashing. It screeched to a halt by the gate, scattering gravel. A figure was standing in the middle of the driveway, barring the way.

The constable stuck his head out the window. "It's okay, miss. Sorry we took so long."

Libby ran around to the side of the car. Her face was flushed. "What kept you?"

"We had to … "

"You're too late. He's escaped."

"Where?" yelled the driver.

Libby waved back along the road. "That way—blue Chevy—Saskatchewan plates, I think. Didn't he pass you?" The Mountie shook his head. "Well, he's gone. I ran down here to warn you. My guess is he beat you to the corner and headed Cardston way."

"Okay, thanks! We'll get him."

Spitting dust and stones, the patrol car rocketed away. Running like a jackrabbit in her clicking western boots, Libby raced back up the drive.

AT FIRST SHE thought he was dead.

When she got the freezer door open, he was slumped pale and motionless on the ice-cold floor. She dragged him out of the dark tomb. As he lay on the kitchen floor, frost vapour rose from his still form. Her heart contracting in anguish, she threw herself upon him, trying to warm his body with her own while at the same time blowing into his mouth: the breath of life.

After a while—agonizingly long—his body gave a shudder. His chest muscles spasmed, and then he began to breathe on his own. Libby massaged his body, rubbed him, flexed him, all the time muttering words—encouragement, apology—of which she was scarcely aware. Finally, she was sure he was out of danger.

But she also knew that the officers who had raced away in pursuit of the non-existent Chevy might give up the chase and return at any time. Or a second patrol car might arrive. She got John to his knees, shoved her shoulder under his, levered him to his feet, staggered with him through the living room and into the corridor beyond.

Then there was the sound of a vehicle approaching on the drive.

The man she was supporting gave a convulsive start, and they both almost fell. "It's okay, John," Libby said frantically. "They won't be bothering you. Please believe me! *I'm helping you now.*"

She got him walking again. Reaching the room where he had slept, she dumped him on the bed and pulled the blankets right up around his dazed and flushed face.

"Don't move," she whispered. "Don't do anything. If I bring anyone here, pretend to be asleep. John—I swear—I believe you now, and I'll look after you."

As Libby ran back through the living room, she could see two policemen coming up the steps to the front door. She kept on to the back. With a shudder, she slammed the freezer door, then rushed into the office and flung open the window.

The front doorbell was ringing. Finally, after taking a moment to catch her breath, Libby went to meet the Mounties.

She was able to satisfy them. She kept the story as close as possible to what had happened, telling of surprising an intruder searching her boss's office, scaring him with a warning shot, imprisoning him in the office but not realizing he'd be able to get out of the window while she called the RCMP. As he fled she had got only a glimpse of his car and gone to the gate to warn them.

Finally she mentioned her "cousin from Vancouver" who'd come to visit, only to get laid up with a case of flu. She took the officers through, showed them John from the doorway. He acknowledged them hazily, and she briskly closed the door.

And that was that.

When they were gone, Libby got herself a shot of whisky and downed it straight. Thus fortified, she returned to the office and re-read the e-mail from Bud Wetherall. Then she went to rejoin the man she had almost killed: the man who, one way or other, appeared destined to change her life.

TWO

Lying in the blissful warmth, John felt a sudden movement beside him. Lazily he opened his eyes. The girl—the girl who had shot at him and—what?—imprisoned him in ice—had now returned and was ...

"Oh, no!" John abruptly sat up.

Libby pushed him firmly back onto the bed. Her voice was quiet but firm. "It's okay, John! Everything's all right. Better than you ever hoped. Your boy's *alive!*"

John came wide awake. "What? How do you know?"

"An e-mail came in from Bud. It must have been there for days but I didn't open it till this morning, After I'd already ... Well, anyway, I printed it out. Listen." Libby produced a printout, scanned it, finally found the place she wanted and started to read.

"Now for the real news. For quite a while I've had our names listed with several child-adoption agencies but, to avoid building false hopes in Mimi, I kept this a secret. Recently, a group in Oregon indicated they might have a child for us, which—though Mimi didn't know it—was the real reason for our trip to the States. Everything went great and we have the child. A three-year-old boy, name of Nate. Mimi is so happy it's amazing. The change has to be seen to be believed. She wants to call him Gabriel. And why not? Would you believe it? Here we are—by some miracle—a family again."

Libby stopped, seeing John's expression. "A family at your expense. I'm so sorry."

John was still trying to take it all in. "At least you can see I'm not out of my skull."

"I'm sure happy about that and even happier that your son's okay."

"But why all the adoption-agency crap?"

She shrugged. "I've known Bud a long time. He's a shrewd old fox. He'd realize they couldn't just produce a child without a cover story."

"Yeah—of course. Is there any more?"

Libby read on. "Lib, before we get home there are some things I want you to do. Gabe is to have the room near you … "

Here! John thought. *This room right here!* And that made him so furious he had difficulty keeping silent as she continued.

" … and I want you to have it redecorated kid style. Call Arch Nielsen in Cardston for that. Also buy a big bunch of toys. Really fill the place, comprende? Good girl, I know you'll do a great job. But remember, he's only three—so no hunting rifles this year. From here I figure we'll move on to Edmonton and stay a couple of days. I hate cities, but Mimi heard about some great water park at the West Edmonton Mall. Thinks the boy might get a kick out of it. From there we'll swing down to Drumheller to call on Will and Beulah—get there Saturday night. Mimi can't wait to see their faces when we haul in young Gabe. After that, I'd like to come on home, but Mimi doesn't want to do that till we're sure everything's ready at the ranch. She wants Gabe to feel like it's his place from day one. So we'll keep on for a bit. I'll keep you posted … "

Libby put the e-mail aside. "I guess that's it. All that matters."

In John's brain one thought surfaced, sweeping aside anger, relief—even joy. *Now I know where they are.*

Libby examined the printout. "This must have come in at least a couple of days ago."

"Yeah?"

"If I'd only checked the e-mail earlier I'd have known you were telling the truth."

"Never mind that now. What's today?"

"Friday."

"And on Saturday they're arriving in—what did he say—Drumheller? Where's that?"

"About an hour east of Calgary, in the Badlands."

"Badlands? Sounds like something out of a Western movie."

"Kinda looks like it too. It's where they found all the dinosaurs."

"And that's where they're taking Nate. Who are these people they want to impress? You know them?"

"Sure. Will North is Mimi's younger brother. He used to be a Calgary cop, but he got busted out for reasons no one talks about. His wife Beulah's a real nice lady though."

"How long would it take to get there?"

Libby shrugged. "If you're well enough to leave tomorrow, we should have no trouble getting there when they do."

It took a moment for this to sink in. "Did you say we?"

"Any objections?"

"I can't ask you to get involved in this."

"I'm already involved, mister. Have been, ever since I shoved you in that awful freezer."

"But that wasn't your fault. I mean—I was acting like a crazy man."

"No argument there," Libby said with a brisk laugh. "But I did almost end up turning you into frozen steak. How do you reckon that makes me feel? And all because of some sick stunt Bud and Mimi pulled. I'm not only angry, I'm sad and embarrassed too. I don't just work here, John. I've always been made to feel like one of the family."

"Mmm—I'd suspected that."

"If you want to know, I used to be part of a different kind of family altogether, but I escaped from that."

"Escaped?"

"Yeah. I used to be a Mormon."

"Really?"

"Brought up in Cardston. Ran away when I was 16. Didn't fancy the notion of marrying some old man. My folks cut me off and I got in some trouble in the city. Then the Wetheralls took me in. Before Mimi went off the deep end, she used to be almost like my older sister, and Bud taught me how to do most of the stuff around here, took me on hunting trips and all kinds of things. I imagine the way I feel about them was obvious enough. Is that why you didn't tell me the truth right off? You thought even if I believed you, I'd want to help them?"

He shrugged. "I'm a stranger here. I knew Bud was rich, probably with a pile of influence and connections. As a matter of a fact, for a while I thought he might be a Mormon. Till I could prove Nate was alive, my one advantage was that they didn't know I was on to them. I was really scared of blowing it."

"I understand." Libby began to pace. "Okay—I'll be honest. After I read that e-mail and realized you were telling the truth, I did sort of wonder how I could stop my friends from being punished. But not how they could keep your boy from you. Do you believe that?"

Looking at those fierce eyes and the straight jaw, he didn't need to consider. "Yes. Actually, if I'd followed my gut feeling, I'd have told you right away."

Her eyes stopped being fierce. "Thanks, John. Now I'll tell you something. Yesterday you asked me if I had any children."

"Yes?"

"Well, I wasn't completely straight with you. After I ran off, I did have a baby. Gave it up for adoption. I still think I did the right thing but I'll never forget the feeling of—emptiness. Do you hear what I'm saying?"

He nodded.

"Though I understand Bud and Mimi's need, I could never condone what they did to you—or your wife."

"*Ex*-wife," John said, hastily. "I'm glad. Thanks."

She sat down on the bed. "But there's another reason I want to come along. As I said, Bud and Mimi have been like family. If there's one thing I do regret, it's that I didn't know them when I gave up my own baby. What they've done is truly wrong but they're not bad folks, and I know I can persuade them to give up your boy without a fuss."

"I'd certainly have no argument with that."

"We do this together?"

He found her hand and squeezed it, feeling better in the presence of this woman than he had in a very long time. "It'd be a privilege."

Libby left her hand where it was for a while, looking into his eyes. Then she rose. "Now your worries are over. We'll get Nate back pronto, count on it. You get some rest." She moved to the door, then turned back, grinning. "Oh—there is one other reason why I offered to help."

"Yeah—what?"

"John, you're a nice guy, and you've been doing your best. But from what I've seen, to let you loose again alone would be—how can I say it—negligent."

THREE

On Saturday John awoke feeling remarkably fit, considering the mayhem of the day before. Since the Badlands region was less than three hours away, and it was imperative that they not arrive before their quarry, they didn't start out until the mid-afternoon.

Libby's 4x4 was not a Jeep, as John had first believed, but a sturdy old Toyota Land Cruiser. She insisted on taking it instead of his MG, and he had no objection. As they went to get in, she tossed him the keys. "Here—you drive."

Since she was not the kind of girl to ask a man to take the wheel because she thought it was feminine or proper, he looked at her in surprise.

"I figured your mind must be pretty fired up with seeing Nate tonight. Driving will give you something to occupy it."

"Thanks."

"You're welcome." She patted the flank of the vehicle as if it were a horse. "Just don't make me regret it."

"Yes, ma'am, I'll do my best," he said, switching on the engine. It turned over lustily but didn't catch.

"Sorry! Should have told you. This model's got a hand choke. It's old-fashioned but great for starting in the cold."

John smiled. "Yeah, I know—the MG's got one too." He felt guilty about the stunt he'd pulled two days earlier, which had made him seem dumber than he really was about engines, but the time for that was long past. He pulled out the choke and the engine caught instantly.

They drove into Cardston, passing the giant stone sentinel of the Mormon temple, then turned north. Libby had suggested they avoid busy Highway 2, following a parallel route to the east instead. It would be quieter, avoiding Calgary, yet take them fairly directly to their destination.

Leaving the foothills, they travelled across country as flat as the sea and the colour of burnt brick. The sky was a hard, metallic blue, the sun a blazing hammer. It was brutally hot, even for a southern Alberta summer: 35 degrees Celsius, and no letup as the afternoon wore on. Endless expanses of wheat and parched grass shimmered in the windless oven, cattle that could not find shade slumped and baked. Though sturdier than his MG, the Land Cruiser also lacked air conditioning; the open windows brought little relief, as the wind poured in like a blast furnace.

Accustomed to the mild coast, John began to feel as though he might melt into a grease spot. The excitement of the imminent reunion was scarcely enough to distract from his growing discomfort and even Libby, used to the near-desert conditions, eventually started fanning herself with her hat. Finally, on the edge of a town with the apt name of Vulcan, John spotted a small roadside café. Libby saw it too. When he threw her a glance, all she said was, "Oh, *yeah!*"

He swung the Land Cruiser into the lot. The café was empty, and no servers were evident, but it appeared to be open. They sat at a table, soaking up the blessed coolness, not caring whether anyone came to see what they wanted. But soon a homely woman, who looked as though she belonged in a farm kitchen, appeared from the back. "Hello, dears," she said cheerily. "Warm enough for you?"

They ordered Cokes, which could be seen in a nearby cooler. These disappeared with near-mystic speed and they ordered more. Only then did John's brain start to function properly again. He stared out across the endless sea of grass to where, somewhere beyond the horizon, his son was being borne toward their rendezvous. John took out the photo of Nate, snapped in the vehicle that was used to steal the child and was now bringing him back. But instead of relief, he felt unease. Picturing the confrontation ahead, he was filled with sour foreboding. Something was wrong, or going to go wrong: the feeling was very strong.

Libby looked at the Polaroid, then at John. "Getting the jitters?"

"I don't know. Maybe I'm overexcited—or maybe it's this damn heat—but suddenly it seems that it can't be this easy."

She nodded seriously. "I understand. After all you've been through, it must be hard to believe it's almost over. But look at it this way: Nate is your son. You can prove that and Bud knows it. He may be rich and clever, but this is Canada, not some place where he can do whatever he likes. Once we meet up, the party's basically over. How you handle things after that is your business. But, believe me, the only ones in real trouble are Bud and Mimi. It's in their interest to cooperate."

She was right, of course. As they sat a while longer in the cool café, preparing for the last leg of the journey, John began to feel better. They had sandwiches and coffee and it was 6:00 when they finally got back into the Land Cruiser. Evening had brought some moderation in the heat; it was far from comfortable but bearable. They continued north on the straight, flat road, at one point crossing the Trans-Canada Highway. At 7:30, after the route had finally veered east—a relief if only because of the direction change—Libby pointed to a side road off to the left. "Turn here!"

John did as he was told, though at first he couldn't see why. Ahead, the prairie continued uninterrupted under a purpling sky. They came upon a parking lot with a number of vehicles, which was surprising since there didn't seem to be any reason for someone to stop. As they entered the lot John looked enquiringly at Libby, "What's this?"

She smiled mysteriously. "Wait!"

Beyond the cars, a small group of people stood in a ragged line, staring northward, apparently at nothing. John scratched his head. "What's going on?"

She got of the car. "Come and see."

He followed her toward the line of people. No head turned as they approached. Everyone kept staring, and only when he stood beside them did John see why. The earth didn't continue on, as it had appeared. Instead, at John's feet, so sudden that the sight brought a jolt of stomach-turning vertigo, was a chasm. How wide it was, or how deep, it was hard to tell in the fading light. But John had seen pictures of the Grand Canyon and it certainly reminded him of that. The huge erosion-scar clawed its way through the ground, from east to west, as far as the eye could see: a profusion of gullies, draws, cliffs and canyons, filled with deepening shadows; some smooth, many gouged into shapes fantastical. Beyond, in unfathomable distance, the sea-flat prairie continued undisturbed to the horizon.

Libby said quietly, "What do you think?"

"Awesome! This is the Badlands?"

"Yeah."

He nodded, contemplating the strange scene: an all-too-appropriate place for the ending of his even stranger quest.

A short time later they drove down into the canyon itself, entering Drumheller. It was a surprisingly large community: originally a mining town, Libby said, now a tourist Mecca, living off the profusion

of ancient fossils found in the valley. The Dinosaur Capital Of The
World, it called itself, evidence of which was all around. Enormous
replicas of beasts lurked everywhere, disturbingly real in the fading
light. In the town centre towered a 100-foot Tyrannosaurus Rex.
To John, the place had a surreal quality, a dark-carnival aura that
somehow attached itself to the anxiety building again in his gut.

It was after 8:00. By now Bud and Mimi must surely have
arrived. Their destination was Mimi's brother's house, a few blocks
away. But since John and Libby were low on gas, and might not be
able to get it later, they made one last stop. While John was filling
up, Libby took a small bag and disappeared out back. When she
returned he got a shock.

The figure that approached was dressed in a light skirt, sleeve-
less top and sandals. Dark hair, held to the back with two combs,
flowed across shoulders of Indian brown. Unencumbered at last by
jeans and boots, it moved with the willowy grace of a dancer. She
was right beside John before he realized who she was. He stared and
she smiled self-consciously.

"What are you staring at?"

"You look sensational."

"Thanks." She smiled, but then her face sobered. "You see, Bud
likes me to be dressed as what he thinks of as 'ladylike.' And Mimi's
brother, Will, creepy though he is, always did have a bit of a crush
on me. So I figured—with what you've got to do, every little bit
would help."

"Yes," John said. "Of course. Thanks."

Then he surprised himself by kissing her firmly on the cheek.
She put her hand up, touched his own cheek lightly and smiled
again. "Come on, John. It's time."

It took only minutes to reach the residential area, a few square
blocks of homes, modest but well kept: lawns, board fences, large

shade trees. Away from the tourist hub it was quiet, streets deserted, cheerful windows aglow; a cosy village haven, with little hint of the tortured waste that lay beyond. Libby directed him into a street with several slightly larger houses. In the driveway of the farthest was an enormous motorhome.

They pulled in alongside, shutting off the engine. Libby and John turned to each other. Libby said, "You ready?"

"As I'll ever be, I guess."

"Good luck, John."

They got out and walked together to the door.

FOUR

Will North opened the door. He was a dark-haired man about 40, not tall but with unusually well-developed chest and arms. He had a flat pale face with brown eyes, which, even though they were large, managed to look cold. Immediately obvious was the likeness to Mimi Wetherall. He seemed to be drunk.

Will's eyes grew rounder when he saw Libby, and he leered at her. "Well—hey! Bud didn't say you were coming." He eyed John, not exactly kindly. "This your guy?"

Libby ignored the question. "Can we come in, Will?"

"Sure! Why the hell not," North said, in a tone that was, oddly, both expansive and surly. The front door opened into a small hall, which led to the rest of the house. North went first and they followed, with John at the rear, moving into the living room.

Bud Wetherall was the only one there, sitting with a drink in his hand on the far side of the room. He saw Libby first and looked surprised. Then his eyes moved to John. He gave a little frown, as if trying to recall where he'd seen the familiar face. Then his mouth dropped and the drink fell from his hand. He leaped to his feet, and his shoe came down on the glass, crushing it to rubble.

"Jesus Christ!" Bud whispered.

He looked as though someone had just pronounced a sentence of death.

Mimi and Nate were asleep in the motorhome. After he had recovered a little, Bud told them that. Also he begged that they not be awakened, at least until he had a chance to tell them how it had all come about.

"Let me see him," John snapped. "I'm not going to listen to anything till I've seen that my boy's okay." He turned and headed back for the motorhome.

To find Will North barring his way. "Where do you think you're goin', mister?"

"To see my son," John said coldly.

"Oh, yeah? Bud here tells me the kid was adopted."

Libby moved between them. "Will, don't be stupid! The boy is John's, there's no doubt. Bud and your sister are in very deep trouble. And if you don't want to be charged as an accessory to kidnapping, you'd best move aside."

North gave Libby an evil look, mixed with lust. Bud spoke curtly. "He *is* the boy's dad, Will. Let him by."

North reluctantly obeyed, but of all of them he looked the most put out.

"Go on, John," Libby said quietly. "Go to your son."

John went.

Outside, he saw that a single light was on in the living room of the motorhome. He went to the side door, opened it quietly, walked in. Everything was as he remembered; a most elegant gilded cage for a stolen bird. On the front couch, with a little lamp burning and a child's book nearby, slept Nate.

He was splayed on his back, legs and arms flung wide. His face, unmarked by fear or dream, looked angelic. Clutched firmly in one hand was a Teddy Ruxpin bear identical to the one John had given

him a thousand years ago. Blinking back tears of relief and unexpectedly savage joy, John stared at his son.

"Hi, Nate," he said quietly at last. "I missed you." He reached
down and brushed the boy's hand where it clutched the paw of the
bear. Nate sighed, and jerked into a new position.

Unable to stop himself, John moved to the master bedroom.
Mimi Wetherall was sleeping as peacefully as her purloined child.
One angry corner of John's heart longed to awaken her, to tell her
that her cruel charade was over, to revel in her shock and fear and
disappointment. He dismissed that, but not because of the pleas
of her husband; now that he'd found Nate again, he couldn't bring
himself to let bitterness and spite mar the moment.

"Back in a second, kiddo," John whispered to his sleeping child,
and hurried into the house. "First thing," he said, "before anything
else, I'm going to take my boy out of here. If you don't want to wake
your wife, it's okay. But I want Nate right away."

Bud Wetherall seemed so overwhelmed as to be close to tears.
"Sure," he said hastily. "Of course. But please—John—let me tell
you how this terrible thing happened."

"It doesn't matter."

"But it does! I need you to understand. The abduction was
my wife's doing. It was she who planted those fake clues, making it
look like Nate'd gone in the river. While all of us were sleeping, she
drugged him and hid him away in the motorhome. I didn't even
know we *had* your boy until two days had passed and we were almost
home. By that time everyone thought he was dead. I figured that if
we returned him then, no one would believe that I hadn't been
involved and I'd be ruined. So I'm afraid I went along with it. Another thing that made it easy was that you, and particularly the kid's
mum—excuse me for saying this—seemed like folks he'd really be
better off without. I've seen those marks where it looked like he was

beaten. And although I realize that's no real excuse for stealing him, at least you'll be able to see that we weren't completely wicked."

"Bud, what's the fucking matter with you!" a voice said with drunken suddenness. It was Will North, slouching nearby, nursing a beer. "Why in hell are you letting this happen?"

Wetherall ignored him. "I misjudged you, John, I can see that now. Instead of accepting your son's 'death,' you turned out to be some sort of super-sleuth and tracked us down. That in itself tells me how strongly you must feel about him."

Before John could respond, Will lurched forward, waving his beer. "Bud—are you crazy? Why are you making nice with this asshole?"

"That's enough, Will."

"No it ain't! You don't have to give up the kid. I used to be a cop, for fuck's sake. I know stuff that can be done … "

"I said *shut up!*"

Bud Wetherall rose and gave his brother-in-law a resounding slap across the face. North didn't react, stood swaying stupidly.

"I'm sorry," Bud said. "Please don't take any notice of my brother-in-law. His wife ran out on him yesterday. Wants a divorce, apparently. When we arrived he was half drunk and crying the blues, which is why Mimi went off to bed so early." He put his hand on the other man's shoulder. "Sorry I belted you, boy. But you're drunk and out of line. And making things worse for me. Now get! Off to bed!"

He turned North and shoved him toward the back of the house. The man went, disappearing into a bedroom. There was a creak of bedsprings, a groan, silence. Will North was at last out of the picture.

FIVE

Bud Wetherall **went** to a drinks cabinet across the room and poured himself a whisky. He took a swig, then faced them. He said quietly, "I'm not going to apologize for what we did to you—that would be hypocritical and sickening. You've won, John. Our worst punishment is that we've failed. And tomorrow, when Mimi wakes up and I have to tell her what happened to what she now thinks of as her son, she's gonna go crazy again. If she doesn't try to kill herself, she'll at least need care for the rest of her life. That's what we have to look forward to.

"Now—I understand that some kind of charges will have to be laid. And I'm perfectly willing to give myself up to the authorities. But please, not here. Not in this town where I'm a stranger. Tomorrow, if you agree, we'll all go back to Cardston and I'll turn myself in there. Where we're known, where people understand what we've been through, Mimi will stand a chance of gentle treatment. I know, under the circumstances, I've no right to ask this. But—for Mimi's sake—I'm asking anyway." He grimaced, with a crooked smile. "In fact, you could say I'm begging. Well, John—how about it?"

Uncertain, John glanced at Libby. She was looking moved, but the moment her eyes met his they fell away. Even feeling about Bud

as she did, she wasn't going to try to influence him. That understanding—coupled with the generosity engendered by the sheer joy
of having Nate back—caused him to make up his mind.

"Okay," he said at last. "Cardston it is. But we head back first
thing in the morning."

"Thank you!" Bud looked away, and there was little doubt he
was blinking back tears. He said quietly, "You know, John, you may
be an actor, which some folks might say is a pretty soft way to make
a living, but I'll say this—you're more man than I am. And you make
me feel ashamed."

Bud finished his drink, put down the glass, gestured in the direction that North had taken. "There are plenty of rooms back there.
I'm sure you'd feel happier if your boy was in one of them. Come and
get him. Then I'm going to bed."

He disappeared toward the motorhome. Hastily, with a look of
relief at Libby, John followed him out.

The "plenty of rooms" referred to by Bud turned out to be two.
The larger, which was probably a guest room, had a double bed.
The smaller, a sun porch leading off the guest room, had only a
small couch.

Nate had shown no sign of awakening when lifted from the
couch. As he was put in the big bed—still firmly clutching his
bear—his eyes fluttered open and he smiled vaguely, but John knew
that nothing had gone in. As he was covering him up, Libby entered
the room.

"Where are you going to sleep?" she asked quietly.

John grinned happily. "Right beside this monster."

"And me?"

"There's a couch out on the porch."

She went and looked at it. "How about finding some blankets?
There's probably a closet in the hall."

John did so, discovering blankets and another pillow. When he returned to the bedroom Nate was gone. But from the sun porch Libby's voice called quietly, "John—out here!"

On the porch he found them, Libby sitting on the couch, Nate, dead to the world, with his head in her lap. She smiled at him. "I figured this was a bit more his size than mine," she said simply.

"Then where will you ...?" he began, and stopped, feeling foolish.

Libby didn't seem to notice. Transferring Nate's head to the pillow, she helped tuck the blankets around him. Finally, before putting out the light, she leaned across and ruffled the little boy's hair. The gesture was quick, a flick of her supple brown hand, but in it was all the gentleness of a kiss.

With the Wetheralls in their motorhome, Nate asleep in the sun porch and North passed out, the house was theirs. Incredibly, at the end of this arduous quest, they had ended up in a sort of haven. What problems still existed were for the morning.

Since they were both frantically hungry, Libby rooted around in the kitchen, finding sausages and bread and cans of tomato soup and coffee. After all they'd been through, it tasted like a feast. When they were finishing up, she said, "It was decent of you to let old Bud go down home to take his medicine."

John shrugged. "I guess having Nate back makes that easy."

She looked at him seriously. "When all this is over, I hope you give him the same sort of break."

"What do you mean?"

"By keeping an eye on him, spending more time with him. By sticking with your boy, for Christ's sake. And, divorced or not, being a proper dad."

John nodded seriously. "Oh, I'll do that, don't worry. Ever since I've known Nate was alive, I haven't been able to think of anything else. For a while I got it into my head that Val was abusive, but I'm not sure that was true. When I picked him up he did have some bruises, but she denied hurting him. And her husband said something about a fall from a swing. I was just so angry—and feeling so damn guilty—not just for losing Nate, but for neglecting him earlier, that I had to load some of it off on her. Val hasn't made it easy for me, that's for sure. But I know I could have tried harder to see Nate. Actually, I could have done better in a lot of ways. But it's so easy to let time go by, to get distracted, especially in the work I'm in, and to shift blame ... " He stopped, looking embarrassed. "I'm sorry. I don't know where all that come from."

Libby, whose blue-green eyes had been regarding him seriously, broke into a smile. "Never mind. I'm happy you felt you could talk about it with me."

John looked both awkward and pleased. "It was easy. Seems like you've been making a lot of things possible for me lately."

"C'mon—it's no more than anyone would have done."

"You're too modest. None of this, especially tonight, could have happened without you. I just want you to know that I know it. Thank you."

"Mister, you're very welcome."

After they ate, they cleaned up as much as possible in the wife-deserted wasteland of a kitchen. Then, as if it was part of the same ritual, Libby moved to John, put her arms around him and kissed him. It was neither a peck nor an outpouring of passion, but a solid, honest kiss with all the trustworthy indications of a fine summer morning.

"Come on, John," Libby said. "Let's go to bed."

He didn't feel foolish or awkward any more. He took her hand and they proceeded to do what she had suggested.

LIBBY, WHEN SHE removed her clothes, was a thorough delight . Everything about her was spare and well muscled, but she was wonderfully
rounded too, with curves in her breasts and stomach and thighs that
woke all the good fires that John might ever have desired.

The feeling of her, making love, was even better. She had
strength and gentleness and enthusiasm. Loving her not only made
his body feel splendid, he was aware of a wholesomeness, a sense of
more-than-physical connection, rare in the free and easy world that
he inhabited. Far from being casual, this encounter caused an inner
vibration of such intensity that he found himself wanting to sing or
to laugh aloud.

It was all very fine. When it was finally over, they slept soundly.
They slept till they were both wakened, not by morning but by a
bright light.

And—six inches from their still-nestled heads—the long barrel
of a gun.

PART FIVE

ONE

When Bud Wetherall went back to the motorhome he did not go to bed. He poured himself a drink, turned out the lamp, and sat slowly sipping, thinking very deeply, going over all perspectives and possibilities, sifting a host of solutions. He sat thus for three hours.

Finally he rose and looked in on Mimi in the bedroom. Last night, after the shock of finding out what had happened to her brother's marriage, she had done what was now a rare thing; taken a pill. She was sleeping like the dead and would remain so till morning but Bud closed the door anyway. No point in taking chances.

After that he turned on lights in the kitchen area and started a powerful brew working in the coffee machine. Finally, padding quiet as a mountain cat, he went back into the house.

The door to the spare bedroom was closed. Libby, the child's persistent damn-fool of a father and the kid were comfortably ensconced in there; already, he thought grimly, forming into a neat little tribe all their own.

Resolutely he went into the kitchen. There he found a plastic pail, which he half filled with water as cold as the tap would run. To this he added a couple of trays of ice from the freezer, stirring till he had ice-water and lumps. Then he walked into the master bedroom, snapping on the light.

Will North was lying face down, still fully dressed, just as he had fallen when he had staggered off to bed. Bud looked at his watch, noting that it was 2:30. Will had had four hours to sleep off the worst of his drunk. Bud lifted the pail and, concentrating on the nerve-cluster at the back of the neck, sloshed the ice-water in a merciless stream over the sleeping man.

The effect was instantaneous. The body on the bed jerked and convulsed, as if it had been fed 10,000 volts. It flipped from belly to back. Then, like a monster in an old horror movie, mouth open, eyes saucer-wide, it sat up. North's lungs suddenly sucked in air, in preparation for letting out a yell, but Bud sat beside him and thrust a pillow over his mouth.

He stuck his face an inch from North's and glared a fresh dose of ice. "Shut up, Will," he whispered. "Don't move, don't yell. Don't do anything. Understand?"

North twitched and lifted his arms, about to struggle, and Bud's other hand flew up behind. Holding Will's head without apparent effort, he shook the younger man like an animal. "*Do you understand?*"

North finally seemed to get the point; he nodded as best he could. Only then did Bud let him go.

"What the fuck's going on?" North muttered.

Bud lifted his fingers to his lips, then pointed to the other part of the house. "From now on you must be very quiet."

In North's face, shock was at last edging into curiosity. He whispered, "Why?"

Bud's glacial demeanour permitted a small, grim smile. "Why, brother-in-law—so you can get very rich!"

When North arrived in the motorhome 20 minutes later he had

dried off and changed. Though far from sober, and suffering much discomfort, he was awake and rational enough for Bud's purpose.

A mug of steaming black coffee and two double-strength Anacin tablets were laid out neatly on the counter. North took the tablets as instructed and drank the coffee. Bud poured him more, along with some for himself, and at last sat opposite the man at the kitchen table. It was 3:00 AM.

Bud began the conversation obliquely. "Okay, Will, tell me something: working as a foreman with the highway crew, 40 hours a week, out in all weather, how much do you make exactly?"

"What the fuck's that got to do with anything?"

"I'll tell you. Whatever it is, how would you like it multiplied by ten—for the rest of your life?"

The other man sat up straight. "You messin' with me?"

"Never been more serious. There's only one question—can you do it?"

North's eyes narrowed. "Do what?"

"Now, Will, don't mess with *me*. You know exactly what I mean."

Looking both dazed and excited now, North glanced furtively toward the house. "I've never done anything like that before. Not even when I was a cop."

Bud nodded matter-of-factly. "I know. You're not much of a brain, and from what I've heard, pretty crude. That's why you were busted out of the cops. And I'll bet Beulah didn't leave you just because you couldn't get it up anymore. But it's probable you haven't in fact killed anyone. Which is why I ask you the question."

North didn't have to ponder long. "Yeah. I think I can do it."

"Not good enough."

"Okay! Then I *can*!" Sour resolve was growing in the younger man. "For what you're offering, I know it!"

"It must be you alone. You can't have any helpers in this. No one else to get cold feet, or rat, or try a little blackmail later. It's got to stay in the family—*is that completely clear?*"

"Sure! Shit, I wouldn't want it any other way. So—okay! And a real great place to do it would be … "

Bud held up his hand. "Stop right there! I don't want to know. Just get it done. However you have to but quick, and *final*. For that I'm willing to sign over half of everything I own, making you a full partner in all my enterprises. Since you're my brother-in-law, no one will think that too strange."

North's eyes gleamed. "I guess not!"

"It's a lot I'm offering, and I consider it well worth it. But in return I demand not only guaranteed results but—equally important—to be free of any further thoughts of these people. The girl I'll remember as someone who simply moved on. The man I hardly met. Tonight, the last few hours, never happened. And I took you into the business simply because you're family. Soon that's the way I'll remember it and it's your job to make all this possible. Understand?"

North gave a knowing leer. "What you're sayin' is you're squeamish."

Bud's expression didn't alter, but his hand grasped the other man's fingers in a crushing grip. "What I'm saying, brother, is that I need to be able to live with myself in the future. If you're not capable of understanding such subtlety, just follow instructions. That's it. Well?"

The ex-policeman looked at the other man's rock-hard face, feeling a twinge of fear. His compressed fingers hurt more than he would have believed possible. "You got it, Bud. Both things, I promise!"

"This is your final word?"

"Yeah—*YEAH!*"

When Bud let go of North's hand there was an audible crack. He rose, consulting his watch. "Less than two hours to dawn. By then I want to be long gone."

The house was dead quiet as Bud re-entered it. He put on a

single light in the kitchen and listened. Nothing. He went to the door of the spare room and listened again. Still nothing. He put his hand on the handle and turned, slowly, applying sideways tension to stop any rattle, pushed the door a few inches inwards and listened: breathing, two sets, low, intermingled and regular.

Bud crept into the room, looked at the bed. The two who had come to steal his life were there, sleeping tangled together like puppies. An image flashed across Bud's mind of himself and Mimi like that when they were young. He pushed away the thought and resolutely removed his gaze.

Into the room beyond he drifted, immediately seeing his new son. Gabe was lying on his stomach, hands splayed, covered by a blanket. Bud moved in, picked up both child and blanket. The boy squirmed a little, opened an eye, registered a familiar image.

"Daddy-Bud."

It was a nuzzled mumble. Then came a snuggling, an easy body-to-body adjusting, as Bud held the bundle to him. And, like a wild animal bearing off its young, he slipped back across the bedroom, easing the door closed behind him.

A couple of minutes later the child was back in the bed he would never know he'd left; the restored father, eyes clear, eased into the driver's seat of his big, quiet machine. The engine started, no more than a whine, a cough, then a gentle purr. The motorhome backed, turned and with ponderous grace moved away.

Its driver, who had pushed much bigger rigs but never such a successful one, held the wheel easily and whistled a tiny tune. Once he was out of the Badlands he turned south. It was not yet dawn.

TWO

As John tried to sit up there was a click, and something hard and painful bit into his wrist. His arm was pulled sharply sideways and there was another click. At the same time there came a sharp cry. Libby's voice.

He remembered where he was and saw that the girl was struggling to sit up too. As she did so, his arm was jerked again and only then did he realize that something was holding them together. Amazed, he twisted around to see what it was.

Handcuffs.

Then there was a brisk flurry, and the bedclothes that covered both of them were wrenched away.

"Okay, you two animals," a harsh voice said. "Out!"

John jerked his head up, finally focussing on the figure beyond the bed. It was Will North. The ex-cop was fully dressed, with what looked like a police-issue revolver in his hand.

The next thing John understood, as shock jerked him into full consciousness, was that he and the girl handcuffed to him were naked. Embarrassment rose, to be shoved aside by anger. But it was Libby who got in the first words.

"You pervert!" she snarled. "What do you think you're doing?"

She wasn't looking embarrassed. Fury stretched her slim body as taught as a bow-string, her nipples pointing at North like accusing fingers.

He in turn was staring at her, the lustful gaze that John had noticed earlier now obscenely frank. Like hungry rats, his eyes wandered over her body.

John's anger accelerated to rage. "You bastard!" he yelled. "Let us go, or I'll goddamn kill … "

North hit him, slapping John across the side of the head with his gun. The impact of steel on his cheekbone was like an internal explosion: agony and a galaxy of stars followed by a rush of nausea. As he tried to raise his hand to his head, the handcuffed wrist jerked Libby onto him, and they both tumbled off the bed onto the floor.

Another pain exploded, in the small of his back, this time from a boot. The kick was followed by another sickly-sounding impact and he heard Libby shriek. The pain of the head blow blurred his vision, but he peered around frantically, trying to see what terrible thing had happened to Libby and at the same time to shield her from this senseless unfolding nightmare.

Then something grabbed his manacled wrist. Expecting more punishment, he flinched away. But this time none came. There was a click, and although the pressure on the wrist remained, he didn't seem to be attached to anything anymore. He rolled around and managed to sit up.

North was backing off, holding a small key. Although the handcuffs were still attached to John, Libby had been released. She was hugging her side, and John could see an ugly round welt—a toe-mark—on the ribcage under her breast.

North was now standing with his back to the door, revolver in hand, covering them almost casually. "Okay, assholes," he said.

"That was a little taste. To show you I'm not gonna take any shit. Both of you get dressed."

Recovering his wits as the pain eased a little, John pulled himself across to Libby. "Are you okay?" But before she could reply he remembered something else. He leaped to his feet, yelling as he started to run. "Nate!"

There was a shattering explosion. A wind went by his cheek and he stopped short, staring. North had not moved, but his revolver bled a pale ghost of vapour.

"The kid's not here," North said. "He left with his new folks hours ago. One more move like that, fuckman, and I'll gut-shoot you. Get dressed! You're both under arrest."

Libby rose, recovering quickly. Quite unselfconscious, not even attempting to start dressing, she said, "What do you mean 'arrest,' Will North? You're not a cop anymore and everyone knows it."

Again he was feeling her up with his eyes. "A citizen's arrest. That's what I'm doing."

"What? You're out of your mind."

"I found you breaking into my house and I'm taking you into the RCMP. I've got some buddies at the detachment. They'll keep you busy for a long time. Now get dressed."

"You little creep!"

Libby began to advance on North, but John caught her arm. The shot the man had loosed off had made him understand how dangerous this jerk was. To Libby he said urgently, "No, don't! The police won't hold us up long. Let's do what the man says. Get dressed."

Libby looked from North to John, and she too acknowledged the real peril of the situation. She reached out to John. "Are you all right?"

"I'll survive. You?"

She gave a wry grin that twisted his heart. "Fine."

"Okay, Romeo and Juliet," North sneered. "Stop havin' it off and get those clothes on. Move it!"

Finally they both began to obey.

As they dressed John tried to get his head working. The most important thing was that Nate was gone again. If the motorhome had indeed left "hours ago," by now it would be miles away, vanished once more on the boundless highway system of North America. The whole business about the abductors giving themselves up in Cardston had only been a trick, a scam to keep them from leaving until Bud—who'd never for a moment intended to surrender—could figure out what to do. John began to feel guilty at being so easily hoodwinked, but he knew he had no time for such indulgence. The focus must be upon getting on the trail again as quickly as possible.

One thing that was no surprise was that Will North was acting as the heavy. From the first, Mimi's brother had made it clear where his sympathies lay. Now, evidently, he planned to use whatever influence he had with the police to hold them up as long as possible.

With the respite thus afforded, what would the Wetheralls do? Disappear with the child altogether? Hardly practical, unless they meant to move to some other part of the country, or out of it. No, much more likely was what John had feared most all along—disposal of the evidence.

But he couldn't let himself think about that.

Dressed, John concluded that there was only one thing he could do. The instant they got to the RCMP detachment, he must tell the whole story as quickly as possible. Libby was now dressed too, in the outfit she'd worn the previous evening. That was a good thing, for in it she looked feminine and vulnerable and, considering their ordeal, remarkably attractive. All of which could be helpful when they arrived in custody.

Now North moved to the girl. With his left hand he grabbed

her right wrist and led her across to John. Deftly he grabbed the dangling handcuff and attached it once more to Libby. He glanced about, picked up Libby's handbag, took something out, tossed the bag aside and said, "Let's go. Move it!"

Only when they began to walk out did John realize that something was odd. Earlier, his right wrist had been handcuffed to Libby's left. This time North had put the cuff on her other wrist, so they were manacled right to right. This meant he either had to walk behind her, or at her right side with his hand across the front of his body. He settled for the latter method as they moved awkwardly through the house.

Dawn was breaking as they emerged out the front door. To the east the sky was growing light over dinosaur country.

"Okay, lovers—this is it!"

They had stopped by Libby's Land Cruiser. North opened the passenger door and motioned to John.

"Get in. Right in back."

John obeyed, clambering awkwardly between the front seats. The back seats were mounted at the sides, facing toward the middle. He had to perch on the one behind the front passenger seat where Libby sat, their wrists joined to the right of it.

Immediately North moved around to the rear door of the Land Cruiser, opened it and grabbed John's left arm. A final click. Looking down, John found that a second pair of cuffs, one end already locked onto the auxiliary roll bar behind, now completed his shackling across the seat.

The purpose of this awkward manoeuvre was clear. With Libby partially immobilized in front, and John completely so behind her, North, in the driver's seat, could relax, knowing that neither could bother him. The Toyota was already backing out of the drive before it occurred to John to wonder why the guy would go to so much trouble.

They took only a minute to drive out of the residential area and into the centre of town. Drumheller was deserted, as if the towering Tyrannosaurus Rex had terrified all humanity into flight. Last night the place had been eerie. In the cold dawn light it looked merely a little shabby.

As best he could from his awkward position, John started looking for the red brick of an RCMP detachment. Now he couldn't wait to get there, to be at last in the hands of decent people, proper authorities, to finally tell his story. Then he saw it: there were the lights, the familiar sign, the squad car parked outside. They came right up to it—and kept going.

Without changing speed, the Land Cruiser continued to the end of the street and turned. Then, without looking right or left, without even a token pause for a red light at the edge of town Will North—with his prisoners—put his foot to the floor and headed out of town.

THREE

"Hey, where are you going?" John yelled.

The road they were on, heading east from Drumheller, ran along the bottom of the broad canyon that was the Badlands. As the dawn light grew, outlines emerged of many-layered cliffs, water-sculpted rock pillars and the strange formations called hoodoos, hovering like dark guardians over the ominous landscape.

Since North didn't reply, Libby made a sharp query of her own. John couldn't help noticing that for the first time her voice sounded fearful. "Will—what's going on? Where are you taking us?"

Finally the man spoke. Over the noise of the wind and the engine, his words were crisply clear. "Not to the Mounties, lovers. That's for damn sure."

"Where then?" John said, with a sick feeling that he didn't want to hear. A number of details, unnoticed in the general shock of events, were coming into focus: the time chosen for the "arrest"; the fact that North had taken Libby's 4x4 instead of his own car; the peculiar way they'd been shackled for what should have been a short journey. This wasn't a delaying tactic: it was an abduction. All the talk about the police had been to make them go quietly.

"Christ, we've been stupid!" Libby suddenly cried, and he knew she'd come to the same grim understanding.

North laughed. "You said it, bitch! Stupid you are. But a good fuck to make up for it, I bet."

John could see the vivid flush leap to Libby's cheeks. He strained forward in fury and, since he couldn't move the top part of his body, he began senselessly to kick the back of the driving seat. The vehicle suddenly bucked, screeched to a halt on the pavement. North twisted in his seat, produced his revolver and rammed the barrel against Libby's temple, so hard that she cried out in pain.

But North was looking at John. Earlier his eyes had been cold; now they were like black grapes, empty of anything but savagery. "Listen, prick," North snarled. "Any more shit from you and I'll shoot this bitch right now. Is that what you want, dirtbag?"

In the ghastly silence that followed, anger and horror fought a deadly battle inside John. He dared not even look at Libby for fear of what he might do. He knew that North had been speaking in deadly earnest. At last he got himself under control. "No, of course not," he whispered. "For God's sake, let her be."

The frozen tableau remained for a moment more. Then Will North slowly lowered his gun. The 4x4 jerked forward, gaining speed.

They entered a village, built beside the river that had carved out this lunar landscape. The place was silent, deserted, the tops of the roofs struck by the first pale rays of the sun. John just had time to glimpse the name, Rosedale, before they turned onto a side road, leaving behind the last small outpost of civilization.

Now they were completely alone, following a narrow road through a long and winding valley. They rumbled across a series of ancient bridges, crossing and recrossing a stream bed that looked as though it hadn't held water since real dinosaurs roamed. As they progressed, the sun thrust itself above the surrounding cliffs with summer-swiftness, bringing the first hint of killing heat to come.

Then, as the valley widened, they came upon another place of habitation. But this was ancient, with rotting ruins, empty lots, crumbling mining equipment: a ghost town. The only structure left standing bore a legend on its peeling boards: LAST CHANCE SALOON.

Splayed across the hard back seat, jerked and twisted at every bump, cuffed and helpless, John watched the mouldering wreck go by. If nothing else, North's vicious outburst had put to rest any misapprehensions as to what was in store. They were to be disposed of, of course: on the orders of Bud Wetherall, who'd made fools of them.

Why North was doing this wasn't hard to figure. Apart from being a brute, he was Mimi's brother, and the only other person who knew of John's and Libby's arrival in Drumheller. For silence and services rendered, there would no doubt be a hefty reward, which Wetherall was amply able to pay.

This journey could have only one destination—a remote grave. North, knowing the country, probably had a special place in mind. This blasted land looked tailor-made for getting rid of bodies. But why hadn't North killed them already, as he'd threatened with Libby? Perhaps there was walking to be done at the end of the line. Or maybe North got a kick out of the torture of suspense: he was certainly capable of that. Whatever the reason, there could be little time left to think about it.

Last Chance Saloon. Under the circumstances, it seemed prophetic.

After leaving the ghost town, the road deteriorated into little more than a dusty trail. Minutes later, the canyon divided. What remained of the roadbed continued to the left. The right fork was barred by brush and a broken gate. Without pause, North geared down, mounted a scrubby rise to the right of the gate, climbed over it and down into a dry stream bed beyond. They continued for a while on this bone-shaking trail until at last, mercifully, they returned to the flat canyon bottom.

This new route led into a deep cut that narrowed, curved south, then opened out again. Surprisingly, here was yet another canyon system, more remote and desolate than anything that had gone before. The land, save for a scattering of sage brush in the most protected draws and a blur of lichen on the rocks, was almost completely barren. Fantastical sandstone outcroppings, scrubbed smooth by eons of water and wind, stuck through the skin of the world like bones. Higher up in the layered strata were black seams of coal. Here and there on the scarred cliffs could be glimpsed the dark eyes of caves.

By now the terrain was so rough that the 4x4 jolted and pitched alarmingly, making John's efforts to stay on the seat a growing agony. Even though he knew what it would mean, he found himself actually wishing that they would reach the end of this awful journey.

But it hadn't happened yet. They drove on, through a maze of twisting and intersecting gulches while the sun rose, adding stifling heat to the pain of the ride, until they felt they must surely have travelled out of the real world into some far-off region of time.

Then the journey ended. The 4x4 rounded a bend and without warning, lurched to a stop. They were in a flat area in the shadow of a cliff, strewn with boulders that had fallen from above.

In the rock wall, directly ahead, was a dark opening, an abandoned mine. Farther in, half-collapsed pit-props held up what was left of a hand-hewn shaft. This was the end of the road.

In all ways.

Will North turned off the engine, leaving the keys in the ignition, and got out. Without a glance at his prisoners he walked up to the cave mouth, examining it critically. He nodded his head in satisfaction.

Libby turned at long last to look at John. To do this she had to twist her head awkwardly and peer over her right shoulder. Their eyes met and locked. They both knew what was about to happen and that there was no point in putting words to it. The embrace of this glance was all they had, so it had to be enough.

The moment ended when North returned. And the nightmare began.

FOUR

North strode to the passenger door of the Land Cruiser, threw it open and unlocked the cuff that attached Libby to John. He did not unlock John.

"Get out," North said.

Libby did so. Her eyes were clear, her head very high. She did not look at North. "You'll never get away with this," she said.

North chuckled derisively, pointing to the cave. "With a hundred tons of rock sittin' on you and your pal, I reckon I'm free and clear. Also a fucking millionaire."

"Don't believe it. If we're dangerous to Bud, so are you."

"I'll be the one to worry about that. You better worry about yourself now, whore."

Libby laughed savagely. "That's what all women are to you, isn't it? Whores! That's why Beulah finally left you. Because you're a sadist and a pervert. Well, I'll tell you, mister—all the whore you'll ever know is in your own sick head."

From the back of the 4x4, where the other cuff held him fast, John could hear clearly what was going on. What she was doing took courage but it would only make things worse for her. Desperately he called, "Libby—let it be. It doesn't matter now."

North roared with laughter. "Creep," he called gleefully. "This slut is braver than you!"

For some reason that drove the girl crazy. Or perhaps the fact of imminent death had finally broken through, and she didn't care anymore. For she spat directly in his face.

"Shut up!" Libby yelled. "You're the creep. I'd rather be dead than spend a minute more with an animal like you. So go on, do it! Take your big gun and shoot me now. It'll be a pleasure just to stop looking at your filthy face."

John's throat contracted in distress. Having given up hope, Libby was trying to provoke North to make a quick end. But it was the wrong way to do it. Just how wrong, he was about to find out.

Furiously, North grabbed Libby's shoulder with his left hand and the light fabric of her blouse with his right. With one savage movement his hand slashed down, and the entire top came with it, leaving her nude to the waist. He threw the shredded top high in the air. Before it began to descend, the hand came in again, entered the waistband of the skirt. With a much larger ripping sound, that came away also and was flung aside, leaving only her briefs. His hand then fell on these, ripped them off, leaving her naked.

She began to struggle violently, but he held her easily, a kitten in the grasp of a mastiff. Then he hit her with his huge ham hand, backwards and forwards—once, twice, three times, four—hard, bone-crushing blows that sent the girl's head bobbing crazily from side to side like a punching bag.

John, handcuffed in the Land Cruiser, watched what was happening at first in silent horror. At some point he found himself yelling. There was no point in it, he knew that, but couldn't help himself. He didn't want to look either, but knew that he had to: to bear witness, and in doing so to share in Libby's anguish.

Ten times he saw North hit the girl. Finally she hung limp,

blood oozing from her nose and crushed lips, as if already dead. John hoped that for her sake she *was* dead.

Knew she wasn't.

Their abductor lifted the naked form and carried it to a flat slab of rock to the right of the truck. The girl, a broken doll, was dumped on her back, with her trunk on the rock and her legs hanging off it. North stood back, grinning in satisfaction at his handiwork. John was sure the rape was about to begin, but he was mistaken. The man licked his lips, rubbed his hands together, then turned and strode back to the 4x4.

"Hey there, creep," North sneered. "Having fun?"

Rigid, John simply stared.

"You're gonna get a much better show pretty soon. I'm gonna fuck the bitch, of *course*, all the better 'cause I know you're watching—then I'm gonna shoot her. Finally I'm gonna shoot the audience: *you*, creep! Whadaya think?" He did an obscene imitation of a British accent. "Good fucking show, eh? Afterwards there'll be fireworks. But that bit you *don't* get to see."

He laughed and went around to the back of the Cruiser, throwing open the hatch. He removed some items that he'd evidently packed earlier: a six-pack of beer and a cardboard box. He opened a can of beer and drank thirstily, stowing the rest out of the way under the seat. From the box he removed several sticks of dynamite and a roll of fuse wire. He grinned. "But business before pleasure, eh?"

North slammed the hatch shut. Carrying the dynamite, he strode to the mouth of the cave. And John—even though his brain was reeling from what he'd already seen, and the worse horrors to come—understood everything all too clearly.

And had a wild idea …

North's plan had been perfect and simple. After the murders, he would dump the vehicle and bodies in the mine and blow it up.

He'd have a bit of a hike back home, but it would be worth it. All evidence gone forever: John and Libby just two more in a valley full of deep-buried fossils.

But cruelty and vanity had caused the man to make one small misstep: he'd *had* to let John know what was in store. In giving him time to contemplate his doom while the charges were set, North had also presented his victim with the opportunity to realize something else: he was sitting—albeit shackled—inside a weapon.

Capable of one shot.

If this fact and North's activities could somehow be made to interact, he'd been presented with one opportunity.

IF … !

To cock his weapon, John had to reach the Cruiser's gearshift. He strained forward but his right hand, with its still-dangling manacle, barely reached forward of the seat back. The gear lever was a good 12 inches farther on. Desperately, John examined where he was attached. The handcuff was fastened around the right auxiliary roll bar, which swooped above the back of the seat, joining the main roll bar amidships. John found he could slide the cuff up the auxiliary bar and across the back of the seat, right to the junction at the middle.

Then he could reach the gearshift.

He knew that with the engine stopped, even without being able to depress the clutch, he should be able to get the shift into first gear. He shoved the lever forward and it worked.

At that moment Will North, having finished his preparations, walked out of the mine.

John froze, moving only his eyes to check out the exact position of the 4x4's ignition.

North's head turned, but he took no notice of the truck. He was looking across at where the naked figure lay, unconscious, draped on the rock. To get to Libby, he would have to cross very close to the front of the Toyota.

John barely had time to resume his original position before North started to walk. But the man didn't go directly to Libby. Instead he came up to the driver's window and stuck his head in. "I'm all done," he grinned. "One match and kaboom! Pretty neat, eh? Now I'm gonna fuck your lady. Pay attention, asshole, you might learn something. Oh—yeah—no point, right? You're gonna be dead!"

John gazed at North, willing his own features into a mask, praying that his quivering excitement would not show, or that it would be mistaken for terror. North smiled, savouring the moment, then with a grunt of contempt he turned away. He looked across at the naked girl on the rock, licked his lips again and began to walk, unfastening his belt.

This was it. John knew he had only one chance. As the other man moved—so did he.

North's path brought him directly in front of the Cruiser. Dead centre, he paused, looking in through the windshield.

By that time John had slid his manacle along the roll bar and was stretching for the ignition key. He knew he could reach it, but there would be only a split second to do what was necessary. His fingers strained, fumbled, finally made contact. He looked up, to make sure his target was in range. The eyes of the two men met through the glass.

North froze—in dreadful comprehension.

John turned the key.

Like a demon unleashed, the Cruiser leaped forward. Fueled by the first powerful surge of the starter motor, all four wheels gripped and thrust. The tough steel fender caught North's knees, snapping one like a twig before it could bend. Then the metal monster fell upon him.

The ex-cop went down like a manikin. Yet as he slid under, one of his flailing hands caught the fender. As the 4x4 continued to move, North was dragged along. The journey was brief. Straight ahead, at the mine entrance, was a large rock, half a metre high and many tons in weight. North's body hit the rock first, then the vehicle followed. It ground him onto the stone, pulled and lifted. North screamed—but the sound was immediately cut off.

The fender of the truck, moving but with nowhere to go, rode up and over the collapsing pile of flesh and bone, crushing the rib cage against the rock, still moving, grinding, down, down ...

John turned the ignition off.

The vehicle, released from propulsion, jerked, settled, came to hideous rest. The heavy fender was about an inch from North's jaw. Between the steel and the rock was a five-inch gap. It would have been less, but that was all that the body would crush down to. Blood oozed across the rock in a slow rivulet, like wine from a press.

Beyond the ruin, dust settled. A stone fell from above, bounced against the hood of the Land Cruiser and skittered away.

The canyon was silent.

FIVE

It had to be over a hundred degrees inside the Land Cruiser.

Two hours had passed since Will North had been crushed, but he had not died then. The force that had broken him had somehow left heart and lungs functioning, and—by some perverse miracle—enough room for the passage of minimal air. The result: instead of a swift death, slow torture.

When he sufficiently recovered from his own shock to think, John had tried to release the gearshift, hoping the 4x4 might roll back a little. But, try as he might, he could not get it out of first. From his position, with only one hand and not able to release the clutch, there was nothing he could do.

So North had had to stay there, destroyed but not departed. Every few moments he would become conscious. Though John couldn't see him, he could hear him. What he was doing, quite clearly, was screaming in agony, but what emerged from his mangled interior was like the faint squealing of a rusted hinge, or a small animal held over flames to roast alive. Before death, Will North had found his hell. No doubt he would eventually die. Though John would hate the man forever, he couldn't help praying now for the wretch's release.

Of much more concern was Libby. Since the beating she had
not stirred. Though it was as well that she was unconscious during
North's lingering death, her continued stillness wasn't good at all.

The sun had moved around, bringing her, spread-eagled on her
rock, out of the shadow. Trapped by the canyon, the heat had risen
relentlessly. Libby lay on her back, head lolling, legs horribly splayed,
naked and frying. This, and the fact that she continued to remain
unconscious, drove John to anguish as the time passed.

Perhaps she was dying, perhaps already dead. He didn't know,
couldn't find out; he was inside his own prison. He could see Libby
but couldn't get to her. That was the worst thing of all. It would have
driven him crazy, except for one small blessing: Libby's tool box.

It had been stored under the right rear seat. He had begun to
despair when he noticed it sitting there. It contained a fine set of
tools; he remembered this from when Libby had worked on his MG.
There was only one instrument he needed. If it wasn't there, all the
tools in the world would be as useless as toys.

He tried to reach the box, but at first he couldn't. Then he got
a toe around the back of it and managed to hook it out, dragging it
into the centre of the floor where he could get at it with his free right
hand. He opened the box, tossed tools out on the floor. What he
needed wasn't in the top tray. He had to go rooting on the bottom,
searching, more and more frantically—at last he found them. Two
files: a small flat bastard and a rat-tail.

Salvation! Maybe ...

Using an edge of the flat file to make a V-cut, he went to
work on the manacle chain. The metal was case-hardened steel,
extremely tough. At first it seemed even harder than the file. It was
10 minutes before he had made a mark as deep as the thickness of
his thumbnail.

The handcuffs dangling from John's right arm—the pair once

attached to Libby—kept getting in the way. The effort made him sweat profusely, but in the roasting heat of the cab the moisture didn't stay long enough to cool him. It evaporated instantly, uselessly depleting the liquid in his body. Soon the filing took more and more energy. Now, he had to stop frequently to rest, each rest getting longer, providing less relief.

To add to John's distress, soon after he started filing, North began anew his strange, bleating screams. After a while the awful sounds appeared to coordinate with the movements of the file. As heat and exhaustion began to edge John's mind toward delirium, fantasy worked a bizarre illusion; he began to feel that he was filing directly into the dying man's flesh. Considering his feelings for their would-be killer, this shouldn't have bothered him. But it did. He began to feel guilty, to want to apologize. To want to stop.

He raised his head and fixed his eyes on Libby, grimly filing on, on, on ...

Once the file had moved through the outer case-hardening of the steel, it began to move more swiftly. But even that was little more than the pace of despair. Beside the handcuff was his wristwatch, and he couldn't help being constantly aware of the time. The figures flicked by, seeming to taunt, to change faster as his own exhaustion grew.

When he was halfway through the chain, the time was eleven o'clock. In exhaustion, in near collapse, John paused to rest. His left heel slid back under the seat, and banged against something that clunked. He looked down, seeing what in the press of events he had forgotten.

"God! Oh, dear God!"

Sitting beneath the seat was the six-pack brought along by their abductor. John fished out the five remaining cans and wrenched one free. He transferred the can to his manacled hand, tugging at the tab with his right. As soon as the metal opened, hot beer started to foam out of the can. John cried out, knowing that in an instant he was going to lose half the precious fluid in one wild gush of near-vapour.

Just in time he got it stopped. The fizzing stuff oozed out like soapsuds, but he got his mouth down, sucking up much of it before it fell.

As beer it tasted like piss. As liquid it was straight from paradise.

After swallowing all the foam, John pulled the tab right off. Half the beer was still there. He took two huge gulps. Immediately he felt the liquid working, restoring him, almost instantly passing from stomach walls to bloodstream.

What went with it, of course, was alcohol. Even the small amount in the beer at that moment felt like a jolt of cocaine. His head swam and then he knew fierce exhilaration. He let out a gasp, opened his eyes and found he was looking straight through the window at the frying, dying form of Libby.

That gave him a jolt bigger than the beer. Breathing hard, feeling at the same time high and terrified, he put down the beer can. Then he got the other four cans and placed them beside it.

This beer, this blessing, might save their lives but it was also liquid dynamite. It had the water content his body craved, but the alcohol could break down all inhibition, all restraint. In the state John was in, if he had too much too fast, he could easily lose control. Even now, an insane voice in his head was urging him to just sit and guzzle the lot, to throw away all hope in exchange for a few moments of bliss.

Deliberately he looked out again at Libby. Then he picked up the unopened beer cans, tossed all but one beyond the front seat, onto the floor. Out of reach, unless and until he got free. He took up the opened can and had one small sip. With the buzz of it carrying on, making use of the surge of energy, he grasped the file again and set to work.

The death-wails from below resumed but he ignored them; he also ignored the ache in his arms and the growing blisters on his fingers. He kept his eyes on Libby and the file in the deepening groove—and worked and worked. Some time later he noticed that it was noon. He had finished the first beer and taken a few small sips from the second. There was blood on his hand and on the file.

And he was almost through.

Now he felt totally exhausted, insanely hot, desperate and high all at the same time. He knew that his body was losing fluid faster than the beer could replace it, but the controlled flow of alcohol was a stimulant to the use of energy reserves. And it took the edge off the pain and the fear. If only he could keep the balance long enough to finish.

John gave a sharp tug at the almost-severed manacle. It gave no sign of parting. Not quite yet. He took up the remaining beer can, weighed its contents, looked at the nearly completed file cut. Then he upended the can, finishing the contents in one long swig. He tossed the can down, flattened it with a stamp of his foot.

Under the van North gave a last strangled cry.

On her rock Libby moved. John saw it. He was looking right at her when she did it. She was alive. *Alive!*

John gave a joyous shout, grasped the file and shoved it into the almost-completed groove. Over-excited, he thrust too hard. The tool twisted, slipped from his numb fingers, flew sideways and away, landing in the front cab beside the cans of beer. Unreachable.

He stopped, staring stupidly. A wave of horror began to envelop him; then he remembered the rat-tail.

He knelt, scrabbling amongst the tools and at last found it.

With beating heart, with pathetic care, he applied it to what was
left of the metal on the manacle.

"I'm sorry," he muttered to Libby, without even knowing he was
doing it. "Oh, God I'm sorry … "

The rat-tail file was not nearly as good as the other. It was
more worn and completely round, with no biting edge. Since it
wouldn't fit in the groove, he had to start on the other side. For
a while it didn't seem to be having any effect. Then, at long last,
as anguish was building to despair, he saw that it was working.
A shallow trough had appeared opposite the first cut, perceptibly
lessening the thickness of the remaining steel. With new hope he
kept going. The rat-tail was harder to hold than the bastard file.
In his already lacerated fingers it was making a groove all its own.
A blister broke and fresh blood began to ooze, but now he didn't
even feel it. He filed, filed, filed …

Began to sing.

It was a ditty from a musical he'd once performed in at some
Canadian provincial theatre, Calgary actually, long ago. The words
came in rhythm to the work, driving it on:

> Oh–oh–oh, it's a lovely war
> Who wouldn't be a soldier, eh?
> Oh, it's a shame to take the pay
> Form fours, right turn,
> How do we spend the money we earn?
> Oh–oh–oh, it's a lovely war …

It moved!

Under the pressure, the metal of the manacle began to bend.
John dropped the file. With his right hand he grasped the cuff around
his wrist, starting to pull, to wrench, to twist: in, out, around …

It parted!

The impetus of the last jerk carried John backwards, sending him sprawling amongst the tools; upended and exhausted in the back of the Toyota Land Cruiser.

It was half an hour after noon. And he was free.

SIX

John was unaware of his passage from the Cruiser to Libby, but some time after his release he found himself standing over her. He knelt, shielding her face from the sun with his own. As the shadow passed across, her eyes flickered. She groaned.

"Libby," he whispered, feeling both joy and awful dread. "Libby—it's me!"

She opened her eyes. They tried to focus on him, and her mouth moved in the barest twitch of a smile.

"Libby, it's all right. You're okay. We're both going to be okay. Hang on!"

Now that it was over, with the release of tension, he suddenly felt sick and dizzy. He stood up, swaying, trying to push away the nausea and to think what to do. Ah! The first thing, of course, was to get Libby out of the sun. Yes—that was it.

He moved back to the Cruiser and opened the back door wide. The floor between the seats was covered with the scattered tools, and he swept them aside. The cuffs dangling on his wrists made movement awkward, but he couldn't stop to attend to that now. He went back for Libby.

Her eyes were closed again. He didn't know how conscious

she'd been but he knew he couldn't expect any help. He would have to lift her. John knelt, raised the girl, trying to get an arm under her shoulders. Despite her horrific treatment, he was pretty sure nothing was broken. But the bruises on her face, the blood and sweat and dirt over the rest of her body, made her seem so frail and injured that he was afraid to move her. But it had to be done.

He managed to get her sitting up, then knelt facing her, continuing to lift until her head and arms were dangling over his right shoulder. Then he began to take the weight, sliding her farther back over his shoulder as he rose. When he was finally upright, a new wave of dizziness hit him. He stood wobbling, eyes closed, breathing deeply, willing the wave to pass. At last it did. Before another could come, he walked with her back to the truck, lowering her onto the floor, then gently sliding her back and sideways, until at last she was lying flat.

His next instinct was to cover her. But, though she might be in shock, she could hardly take a chill in this boiling heat. What she really needed was water. What they had was beer.

From the cab he fetched the cans he'd dumped there, opened one, pulling the tab back carefully, letting the gas escape first. But she was in no shape to drink yet. It came to him what he could do. He searched around and found Libby's shredded clothing. He retrieved the garments and turned back ...

To find Will North staring at him.

Since the moment of his release, and in his concern for Libby, John had not given the man a single thought. Now, as if in a trance, he drifted over to the crushed remnant. Though its eyes were open, the gaze was from the other side of death. The process had taken ghastly hours, but the torture was finally over.

Seeing up close what his desperate action had accomplished, the terrible manner in which North had died, John felt repulsed but not sorry: if not for this, both he and Libby would now be dead and buried. It was that simple, and it wasn't going to make him lose a moment's sleep.

John turned away from the ruin and hurried back to Libby. The skirt he folded and placed under her head. From the top he tore a smaller piece, soaking this with some of the beer. With this he bathed Libby's forehead and face and temples. Her eyelids fluttered again, showing she was at the edge of consciousness.

He knelt closer, lifted her head and managed to pour a few drops of beer into her mouth. Her tongue moved, worked. She swallowed. He poured in a little more and this time she swallowed directly, coughed—opened her eyes.

"Hey, Libby, it's me," he said softly. "It's okay. Everything's going to be fine now. Just drink—drink what you can—and I'll get us out of here."

She seemed to listen. It wasn't clear whether she understood or even knew him but she appeared reassured. He put the can directly to her lips, and this time she actually drank a few sips. Then she coughed hard. He held her, rubbing her back, cuddling her head against his shoulder. When the spasm was over she reached her lips forward again, the desire obvious. So he stayed there, slowly feeding her, until most of the can was gone. By then the liquid and the alcohol had done their work. At one moment she was drinking, the next her head drooped sideways in sleep.

He laid her back gently, looking around for something for a cover. Nothing. So he took off his own sweat-soaked shirt, draping her from shoulder to thigh, tucking it under at the sides. It probably wouldn't stay once they got moving, but it would have to do.

He pulled up her legs so he could shut the back door. He refilled the tool box, bracing it against her right hip. This and the fact that she was jammed in quite tightly should stop her rolling around, if he drove slowly.

John then climbed across into the driver's seat, taking with him the half-finished can of beer and the two that were still unopened. Sitting with his eyes closed, he slowly drank the rest of the can. It didn't give him a rush anymore. He tossed it aside and jammed his foot hard down on the clutch. Released from tension, the 4x4 settled backwards, the bumper sliding off the body.

Now it was easy to pull the shift out of first. John turned the key and the engine roared to life. He put the vehicle in reverse and backed up. As he turned, the handcuff dangling from his right wrist clattered against the steering wheel, reminding him he had one last task.

He got out and approached the body of North. It had fallen sideways off its rock, face to the sky, crumpled like bloody trash in a sack. Steeling himself, John felt around, finding a wallet, coins, a cigarette lighter—and finally keys. He removed the manacles from his right wrist, and the remains of the other from his left. These he tossed on top of his dead tormentor. The keys he put in his pocket.

He had turned the 4x4 around and driven about 50 metres when he had a sudden thought. He stopped, sat for a while, then walked back to the body. Where it had ended up was under the lee of the cliff, at the entrance to the mine that was to have been their tomb.

He retrieved North's lighter, walked into the mine and searched about, finally finding what he was looking for. He knelt, flicked the lighter, then made a very fast exit.

The Cruiser had travelled another 100 metres when there was a tremendous explosion and the rocks came down.

SEVEN

Somehow he lost his way. John had no idea how it happened. Despite the terror of the journey, he'd thought he had a pretty clear memory of the route they had come. After half an hour of driving he knew he was mistaken.

He went slowly, never going above second gear, paying careful attention to the terrain, but looking back often to check on Libby. It must have been during one of those moments that he missed a vital turn, for when he should have reached the narrow gap that led back into the lower part of the canyon, he didn't. Instead, he realized he was going in the wrong direction entirely: south.

Also, the canyon floor was becoming harder and harder to negotiate, even for the rugged Land Cruiser. Finally, forward movement became impossible. He managed to get the truck turned around and went back, following his own tracks, searching for an exit from what was a veritable maze of canyons, gulches and steep ravines.

Now, though the going was better, the steering wheel was increasingly hard to turn. He started to feel dizzy again, which wasn't surprising. Though he'd been doing his best to ignore the blinding heat, it was nevertheless doing its work on his body. If he was to get out of here, he had to find water. He was down to the last can of beer. Liquid and alcohol: the double-edged sword. But his need for the first was so great he had to risk the second. He stopped, opened the can, sipped, again grimly resisting the urge to drink it all.

Then he put the 4x4 in gear again and continued on. This time he was headed north, searching for a cut-off that would lead to the exit. But he couldn't find it. Ten more minutes he drove, twenty. He reached down for another sip of the beer, receiving his last nasty shock. Unnoticed, the can had tipped on its side and all but a dribble was gone. He sucked that down, cursing, dazedly kept on.

Now the sound of the engine appeared to be growing louder, a monotonous, mocking tune. John knew he was growing light-headed. The sun-drenched landscape was taking on a shimmer that was not simply the result of the overheated air. The crouching rock-faces were assuming a life of their own. His eyes were beginning to play tricks.

John straightened in the seat, clutched the wheel—now heavy as lead—and squinted desperately to clear his vision. Ahead he saw a fork in the canyon. He drove up to it and stopped. His head grew lighter by the minute and he had to force himself to concentrate.

The right leg veered to the east, continuing as far as he could see. The left led into a deepening ravine. At the last moment he wrenched the wheel left and headed into the ravine. The 4x4 entered cooling shadow from the cliff wall, which was a relief. But this couldn't be the way. It was turning into a box canyon, which grew deeper and steeper the farther in he went. He came around a bend to discover a blind alley: a flat-bottomed depression no more than a hundred yards square. Straight ahead was a line of giant hoodoos, barring his way. The only other feature was a dried-up creek bed. Numbly, without even the strength to berate himself, he stared—then a thought fuzzily took shape: *to form a bed, a stream has to come from somewhere!*

John heaved himself out of the 4x4 and stumbled across to get a closer look. The stream bed was gravelly, flat and came straight from the cliff wall. Pressing on on foot, he came around an outcropping into full view of the canyon end and then it all became clear. Halfway along the line of hoodoos, visible only from this new angle, was a water-carved fissure, 20 feet wide. At the far end was open sky.

Shock and exultation sent a surge of energy through John's body. "Libby!" he yelled, turning to flounder back to the 4x4. "Libby—I've found it!"

But before he reached the Cruiser, he noticed something even more interesting: under the nearby cliff a small area looked damp. John went to investigate. He had not been mistaken. Water was oozing from between two layers of rock, Farther back beneath an overhang, the strata was even wetter. In a deep cleft, actual drops were falling into a small pool.

"Oh, man!" John whispered. He leaned down, thrust his head under the overhang until it came near the pool. He lowered his mouth, letting his tongue dip into the water. Heaven!

"*Libby!*"

Then he was running for the truck, feeling frantic and guilty and horrified and ecstatic all at the same time. He flung open the back door of the 4x4 where Libby lay, covered by his shirt and breathing steadily.

"Water!" he gasped, as he gathered empty beer cans. "I've found water! Libby, hold on."

He filled a can from the rock pool and hurried back. When he dribbled water on her lips, her eyes flickered. A few more drops and her mouth snapped open. He poured the water in, not worrying if it splashed, trying not to make her choke. Soon she was swallowing strongly. A while later Libby sat up.

There were four useable cans in the Cruiser. John also discovered an empty 7 UP bottle wedged under a seat. After they'd both drunk all they could, they filled the five receptacles while John told her all that had happened.

Libby put on John's shirt, which, if hardly stylish, at least covered most of her. The front of her body was an ugly red and the bruises on her face looked dreadful, but resolutely she heaved herself into the passenger seat.

"Do you want to wait a bit before we start?" John said, with concern.

Libby smiled grimly. "What I *want* is for this never to have happened. What I'd *like* is to have seen it when you totalled that bastard North. Now, all I want is to get home. Don't worry about me, John. Get us out of here."

The rock cleft that he'd discovered proved wide enough for the vehicle. Struggling through it on the stream bed wasn't easy, but they'd already travelled on worse terrain. At one point, a large boulder seemed about to block the way, but they managed to squeeze around it. Half a kilometre from the start, the cleft abruptly ended, emptying into a ravine that cut across from left to right. Clearly visible in the dust were tire tracks—their own.

John's heart plummeted. Had they been going in circles? Then—*then*—he recognized it: the connecting canyon that led back to the outside world.

Libby evidently understood too. "Oh, thank God!"

"Yeah!"

"We turn right—right?"

"*Right!*"

The sky, which had been a narrow band as they moved through the cut, opened into a broad bowl and was suddenly radiant. The sun was sliding off toward the west, pointing the way home.

PART SIX

ONE

They got to Will North's house just after 5:00 PM. It seemed incredible that less than 12 hours had passed since they had been summarily snatched. The idea of returning to the scene of the abduction was far from pleasant but they had no choice. The place was empty and they had to have somewhere to rest and recover. Besides, all their stuff was there.

When they arrived on the quiet street, parking close to the house that looked so peaceful and ordinary, Libby gave a shudder. "I can almost feel him still here."

John shut off the engine. Considering their appearance, it was fortunate that the drive was well screened from the road. "I know what you mean. But here's the good thing: as long as Bud believes it's *us* buried in that canyon, he'll think he's safe."

"Which means Nate's safe too."

"Right!"

"Is that why you set off the charge?"

John grimaced. "I wasn't thinking that clearly. It was sort of appropriate, hiding the body the same way the guy had planned to hide us. But it also means there's no way Bud can find out his plan has failed. We just have to figure how to keep it like that till we find him."

The house was locked, but John had North's keys. John's and Libby's things were inside; his suitcase, wallet and keys and her handbag and travelling case were in the spare room. No doubt North had intended to get rid of these things at his leisure.

The house had such a haunted, sickening feeling that John would have liked to gather their gear and get out. Of course, this wasn't possible. Apart from rest and recovery, and the need to figure out what to do next, another factor arose. It was something neither of them had anticipated, but it could mean either disaster or a real breakthrough in the rescue of Nate—and they very nearly missed it.

Once they were safely inside, they realized they were ravenous. Fortunately, Beulah's kitchen was well stocked. While Libby went to take a sorely needed bath, John got busy with supper.

There was brandy in the liquor cabinet. John had a shot and, while canned stew was heating, brought a glass to Libby in the tub. The bruises on her face had deepened, but her burn was benefiting from the warm soaking. She looked almost content. Sipping the brandy, she sighed. "It was just sinking in how lucky I am to be alive. Reckon I owe you one, John."

"Same goes for you."

"What? How come?"

"If it hadn't been for the need to get to you, I might have given up."

He left her and busied himself in the kitchen. Presently Libby joined him. She was dressed in a voluminous nightie, presumably Beulah's, and looked considerably refreshed. John was grubby from his ordeal, but didn't much care. He was realizing the near-miraculous nature of their reprieve, and anyway, he was famished.

As they were finishing their meal, the phone rang. John and Libby both jumped, staring at the jangling instrument. One possibility struck them simultaneously: Bud Wetherall. Was this the kidnapper phoning to find if he was in the clear? That the job had been done?

John rose and approached the phone. "No!" Libby said urgently.

"I'm not going to answer, don't worry," John said. But even after the ringing stopped he continued to stare.

"What?" Libby asked.

John retrieved a scratch pad that had been on the counter, almost hidden by the phone. "Oh, man!"

"What?" Libby asked again.

Wordlessly, John put the pad in front of her. In an ugly scrawl was a brief note: BUD CALLS—6:00 PM—MON

Whoever it had been on the phone wasn't important. The call had drawn attention to North's note, which they might have missed. Bud would be calling in less than 24 hours, and the fact that North had so specifically noted the time probably meant that he would be calling from the road. The reassurance he'd be seeking was vital; after kidnapping a child and ordering two murders, he couldn't afford to approach his home territory until he was sure he was in the clear. Now there was no one to give that reassurance.

Bud Wetherall had proved that he was desperate and deadly. To protect himself and keep the child, he'd condemned two human beings to death. His belief that he'd succeeded was now their only advantage and that would vanish if Bud learned the truth. His only option then would be to get rid of the evidence: Nate.

They were back to square one.

"I guess we can't wait any longer," John said. "We'll have to go to the police."

Libby had been studying the terse message on the pad, her bruised features drawn in perplexity. "And tell them what, exactly? That the animal who wrote this—the only witness, except me, that Bud actually has your boy—is up in the canyon under 100 tons of rock, where we left him after he tried to kill us? Which part of that story, do you think, would interest the police most? What they'd see as a homicide, or your wild tale of a kidnapping? And while they're trying to work it all out—and Bud is getting more and more scared because he can't contact North—what do you imagine will happen to Nate?"

"Oh."

"Yeah."

"So we can't bring the cops in yet?"

With a gesture of distaste, Libby tossed aside the pad. "Face it, John, we can't bring them in at all. Well, not here in Drumheller anyway. You and I both know what happened in the canyon. Our consciences are clear about that, but we'll never be able to prove it. Will was a brute who beat his wife and tried to murder us, and no one will miss him for a minute. It serves no purpose for anyone to know that we were ever here. Can you live with that? After what we went through, I certainly can."

John nodded. "Yes. But that doesn't solve the other problem."

"Bud calling tomorrow?"

"Exactly."

Libby rose from the table. She took a step and swayed, and John moved quickly to support her. "I'm okay," she said. "I just need some rest."

"Well, let's get you to bed."

But she wouldn't let him support her on the way to the room, to the bed where, what felt like half a century ago, they'd both spent the night. As she was sliding in, she smiled tiredly. "If you're planning to join me, John, I'd recommend a trip to the shower."

John glanced at himself in the mirror. He'd washed his hands and donned a shirt before he made dinner, but what peered back at him was a grubby scarecrow with a huge, ugly bruise on the side of his face. Simply seeing the image made him feel exhausted. *Nate, he thought, wherever you are—I hope you're holding up better than this. But I'm coming. I swear, I'm coming!* He turned back to Libby with an attempt at cheer. "Sorry about that, ma'am. I'll get right on it."

"Good," she said, settling down. "Don't take long. And John— about Bud calling ... "

"Yes?"

"Well," her eyes flickered, fighting the onset of sleep, "it occurred to me: didn't you say that you're an *actor?*"

TWO

John thought about Libby's idea half the night. When he wasn't thinking about it, in short periods of fitful sleep, he dreamed about it, the images foolish and fanciful but mostly fraught with menace. He'd never had such jitters in the whole of his acting career, not even before the most demanding opening night. Because this performance was for frighteningly high stakes, the idea being that when Bud Wetherall called the next evening, John should be North. A remarkable plan, if only he could pull it off.

He'd heard the dead man's voice enough, and in such harrowing circumstances, that it still rang with chilling clarity in his head. But externalizing that mind-voice, even for the telephone, was no easy task. Vocal mimicry was not his forte as an actor and though normally it would have been an interesting challenge, now the thought terrified him. If he didn't succeed, if Bud Wetherall found out he was being conned, he would realize the truth—and the result ...

Unthinkable.

But what other choice was there? If Nate's abductor got no answer when he called, that could also be fatal. If John succeeded, the possibilities were enormous. Believing himself to be in the clear, Bud would head home, to be apprehended before he could do any further harm.

So John knew he had to do it. For this performance there would be no Oscars, no glowing notices or cheering fans, but success would mean a reward beyond price: the life of his son. Which was enough to give anyone stage fright.

THE FOLLOWING DAY John and Libby rested and patched themselves up as best they could. Since her skin was already brown, Libby's sunburn wasn't as bad as they feared, but her face was very bruised and swollen. To pass the time they packed their stuff, washed the Land Cruiser and cleared it out, removing all reminders of their harrowing experience in the canyon. They did everything they could think of, some of it several times.

By 5:00 that evening they were both sitting in the kitchen staring at the phone. Suddenly Libby asked, "Would it help to practise?"

"Practise?"

"You know—what do actors call it—rehearse? I can't act, but I could do myself. It might help you get used to doing his voice. What do you think?"

It was a brilliant idea, and also thoroughly repulsive. The notion of bringing Will North into the house before it was absolutely necessary was obscene. "It's great. But I don't think I could do it."

Libby's bruised jaw jutted. She glared almost savagely. "Not even if it made the difference between seeing Nate alive or not?"

John forced himself to put his emotion aside. "Well—if you put it like that, what can I say?"

"Okay—let's go."

They worked for nearly an hour, playing a pretend phone call, with Libby asking questions and John answering as North. After a while he got into it, and at last he came to believe he had it right; over a telephone, this voice might pass.

The phone rang dead on 6:00.

John lifted the receiver. "Yeah?"

"That you, Will?" It was Bud Wetherall's voice.

John gave a nod to Libby. "Yeah! Who else?"

"Well?"

Not a shadow of doubt about what was meant by that.

"Sure! Everythin's taken care of."

"You can guarantee your work? I can be sure that the results are permanent?"

John permitted his character a coarse but brief laugh. "Damn right, brother! Fuckin' *forever*."

There was a pause. John's heart speeded up. This was it, the psychological moment: if any alarm bells were going to go off, it would be now. If they did, if Bud began to sound suspicious, what would he do?

From the other end of the phone came a sharp exhalation. Bud said, "Good—good!" He sounded both relieved and happy. Definitely no hint of suspicion.

To John's surprise, considering that the man had tried to murder him and still had his child, he now began to feel remarkably calm. Of course, it wasn't himself but Will North on the line, so personal feelings were more easily sublimated.

"When am I gonna see you?" John fed into this all the expectation and ill-cloaked greed he could muster.

"Soon, Will. I haven't forgotten our agreement. I'm about a day's drive away right now. We'll start back in the morning and figure to be home tomorrow night. I'll call you from there Wednesday, and we can begin—making plans. Okay?"

"Fuckin' A!"

"Okay. Take care, Will."

There was a click and the line went dead. It had worked. In 24 hours the Wetheralls—with Nate—would be arriving back home. This time John and Libby would be ready.

THREE

The journey back to Cardston, using major roads this time, took a little under three hours. At 9:30 PM they turned west on Highway 5, passing across the edge of town. As the brightly lit bulk of the great temple loomed nearby, Libby pointed to an intersection coming up on the right.

"Hold on. Slow down—turn here."

"What?"

"A friend of mine lives here—a Mountie that I dated a long time ago. He's a real straight guy, and we're good friends. If you tell him your story first, it could make things go quicker in the morning."

At that moment a police cruiser ahead of them swung into the street Libby had indicated.

"Maybe that's him, coming home from his shift."

"Could be. Follow along and we'll see."

John did so, tailing the cruiser till it turned into a driveway and doused its lights.

"That's his house." Libby laid her hand on his arm. "Well—here we are. Are you ready?"

John thought of the big motorhome that would soon be beginning its journey home. Before it arrived, an astonishing story would have to be told, mountains of credibility established and then, when he'd convinced the powers-that-be that this was really happening, careful plans made. So the sooner they got going the better.

"Ready as I'll ever be!"

He swung into the driveway just as the officer was emerging from his cruiser.

Libby's friend was Constable Lyall Petty: he was 35, with a thick black mustache and a figure like the trunk of a medium-sized tree. Seeing Libby, his smile was pure Alberta sunshine and when she introduced him to John, he said cheerfully, "Good to meet you. Any friend of Lib's is a friend of … " he stopped, as Libby moved into light. "Christ! What happened? Did someone beat up on you?"

"No, no!" Libby said quickly "Horse threw me a couple of days back. My foot caught in the stirrup and I got dragged some. Bummer, but I'm okay. That's not why we're here. John's got something very important to tell you. Can we come in?"

Lyall's wife, Marcie, was putting his dinner on the table, but Lyall declared he had no objection to hearing a story while he ate. Marcie, a small, round woman with crinkly eyes, brought them coffee and stayed to listen.

Half an hour later the tale was done. One section only was left out: everything at Drumheller. For the record, John had that day arrived at the Wetherall ranch, to have his suspicions confirmed by Bud's e-mail. Libby had then had a phone call from Bud himself, letting her know he'd be home tomorrow night. They had then realized they must waste no time in coming to the police.

When the story was done Lyall Petty rose and, without a word, lumbered away to the back of the house. When he returned he was looking very angry. "What's the matter, dear?" his wife said, looking as bewildered as the others felt.

The constable shook his head. "Our little girl's sound asleep

back there. I was just looking at her—trying to imagine what I'd feel
like if she was … " His huge fist smashed into his palm. "Damn!" he
whispered savagely. "*Damn!*"

Grimly he turned to John. "I don't know Bud Wetherall all that
well. I do know he's rich, and probably well connected. But I promise
you this—if he's done what you say, all the smart lawyers he can
muster won't do him any good. The kidnapping of a child's got to
be one of the worst crimes I know. When Bud and his missus step
out of their fancy RV tomorrow, and if they've got your boy—they're
going to be toast." With his bear paws he took hold of John by the
shoulders, almost lifting him clear off the ground. "I'm not saying
that as a cop, but as a dad! Understand me, fella?"

Shaken, John allowed that he most certainly did.

John and Libby arranged to meet Lyall at the detachment the
next morning and drove on out of town. Arriving at the Wetherall
place, the lair of the man who'd plotted to have them killed, was
disquieting, but they were too exhausted to let it bother them for
long. Libby's bed was plenty large enough for the two of them. They
undressed and tumbled in and five minutes later, snuggled up against
his back, Libby was sound asleep. John would very much have liked
to sleep too, but his mind was too keyed up. He thought of his son,
who now might soon be restored to him again.

Nate: since the boy was born, how little he had really seen of
him. Two years after his birth, years filled with the pain of a disinte-
grating marriage. Afterwards, contrary to his confession to Libby, he
had tried to spend some time with his son, but isolated afternoons
in playgrounds, trips to Disney movies and a succession of pale little
gifts did not constitute real fatherhood. As he thought about it now,
it seemed remarkable that he and Nate had retained any connection
at all. Yet somehow, despite everything, the bond was there.

One thing he did know: after this, things were going to change.

John realized how wrong he'd been in surrendering custody so completely, but these things could be reversed. It wouldn't be pleasant to take Val to court, but, if necessary, he would do it. Whatever happened, from now on he'd have his proper share of his son's life.

He'd also learned something else: soft and self-centred he might be, and more than a bit of a dreamer, but he cared enough for what was important to go after it. That knowledge was one bonus from this unasked-for adventure.

The other one lay sleeping beside him.

PART SEVEN

ONE

Bud was glad he was going home. The motorhome was all its makers claimed: spacious, comfortable and cool, and it drove more smoothly than the sweetest semi. The campsite near Great Falls, Montana, where they had stopped, was well appointed, almost luxurious, as such places so often were these days. In fact, since the arrival of the child, the trip had been an unqualified success. A turning point in their lives. This last little leg, dipping down south of the US border, although not originally planned had been a necessary precaution. After the unfortunate incident in Drumheller, it had been prudent to be out of the country till the problem was attended to.

The campground had a play area with swings and a huge swimming pool and Mimi and the boy had spent an hour frolicking there the previous evening. Not being a water person, Bud had sat watching, taking occasional photographs with the old-fashioned film camera he still preferred. Mimi looked about 25, lustrously happy; he was sure no one doubted that the little fellow she played so tirelessly with was her own born child. That wasn't surprising since Mimi now believed it herself. The tragedy of 18 months ago had at last retreated to the status of nightmare, repressed so deeply as to be all but forgotten. The new reality was here, an adored, happy little fellow:

the saviour of Mimi's sanity, the answer to his own desperation. The heir to all their dreams.

Watching them, Bud knew that only one thing was missing: they were a family, yes, but without a feeling of home yet. A set of wheels, no matter how well-appointed, was not home. The glue that would really bind everything together was back at the Alberta ranch. A proper house, with a kid's room, a yard, animals: healthy, family stuff to become part of Gabe's new reality, his true and only childhood.

As for the boy himself, the only holdover from the old days was an occasional hankering for "Real Daddy." But even that was passing. In a few months that bozo would have become a distant memory and the real parents would be themselves.

At six o'clock, when he phoned his brother-in-law as arranged, receiving the welcome news that everything had been attended to, the last thing he told Will was that he would be heading home. After his wife and son came out of the pool, he gave them the news.

Now, on Tuesday morning, with everything cleared and stowed, Bud slid the big motorhome onto the highway, heading north for the border on Interstate 15. The sky was cloudless, promising another blistering day. Already the two big air conditioners had started their day-long toil against the heat.

JOHN WALKED INTO the RCMP detachment office in Cardston. Libby was with him, Constable Lyall Petty was waiting. The three went straight in to see Lyall's boss.

Sergeant Norm Oaks was a trimly built man in his 40s who looked as though he would be equally at home running a bank. After they were introduced, Oaks didn't waste time getting to the point. "Constable Petty has already told me the gist of what you're here about. Want to fill me in?"

John did. He finished by handing over a printout of the e-mail from Bud that had finally made an ally of Libby. Oaks studied it, along with the Polaroid of John and Nate. At last he said, "Mr. Quarry, you are a most extraordinary man."

"Oh?"

"Either that or a bit crazy."

"Now just a minute!" Libby cried.

"Hold on, young lady, I didn't say he *was*. But going on a hunt like that with no evidence, little more than blind hope, anyone'd be entitled to think so. John knew that only too well, I'd guess. That's why he went snooping around, not daring to tell a soul his story. He knew he'd be considered a nut. But he didn't care. He went ahead anyway, didn't give up." Oaks smiled at John. "Don't worry, I'm on your side. But I have to tell you, it's a good thing you've got this e-mail. Now—details. What is your son's full name?"

"Nathaniel James Quarry."

"Age?"

"Three. Born on … "

"Never mind that now. What I need is the date of the original incident—when your son was presumed to have been drowned."

"June 12th."

"And that was in the Fraser, north of Hell's Gate, which would probably mean Lytton … " He reached across and clawed open his door. "Hey, Grace!"

A constable with short dark hair and a distinctly native appearance came to the door. "Yes, Sarge?"

"Get on to the detachment in Lytton, BC. Tell them I need 'em to fax me a copy of an incident report." He gave her the details. "No need to say why, right now."

The constable grinned. "Don't imagine I *know* why, Sarge."

"Oh, yeah—well, you will. All hell's gonna break loose round here pretty soon. For now tell 'em it's urgent. Okay?"

After an enquiring look at John, the constable turned briskly away. "Sure, boss! On it!"

When she had left, John said, "What's that about? Don't you believe me?"

Oaks raised his eyebrows. "On the contrary. But we're not only the cavalry here, Mr. Quarry, we're also a bureaucracy. Kidnapping is one of the most serious crimes there is. I must make sure I've got all my ducks in a row before apprehending these people. But I wouldn't be doing this if I didn't think it likely that the child is yours."

"What do you mean 'likely,'" Libby snapped. "Of course he is."

Oaks smiled patiently. "Yes but you've only got that e-mail. All it says is they've 'adopted' a boy called Nate. Now I agree it would be the wildest coincidence if that lad wasn't Mr Quarry's son. But till we've actually seen the child, we can't be 100 percent sure, can we?"

"But, " John began, then snapped his mouth shut smartly. They were 100 percent sure, of course, but considering all that had happened, there was no way they could admit that. Only by the greatest effort did he prevent himself from shooting a guilty look at Libby, before he continued lamely, "Oh, yeah—I see what you mean."

Oaks continued, "What we're doing here is playing it by the book. Until we prove otherwise, Bud Wetherall has all the rights of a solid citizen. As well as covering—beg pardon—my own patootie, I want to have done my homework before we confront the guy. Okay?"

John did venture a glance at Libby then. She smiled, and he said to Oaks, "Yes, sure."

"Good. Now Mr. Quarry, I've got kids, so I've some idea what you must be going through. But do your best to relax. If we're going to be at the Wetherall place, set up and prepared by the time these folks arrive, there's a lot to do. You have the most at stake here, I know. But the best way you can help is by keeping out of the way."

"Any alcohol or tobacco?"

They were at the border crossing at Coutts.

"Nothing at all," Bud said.

The girl in her Canadian Customs uniform smiled up at him, neat and composed and efficient. He realized she looked considerably like Libby McGrew, dark-haired and tanned with blue-green eyes, and for an instant Bud thought it was. Then he remembered why it couldn't be Libby and felt sick.

Mimi must have been watching, because she called across. "Bud, is anything the matter?"

Bud was furious at himself for being surprised into such a reaction. He pulled himself together and smiled at his wife. "No, I'm okay. Getting a little hungry, is all."

Bud answered the rest of the girl's questions and acknowledged her cheerful welcome home, but he did not look directly at her again. As they were driving away, Mimi said, "Do you feel better now, dear?"

He nodded, trying to banish the grimness from his thoughts.

"It's getting on to noon. As soon as you can, why don't you pull over and I'll make us all lunch."

"Great."

Now that she was her old self, Mimi was a fine organizer. Nurturing her family was what gave her the greatest joy. She said happily, "Afterwards, Gabe and I can play while you rest a bit. It's lovely to be going home but we're not in all that much of a hurry, are we?"

"Right."

Then without warning, Mimi said, "Oh—*Libby!*"

Bud gripped the wheel, feeling his blood run cold. Had she been reading his mind? "What about her?"

"I just remembered we haven't let her know when we'll be home. You didn't call, did you?"

Bud tried to relax. It wasn't easy. "No."

"Then I should do it now."

He shook his head. "Cell's not working. I forgot to put it on the charger. Probably out of range anyway."

"Then perhaps we should stop somewhere and call."

His mind was awhirl but he managed to say, "No—you know Libby. She doesn't get in a sweat. Let's surprise her."

"All right, dear," Mimi said contentedly. "Why not?"

Bud said nothing more. He drove on through the flatlands, heading northwest toward Lethbridge. It was going to be a relief when this last day was over.

BY MID-MORNING JOHN was very tense. He realized that his was not the only problem the detachment had to deal with: despite the seriousness of the situation, normal police life had to go on. But after all this time of personal action, having finally—and necessarily—put the reins into the hands of others, instead of relieved, he felt increasingly frustrated and useless.

It was not much more than half an hour's drive to the ranch. The Wetheralls would not be back until, at the very earliest, late afternoon, so they had plenty of time. What John wanted, what his heart needed, was to have a whole squad of Mounties out at the ranch, prepped and concealed, bristling with fire power—*now*. What he had to settle for was a much more realistic contingent, which was ready to move just before noon.

Sergeant Oaks, John and another constable called Pete Crow got into a patrol car to drive out to the ranch, Lyall Petty at the wheel. Libby followed in her Land Cruiser. On the way Oaks told John the plan.

"We're going to keep this clean and simple. We'll conceal all the vehicles, make the place look exactly like he expects to find it. When

STOLEN   **197**

they arrive and come in the house, we'll be waiting. No drama. No big deal. Nobody gets panicked. By the time they know what's happening, it'll all be over. And if the child with them is indeed your lad, they will of course be arrested. How does that seem?"

"Great." John said. "I must admit, though, that what I had in mind was a bit more dramatic."

Lyall Petty grinned from the driver's seat. "Think we were gonna send in the SWAT team, John?"

Constable Crow, beside him, chuckled. "We keep them for the grow-ops."

The small procession had passed the temple and was now well out of town, heading west across the burned-grass prairie, with the foothills in the near distance and the jagged line of the Rockies rising beyond. "Take no notice, John," Sergeant Oaks said. "They're joshing to keep it light. But we know how serious this is."

John had realized this. They weren't exactly humouring him, but, understanding a parent's fear and potential panic, they were doing a professional job of putting him at ease. What they didn't know was what could never be told: that apart from being a kidnapper, Bud Wetherall was dangerous, to the point of coldly ordering a double murder.

But things were well in hand, he was sure of that. Apart from their training, the weapons they carried, and the general air of pleasant camaraderie, these guys were professionals and they would be able to handle anything that came down. Despite this knowledge, however, and the calm he did his best to exhibit, on the inside he was seething. There could be no relaxation now, no real ease, until this thing was finished. So, though he smiled for the benefit of the RCMP cavalry, one thought grew steadily in John's mind, blocking all else: *Please, let it soon be over!*

ON A RIDGE off to the west there were windmills. Hundreds of them were turning, netting the tireless winds of the Rockies for the Alberta electricity grid. Looking up, Bud was reminded of old movies, shots of Indians appearing in menacing lines against the sky. That made him feel uneasy. He began to get the feeling that he was being watched, which was ludicrous. But the more he tried to dismiss it, the stronger grew the sensation: of threat, of danger.

The windmills, of course, had nothing to do with it. They were just symptoms of the disquiet that had been with him since he had seen the woman in the Customs post. Not that he wasn't sure that Libby was dead. Will North had seen to that. What Bud hadn't expected was for the bitch to haunt him. And there was something else he hadn't considered until his wife's mention of Libby. All the girl's stuff was at the house. Since she could never return to collect it, Mimi would start to worry. Eventually she might insist on making enquiries.

Driving north, approaching the cut-off that would take him west to Highway 5, Bud had an idea. This would involve changing their plans yet again—say, driving straight on to Calgary. For what reason? A great toy-buying expedition for Gabe. That would do it. Then, during the time before they finally arrived back, the girl's stuff could be got rid of, making it look as if she'd upped stakes and left for another job. Only one person could be trusted for this—Will North would have to make a quick trip from Drumheller. All things considered, he could hardly object.

Bud decided to talk to Will before mentioning the Calgary trip. He took the cut-off anyway and stopped at the little hamlet of Raymond. Telling Mimi he'd decided to contact Libby after all, he went to a pay phone and called Will North's number.

There was no answer, meaning his brother-in-law was probably at work. Strangely, Bud hadn't thought of that. He'd somehow assumed that, having been promised riches, Will would have up and quit. But that would seem odd, he realized. Considering what he'd recently done, Will couldn't afford to be seen to be acting differently. Mmm—maybe the guy was brighter than he'd given him credit for.

Bud hung up and stood in the booth staring across the road at the motorhome. Gabe was sitting on Mimi's knee, listening intently as she said something into his ear. He giggled—and suddenly all of Bud's dark feelings dissolved. What the hell was he doing, fretting like this, worrying about details, planning extra trips, for God's sake, when everything was just fine. All they really needed was to get home.

The fact that Libby wasn't there and would never be returning could be handled, surely. He could make up some story, claim later that he'd had a communication, that she'd moved on. Hell, how hard could it be? And Mimi would be too engrossed in her new son to worry for long. *Okay, get a grip*, he thought. *This is where it ends. We're going home.*

Putting on a cheerful face, he returned to the motorhome. "No answer. Must be out in the barn or something," he said, smiling at Mimi and ruffling Gabe's hair. "We'll have to surprise her."

He started the engine. They were just over an hour from the ranch.

THEY WERE ALL in the house. The vehicles had been made invisible; the Land Cruiser and John's MG in the barn, the police car parked well behind it.

Coffee had been made and they had settled down to a period of waiting. In a front window from which the approach road could be seen, Lyall Petty kept a constant and discreet watch. In the kitchen Sergeant Oaks and Constable Crow talked in low voices. Libby sat and watched John pacing, keeping quiet, knowing she could do nothing for him now. John went from restlessness to purgatory to a fever of anxious anticipation that was excruciating, eventually concentrating on staying sane.

While time slowed to the pace of winter molasses. Nonetheless passing.

THE BIG RV reached the intersection of Highways 5 and 2, entering Cardston. It passed the massive temple and kept on going, heading west.

Now the Rockies could be clearly seen, a dark, ragged band across the horizon. The motorhome moved steadily, smooth and fleet, driven by Bud who handled it with confident ease: going home.

IN THE KITCHEN a phone rang.

John jumped, Libby swung toward the sound. It was Sergeant Oaks's cell. The sergeant listened, spoke three words, then put away the phone. His face was expressionless, but his eyes gleamed. "The motorhome just passed the junction at Elk Corners. They're on their way."

They all moved to where they could see Lyall Petty at his window watching-post.

Waited.

BUD TOOLED THE motorhome down the last kilometre toward the ranch. She was a fine machine, giving not a speck of bother since the morning they'd left. He remembered that desperate time, and couldn't help marvelling about the changes that had happened to them all. Since Gabriel.

Bud looked across at Mimi, warmly serene in anticipation of

homecoming, then back at little Gabe, who had fallen asleep on the couch. Mimi caught his glance. Her smile made her seem not a day over 18. "Oh, Bud dear," she said. "It's so wonderful. We're all going to be so happy."

He nodded. Grinned. Reached across his hand, which she took and squeezed. "I do love you, my dear," Mimi said.

Bud smiled, feeling very content, all trace of his earlier darkness of mind quite vanished. "Yeah, honey. Me too."

They topped the last rise—and there across the valley was the house.

"Here they come!" Constable Petty said.

Nobody moved, but tension crackled in the room. Then Sergeant Oaks moved swiftly, joining the constable at the edge of the window. John got to the window in time to see the motorhome reach the drive. He felt numb.

"Okay," Sergeant Oaks said. "Everyone very quiet now."

The motorhome slid up the drive, travelling the last yards with a sway and bounce of final grace before coming to a stop outside the house. Bud stood up, stretched. Mimi unhooked her seatbelt and went back to Gabriel who was still asleep. She stood smiling down at the child, obviously reluctant to wake him.

Seeing them there gave Bud an idea. "You know, I'd like a picture of you two, at the moment Gabe wakes up and sees his new home."

Mimi thought that was grand, but remembered they'd used the last shot on the roll yesterday, at the water slides. Bud recollected that he had some film in his office. He said he'd go get it, at the same time having the sudden desire to kiss her. But he didn't. That could wait for later.

Leaving Mimi to wake the boy, Bud left the motorhome, strolling without hurry to the front door. He opened up and went inside. As he crossed through the house, heading for his office, Bud found himself humming a little tune. He walked into the living room.

"Welcome home," the child's father said.

TWO

Bud's reflexes were so fast that no one had a chance to stop him.

Whether it was because of a natural instinct for self-preservation or because his earlier paranoia had not quite departed, when he was confronted by the ruin of his life, part of him was quite unsurprised. That part instantly took control; it pumped adrenalin, marshalled nerves and muscles, took charge of his healthy physique and set it to work.

After barely a second's pause, Bud twisted, ducked, bolted for the front door. Someone was in front of him: Constable Crow, who made a grab. Bud caught the man off balance, shoved him savagely aside and raced out of the house.

Taking the steps two at a time, he crossed the 10 yards to the motorhome in half that number of strides. He got there just as Mimi, carrying a sleepy Gabriel, was descending the steps. He didn't pause but leaped right at her, grabbing the child and pushing his wife backwards at the same time. With a startled shriek Mimi landed on her bottom at the top of the steps. Bud had the child secure, and immediately pulled up his own legs, slammed and latched the door.

His final act was the natural conclusion. Thrusting Gabriel at

Mimi, he crawled swiftly across the floor to the driver's seat, taking from the clip the Colt .38. Only then did he lift his head to peer outside.

The people who had been waiting in the house were pouring out. Bud recognized Sergeant Oaks from the Cardston detachment and another young cop whom Libby had once dated. Then came the constable he'd had to knock down, then Gabriel's father and, finally, Libby McGrew.

In the RV, it was the child who first found voice. Of all that had happened in the last few violent seconds, one thing impressed him. "Wow, gun!" Gabriel cried, crawling toward Bud gleefully. "Daddy-Bud has a gun!"

"No!" Mimi shouted, grabbing the boy, hauling him back, her face a mask of outrage. "Bud—what's going on?"

As if in answer from outside came the loud but dispassionate voice of Sergeant Oaks. "Okay folks—come on out of there now. It's all over."

It was over all right. After everything that had happened. After being so near. Over!

Bud, on the floor of the motorhome, looked across at Mimi who sat clasping the child. Did she understand what was going on? Her eyes were glazing with something that was part shock, part defiance. As they crouched there, their whole life was draining away like water down a plughole. Mimi must know that, but she was fighting it.

"Mr. and Mrs. Wetherall—please—you can only hurt yourselves now. You must give up the child."

At these words Mimi whimpered like a hurt animal and Gabriel, catching the emanations of anger and despair around him, began to cry. That sound, for Mimi, was a trigger. She hugged the boy savagely and rose straight up, stood with legs apart, glaring at the people gathered out there. "No!" Mimi growled, the sound utterly feral. "No! No! NO!"

Bud, who'd risen too, saw the sergeant move purposefully to

the door. The handle turned, the door jerked, straining against the catch. Mimi screamed. Calmly, Bud flicked the safety off the automatic and put a shot through the door.

Outside, they scattered like rabbits. Bud watched them. Mimi, shocked into silence by the explosion, watched too. The boy, eyes round in awe, watched Bud. "Wow!" he whispered. "Daddy-Bud shot the gun!" For a moment everything was frozen.

Bud acted swiftly. He went into the rear bedroom compartment and closed the drapes, then closed all the other curtains in the RV, except those separating off the cab. Finally he went to Mimi and led her, still carrying the child, into the bedroom.

"Stay here," he said.

Sitting on the bed, embracing the child, Mimi looked up at her husband. All the knowledge of a life shattered was somewhere back behind those haunted eyes. But on the surface something else was forming, hardening: a last fantasy to cope with the horror that was overtaking them.

"The devil," Mimi whispered.

"What, Mimi?"

"The slut-demon who stole Gabriel for her own belly. She has sent her beasts to steal him back."

Hearing this from his wife's swiftly deranging mind was somehow the worst of all. But he managed to smile and sat down beside her, arms around woman and child. "Don't worry," he heard himself saying. "I won't let them take him."

Between them, Gabriel suddenly squirmed. "Mummy-Mimi— I'm hungry!"

Of course the little boy had no idea what was going on. And now that the excitement was over, he'd remembered it was supper time. Routine, pathetic and ordinary. Far from routine, however, were Mimi's next words, "I'll kill us both if they try."

Black depression hit Bud like a hammer between the eyes. He thrust Mimi from him, got up. "You two stay here. I'll make supper for Gabe. Don't worry, it'll be all right." Which was a monumental absurdity. But what else could he say?

Bud moved through the motorhome to the cab. Sitting in the driver's seat, he realized that something had changed in the yard. A police cruiser, which must have been concealed somewhere, had now been pulled across the driveway, blocking any possibility of escape. But that hadn't been what he had in mind anyway.

Bud turned on the headlights, began flashing them on and off until he had their attention. He took the automatic from his pocket by the barrel, ostentatiously placed it on the floor, displayed his empty hands palm outwards, then picked up the CB mike, held it up and mimed talking.

After a moment a figure appeared warily from behind the cruiser. It was Constable Petty. Keeping his eyes steadily on Bud, Petty walked to the cruiser and got in.

Bud turned on the radio, flipping over to the emergency band. After a second there was a crackle and a voice said, "Yeah—I'm listening. Are you talking? Over."

"I'm talking!" Bud said.

"Are you folks ready to come out of there?"

"Not yet."

"We know you've got the boy, Mr. Wetherall. There's nowhere you can go."

"I know it, son," Bud said. "Sorry about the shooting. I won't do it again unless you guys make me. Okay?"

"Understood. When are you going to come out, sir? You can't stay there forever."

"Sure, sure. But we're going to need some time."

"What do you mean," the policeman began angrily, then

stopped himself, thinking better of the rough approach. "Is young Nate all right?"

"He's fine. And he'll stay that way, as long as you don't do anything stupid. Understand, Constable?"

Petty's voice was now subdued. "Of course. How much—er—time are you going to need, sir?"

"I'd say all night,"

Petty sounded scandalized. "All *night?*"

"We need that to say our goodbyes."

Now Petty came back ripe with indignation. "After what you did, you think you've got that right?"

"I'm not talking rights, son," Bud said crisply. "We've got the boy, who everyone wants kept safe, correct? So this is more like a demand. Am I getting through to you?"

"Yes, sir, I believe you are."

"Then have I your word that we'll be left alone until we're ready?"

"I'm not the boss. I'll have to get back to you on that."

"Then do it. But don't take all night. Over and out."

He put down the mike but left the radio on. He watched the policeman walk back toward the house. At the same time another patrol car, lights flashing, came roaring up the drive. Bud hardly gave it a glance. Now that contact had been made and some rules set down, no one was going to try anything stupid. He knew the Mounties well enough for that.

Bud walked back to the kitchen to fix the child's supper. His hands moved with calm efficiency and his eyes were hooded, as if he were half-asleep. His mind ran in overdrive.

THREE

The place had turned into a circus. John was not sure exactly when it happened, it was a gradual accumulation, but by early evening he realized that the house was alive with people.

The police presence had grown only slightly: how many officers did it take, after all, to contain two civilians and a child in a motorhome? But eventually the media started to arrive, first from Lethbridge and then Calgary, though to John it was a mystery how the story got out so quickly. It was going to be a big one, little doubt of that. After a while, the main job of the police was simply to keep order as the number of people—officials, media and sightseers—grew.

Meanwhile, as the hours passed, the motorhome—the image of which would tomorrow be on every newspaper and TV screen—remained quiet and dark.

Just after 10:00 John found himself in a window of the house opposite the silent vehicle. Nothing had moved there since Bud Wetherall had received the promise to not be disturbed till morning. Around the RV the yard was clear, brightly lit by floodlights. At the edge of the lights, barriers were set up to keep onlookers back. At the far end of those, in a position best suited to watch the motorhome door, sat a TV van with its camera on top. The scene was almost festive. John thought it looked as if they were waiting for the appearance of a movie star, rather than this grim saga involving a hostage.

Nate a hostage!

But what had Bud gained? A last night alone with his wife and the child. To John all it meant was a slightly longer period of nail-biting before the final reunion. The Wetheralls might not deserve those last stolen hours, but in the end it really didn't matter. So why was he so bothered? What it boiled down to, he supposed, was that—knowing how devious Bud could be—he couldn't believe that it was really over. Gut instinct told him there had to be something more.

Libby brought him a beer and lingered by the window. For a while they both stared across at the vehicle that had caused so much grief. After a while she said, "John—you should get some sleep."

He did his best for levity. "Is that an invitation?"

"Goodness knows, yes, if it'd help, but I doubt either of us could put much heart in it."

He held her and they stood together. Finally she said, "Let's not hang around here. I know why you've got to sort of stand guard. But I know a better place. Come on."

Libby led him out the back, into the barn where their vehicles had been hidden against the Wetheralls' return. The light from a single bulb was enough to pick out a ladder leading to the hayloft. Up there, a walk beside stacked bales brought them to open doors beside the hay winch. They were high, overlooking house, yard and the dark hulk of the motorhome. Above was a star-filled sky, and to the south a gibbous moon, on its way to a rendezvous with the Rockies.

"At the compound outside Cardston, where I grew up," Libby said, "We had a barn even bigger than this. The loft was my favourite place. I used to sneak away there and play wish games."

"What did you wish?"

"Oh, you know, the usual—that I was someone else, that I could meet boys—but mostly, just to get away." She shrugged and looked at the motorhome that was almost at their feet. "Nothing as important as what we're both wishing now."

Libby pulled up a bale and they sat gazing out into the night. From this angle, the RV did not look quite so prison-like. John thought of Nate, spending his last night, unaware that he was the focus of a drama more incredible than he could understand, oblivious to everything that the dark cross-currents of love and need had brought about. Up here, John felt that he was watching over his son. And in that more pleasant frame of mind, he at last fell into a doze.

HE WAS AWAKENED, it seemed only a minute later, by Libby shaking him. "John. Wake up—I think you're needed at the house."

He sat up. The moon had vanished and there seemed to be fewer people around. "What time is it?"

"Nearly 1:00. Come on, I'm pretty sure I heard people calling for you down there."

They got up and returned quickly to the house. In the living room Sergeant Oaks and a new officer in street clothes were conferring in urgent tones.

"There's very little precedent for this kind of thing," the plainclothes man was saying. "In each case you've got to play it by ear."

They both turned quickly when John entered, looking uneasy. John felt sudden apprehension. Was this it? The nameless dread that had been bothering him? He said, "What? Did something happen? Is Nate all right?"

"From what we know, he's fine," Sergeant Oaks said. "But—well—a few minutes ago Bud Wetherall came on the radio again."

"What did he want?"

"You, John."

"Me?"

"That's right. But he put it in a kind of odd way."

"How?"

"Well, he was angrier at you than anyone. He said it was totally illogical for you to hunt him down on the evidence you had. That if you hadn't been such a—how did he put it?—a 'stubborn, crazy bastard,' he wouldn't be in this trouble. He said that before he gives himself up tomorrow he wants to meet you once more, face to face. 'And if he ever wants to see his son alive, he'd damn well better come.' "

John gaped. "He said that?"

"His exact words."

"Well then, I suppose I have to go."

"There's one thing you should consider," Oaks said quietly.

"Yeah?"

"He called you crazy, but considering the fix he's in, *he* may be the one going off his nut. He got himself into this mess, but he blames you. He may not want to just slap your wrist and call you names. He may mean to really harm you."

"And if I don't go?"

The sergeant looked pained. "Then he may very well harm your boy."

John looked from Oaks to the plainclothes officer. "So—would you say I have a choice?"

Neither made any attempt to answer.

John turned to Libby. Her expression was unreadable, but their eye contact worked like warm fingers on his heart. The rest of him, however, felt very cold.

He said, "Someone better get on the radio and find out when he wants me."

FOUR

After Gabriel ate his supper, Mimi changed him into his pajamas. Then she took him into the big bed with her and read him a story. It was one of his favourites, *The Little Engine That Could*. Mimi read the story beautifully, making all the sounds of the engine, in its doubt and discovery and triumph, as if nothing unusual had happened, as if the great darkness that waited outside to smash their lives did not exist. "*I think I can, I think I can, I think I can …*"

Listening from the kitchen, Bud smiled while he mixed the special drink. It was hot chocolate made very strong, with half-and-half cream and a lot of sugar, just the way Mimi liked it. What made it special tonight was an extra ingredient: the contents of the 19 sleeping capsules remaining in her bottle. When it was finished he put it beside the microwave, ready to reheat, and went into the bedroom.

Little Gabe was already sleepy, but he was valiantly keeping his eyes open for the end of the story. The last words came as Bud sat on the bed. Mimi tossed the book aside, pulled Gabe into her arms and hugged him. Then she laughed and lifted the child to arms' length, lowered his neck onto her face and blew the big farting air bubbles that always made the boy hysterical with laughter. Finally, she held the squirming figure out again, looked at the child intensely, as if registering his image forever, and said, "Goodnight, darling," and then very softly, "Goodbye."

Mimi turned her gaze away, not looking at Gabriel again. She held him out to Bud. "Okay, Dad—how about you get this rascal to bed?"

"Sure. Here we go," Bud said, his great laugh as jolly as a tomb. He swung the boy around, carried him to where his bed was already made up at the far end of the motorhome and slipped him in. "Okay, that's it, young buck. Sweet dreams."

Gabriel settled down, smiled at Bud sleepily. "Wow," he whispered. "You shot that gun, Daddy-Bud."

"Yes, son. Goodnight."

The boy's eyes flickered, already nose-diving into the instant sleep of cats and children. "Shot it good ... wow!" he mumbled, and was gone.

Bud stood watching him for a moment. He adjusted the covers and bent down, as if about to kiss the boy's head. But he did not. He stopped in mid-movement, paused, straightened. And now his face was quite blank.

Without hurry, he went back to the kitchen and put Mimi's drink in the microwave. As it heated, he stood motionless, impassive. When it was done he took it out, walked into the bedroom and handed the mug to his wife.

"Thank you, darling," she said brightly, and started to sip at once. "Oh, it *is* hot," she said. "And bitter ... "

"You think?"

They stared at each other for a long moment. At last Mimi gave a nod, a small strange smile. "But it's fine. Just what I need. Thank you. Darling, you always know what I really need."

"Doll—that's my job."

She reached out for his hand. "And you'll—take care of Gabriel?"

"Depend on it."

Mimi nodded and finished the drink. She passed her husband the mug, settled back. "Will you be long?"

"A while. I've got a few things to do."

"All right. Goodnight then."

"Goodnight."

Bud bent and kissed his wife slowly. He left the bedroom, closing the door, not looking back.

At the sink, he washed Mimi's mug, dried it and put it away. He poured himself a Scotch, sat sipping and thinking, now and then letting his eyes wander to the sleeping child. He thought for a long time. Then he rose, found a pencil and paper, turned on a lamp beside the dining table and started very carefully to make a list.

FIVE

John knocked on the motorhome door.

"Who is it?" Bud Wetherall's voice.

"John Quarry."

The door curtain was pulled aside. Then the inside latch was undone. "Come."

John opened the door. Bud was standing at the top of the steps, automatic pointing steadily.

"Close the door. Lock it. Now come up and sit down."

John climbed the steps, pausing at the top. To the left was the couch used for Nate's bed. In the light from the one small lamp, John could see the little curled-up bundle that was his son. It seemed very little. But alive.

Opposite were armchairs. Bud was already seating himself in the one immediately behind the driving compartment, the chair nearest Nate's head. He pointed to the other.

"Sit down, John."

Wetherall emphasized the command with a significant flick of the gun, but John ignored it and moved straight to Nate. Up close he could see the boy's breathing. In sleep his face looked sweet and peaceful.

"The boy's all right," Wetherall said. "Now sit down, please."

John did so, feeling unreal. Meeting again this monster, the man who'd stolen his son, cynically tricked him and even arranged to have him murdered, he found himself oddly devoid of emotion. If—as was very possible—Bud had brought him here to exact revenge, he knew he should be terrified. "What do you want?" he asked calmly.

Bud didn't answer right off. He just stared, holding the gun lightly, very relaxed and alert. Finally he said, "Christ!"

"What?"

"Well, just *look* at you."

John looked at himself. In any other situation his shrug would have been comical. "You mean I'm a mess? You've been keeping me kind of busy."

The older man made a sound that was both a laugh and a groan of frustration. "John—do you know how much stuff I own? How many men I employ? How much money …?"

He trailed off. John said, "Are you going to let Nate go?"

Bud didn't reply.

"You can keep me, if that's what you want. Do whatever you think you have to. But please, let Nate go."

"Why?"

"Damn you—because he's a little kid!"

Bud leaped up, making a savage gesture with the gun. "*No*, you stupid fool! *Why did you have to come after us?* You had no evidence that any reasonable man would believe. It was ridiculous. Mimi may have been crazy but her ruse was terrific. It was the perfect crime, because no one believed there was one. *Except fucking you!*"

Bud looked at John, at Nate, at the luxurious vehicle that encased them; he shook his head, in irony too great to be expressed. Finally, since there was no more to be said, John came out with the same question. "Will you let Nate go?"

Bud blinked and shook himself. He looked at John pityingly. Crisply he said, "Don't be ridiculous."

There was a long silence. Finally John said, "Then what do you want?"

"When we first met," Bud said, "I thought you were a kind of weak bastard. Yet somehow you've caused me more trouble than anyone in my whole life."

"So what now? Revenge?"

"Better than that."

"What?"

"Cooperation!"

John's jaw dropped. "Are you kidding?"

"Not at all, John. I'm tired of being cooped up here. I want out but I'm not going to do a thing about it."

"What are you talking about?"

Bud passed his gun from hand to hand. "All right, here's what's going to happen. When you leave here you'll be carrying a list. These are the things I require. At the top is Libby's Land Cruiser. Then I want cans of gas and water, food, clothing—a whole lot of stuff I'll need after we leave."

John was flabbergasted. "But they're never going to let you and your wife leave."

"I didn't mean Mimi," Bud said calmly. "By *we* I meant *us*."

"You and me?"

"And Nate."

"You're out of your mind!"

Without warning Bud Wetherall leaped up, but not at John. The move took him to Nate and then the gun was poised an inch from the child's head. Very quietly, and with hardly any emphasis he said, "As a matter of a fact, John, you're probably right. Also I've got nothing to lose. This lad was going to be my son, but now—thanks to you—that can never be. If he can't be a bargaining chip, he's nothing. A bullet through his brain, and yours, and mine—I wouldn't mind that too much. A heap better than what'll come down if I don't get out of here. Is that the way you want it?" He pushed the muzzle closer to Nate's temple, his eyes suddenly ablaze. "*Just say the word!*"

A bolt of pure horror shot through John. He knew the man meant everything he said. The conversation had seemed so reasonable that he'd been lulled into forgetting the real insanity of the situation. Had he gone through all this to recover his son only to foul up now because of a stupid lack of imagination? "No!" John said, desperately. "Of course I don't want that. Please—give me your list—I'll get whatever you need—do anything. But please, put down that gun."

Slowly the fire in Bud's eyes abated, not vanishing but staying at a gentle smoulder. Finally he did turn aside the gun and return to his chair.

"All right, John," he said. "Now that we fully understand each other, you'd better pay attention."

SIX

The first reaction of the plainclothes officer, when he heard Bud's demands, was an emphatic "No way!"

Fortunately, Sergeant Oaks was of another mind. "Listen, everyone. Even if Wetherall does escape, we'll catch up to him sooner or later. The number one priority here is saving the child."

The officer grimaced but nodded reluctantly.

Oaks took Bud's list and scanned it as he continued. "John here has put himself to a lot of trouble to help his boy. If he's willing to keep at it, I don't think we've got the right to stop him. And if that means giving help to Wetherall—well—I figure it's a small enough price to pay."

There was silence. They could see that the suit knew the sergeant was right. But as a last gesture, he took the list, tapping it emphatically. "Okay—but not the rifle."

Oaks shrugged. "He's armed already. Maybe he wants it for hunting when he gets to the mountains since that's where he's probably headed. But right now he's setting the rules, so we've got to go along. And let's face it, one gun more or less isn't going to make much difference."

The suit said nothing more.

By the time everything was found and packed in the Land Cruiser it was dawn. At that time Bud came on the radio again, giving final instructions about their departure. Then he demanded to speak to Oaks. The sergeant came to the squad car and took the mike.

"Oaks here. What is it?"

"Hi, Sergeant," Bud said coolly. "Did you get everything I asked for?"

"Yes. Now you didn't ask for advice, but here's some for free. This is not going to work, Mr. Wetherall. We know you'll try to head for the border, but you'll never make it. And even if you do, sooner or later the Yanks will catch up with you."

"You don't say."

"Yes—so why not let the boy go? Give it up."

"Was that the advice?"

"You got it."

"Okay. Now here's some for you. And I'm only going to say it once. If anyone tries to follow me—by car, ATV, anything—if I see a roadblock or even *hear* a helicopter—the kid will get a bullet. And I'll still have a hostage to bargain with. Understand?"

"Yes, sir," Oaks said quietly.

There was no parting word, just a click—then dead air.

A few moments later Oaks took John aside. The only advice he could give was of pitiful simplicity. "The best chance, for you both, is to do everything he says. The more useful you are the longer you're likely to be unharmed. Hopefully—if he gets what he needs—he'll eventually let you go."

John nodded mutely. Neither of them wanted to put words to how possible this might be.

"If you should get free," Oaks concluded, "the sooner you make contact, the sooner we can move in on him. On that score, we have some extra options to help keep track of him, but you don't have to worry about that. Your first responsibility is to your boy. Now—one last thing." He dipped his hand in his pocket and brought out a tiny, blue-black Beretta .22 automatic lying flat in his palm. "This is an option I must offer. But from what I've come to understand of Bud Wetherall, I can't in conscience advise you to take it. If he found it before you had a chance to use it, I've no doubt it would be fatal for you both."

John studied the gun. Tempting as it was, he had to agree with Oaks's assessment. He waved the thing away, and there was little left but a quick shake of the hands.

Libby and John had a last moment together. Libby held him briefly and very hard, saying nothing. Just the feel of her told him many things, but right now there was no time to contemplate a single one of them.

When it was time to leave, all but Sergeant Oaks and a couple of officers were behind the restraining barriers. The media people who remained had been warned that from this moment they must stay back and be absolutely silent.

John got into the loaded Land Cruiser and, as arranged, turned and reversed it so that its back door was almost flush with the side door of the motorhome. Just enough room was left for both doors to open. When they were, an almost completely enclosed passage would be created from one vehicle to the other.

John knocked on the motorhome door.

"Come in, John."

Entering, the first thing he saw was Nate. His son, though now fully dressed, was sound asleep.

Bud made no greeting. He looked fit, rested and alert. With his gun he pointed to the floor. "Lie down. Face down."

John obeyed, then deft hands were patting all over him; he was being frisked. Sergeant Oaks's advice had been golden. Satisfied, Bud told John to go outside and open the Cruiser's back door. John did so; now the path between the two vehicles was completely shielded. In fact, there was no marksman waiting to try an unlikely shot, but Bud was taking no chances.

In a moment, carrying the blanket-wrapped bundle of the sleeping child, the prisoner who was a prisoner no longer came through. When he was inside, John closed the back door. Then he went round front, got in and started the engine. He put the 4x4 in gear and at that moment Nate, who must have been half awakened by the trip out, stirred and sat up.

The child looked sleepily at the driver of the Cruiser. He didn't cry out or look surprised. But petulantly, as only a freshly awakened toddler can, he said, "Daddy—where've you *been?*"

John tried a grin, but it didn't work. He turned away, let out the clutch and began to drive. "Away, kiddo!" John said. "But I'm back now."

PART EIGHT

ONE

Libby watched her Land Cruiser, carrying the man and the child and the abductor, disappear up the road. For the first time since the beginning of this adventure she felt the onset of bitter anger. At the root of it, strangely, was not what had happened to her personally, the assault and attempted murder by Will North. It was not even that Bud, who was responsible for all of it, appeared to have won. No, what had tipped Libby over the edge was something else, a heart-rending detail that nobody had expected: in the abandoned motorhome, immediately after the departure of the others, they had found the body of Mimi Wetherall.

Whether the woman had killed herself or Bud had done it was not clear, but to Libby it didn't matter. The casual abandonment of this sad creature by the man with whom she'd shared half her life was like a final act of wickedness. More than anything else, it told Libby that Bud—someone she had once cared for and trusted—was truly a man without mercy. She then understood that she was never likely to see John or his son alive again.

Now that the centre of the drama had shifted from the ranch, many of the policemen and most of the media had departed. There were plans afoot to set up surveillance and interception, Libby knew.

But how that might be done she had no idea. She went into the kitchen where, to her surprise, she found everyone clustered around the table, staring at a laptop computer.

Libby came in behind Constable Petty. "What's happening, Lyall?" she said, almost in a whisper.

"Marvels of modern science," Petty said, stepping aside and indicating the laptop. The screen showed what looked like a map. "Cool, eh?"

Libby moved closer. The map, she saw, was of the surrounding area. At the bottom was the US border. In a broad crescent to the south and west, the unmistakable uprising of the Rocky Mountains. Halfway between the map's centre and the mountain chain she could see a flashing blip of light.

"What's that?" Libby asked.

Petty grinned. "It's *them*. We hid a GPS beacon in Bud Wetherall's gear. Now it's being tracked via satellite. That guy may think he's given us the slip, but as long he's in that vehicle—and if we're lucky even afterwards—we know exactly where he is."

TWO

Nate was in heaven. He had both of his daddies with him at last. His Real Daddy and Daddy-Bud. They were going on an adventure. And together they were going to have a good time. Of course, he had always known that Daddy would come back one day. Daddy-Bud had told him that, and when he said something would happen, it always did. It would have been nice if Mummy-Mimi could have come along too. But he guessed she had to stay back and make supper for when they all came home. As they drove away from the big house, which was going to be their home forever, Nate's only disappointment was that he hadn't yet got to play with the toys that Daddy-Bud had promised. But Real Daddy coming back made up for that.

They rolled out of the drive, passing some police cars with lights flashing and policemen and other people standing around. Nate waved to them, but they only stared. They looked sad, maybe because they weren't coming on the adventure too. Nobody waved back.

Then they were away from the people and Daddy-Bud told Daddy to drive quicker. He didn't say it nicely, didn't say "please," as Nate was always being reminded to do, but Daddy did it anyway. He drove very fast, and Nate laughed in glee. He remembered then how much fun Daddy was, and how he had missed him.

He and Daddy-Bud were in the back of Daddy's new jeep car. Nate decided he wanted to be in the front with Daddy, so he could sit right beside him. He started to crawl over and got a real shock. Daddy-Bud shouted at him to get back. His voice was different, loud and scary in a way Nate had never heard. He gaped bug-eyed at Daddy-Bud, and saw that he had that gun again.

"Wow!" Nate said, remembering yesterday. "Daddy-Bud shoot!"

Daddy-Bud didn't smile. The scary expression stayed. He told Nate to sit down and stay there, not to try to go into the front with Daddy again. Nate started to cry. Then Daddy, driving fast, reached over and managed to find his head, patting clumsily because he couldn't see what he was doing. But the touch was so good Nate felt a bit better. And over the engine's roar, the words came strong and clear.

"Don't worry, kiddo. It's okay—I'm here. Be good and do what the guy says."

Daddy-Bud reached out swiftly. With the side of his gun he hit Daddy's hand very hard. The blow glanced off and stunned against Nate's shoulder, taking his breath away.

"Never mind that shit. Just drive," Daddy-Bud growled.

And then, although he was only three, Nate understood that this was not a fun adventure at all. It was turning out to be a very bad time.

BUD KNEW THAT the beginning would have to be quick. Although he had bought the ranch only a few years back, he had come to know the area intimately. The Rocky Mountains, which swung in a jagged arc a few miles to the southwest, were not only a vast area in which a man with sufficient expertise could hide indefinitely; they were also a perfect passage across the US border. Waterton Lakes National Park and its American counterpart, Glacier National Park, were separate in name only. The reality was a seamless wilderness of mountains and lakes, valleys and passes, through which ran a maze of hiking trails, providing, at least in summer, a veritable sieve for passage between the two countries.

A man with toughness and patience and skill could vanish into the mountains in Alberta, emerging in Montana when he was good and ready. After that, with the US contacts and money he had access to, he could have a whole new life. All he had to do was make it to the mountains.

Although he had been allowed to leave and given promise of free passage, Bud knew he couldn't count on that for long. As time passed, and they got their act together, they'd begin to hunt him, hostages or not. Also, he had little doubt they'd be up to some tricks he didn't know about.

Right now he had two advantages: it was slightly after 6:00 in the morning so it would take a couple of hours for efficient pursuit to get organized, and he'd taken a route that they had probably not anticipated. Instead of going north to fast-but-vulnerable Highway 5, he was on the back road that wound south into the foothills behind his property. On maps, this didn't appear to go anywhere, not even as far as Highway 6, the Chief Mountain Parkway, which led to the US border, but there were connections, little more than trails, which an off-road vehicle could negotiate. These could get him to the Blood Indian Reserve beyond the parkway. Crossing that road itself would be the tricky part; no doubt it would soon be under surveillance. But once they were beyond it, there were routes that could be driven quite far into the higher foothills. To guard against eventualities, he would keep the kid and his father to that point.

Then he'd be on his own.

Meanwhile, he had one calculated purpose: to make life as unpleasant for the others as possible, thus keeping them off-balance and pliable. When he reached the wilderness, where hostages were no longer of value, he would do whatever was necessary. It was a pity about the kid. Had things been different it would have been good to have him around, even though he wasn't flesh and blood. But the real need had been Mimi's—dear, mad Mimi, who'd caused all this damn trouble in the first place—and she was gone.

The kid's father, though—it was no pity about him. Bud hadn't changed his mind about John. Sure, the man had exhibited tenacity, but that was purely an emotional reflex. Essentially, he was weak. Bud resolved to use that weakness to the last, keeping him in constant fear, especially for his son, so he wouldn't try to get smart and would do exactly as he was told, hoping against hope to earn his freedom. When the time came, disappointing him would be a pleasure.

THOUGH PAINFUL, THE blow that Bud delivered did John a service; it made him stop kidding himself.

At the start of the journey, John had clung to one small hope: that, having used the two of them to extricate himself from the trap, Bud would reciprocate by letting them go. But after they were under way, alone together, the truth began to dawn. After the first blow was struck he was coldly sure.

This was no Boy Scout expedition with rewards for good conduct. Their direction of travel, plus the equipment their captor had ordered, made it clear that Bud intended to vanish into the wilds of the Rockies. At that point he'd have no further use for hostages. Leaving them behind to point out his trail would be dangerously sentimental and Bud wasn't sentimental. He was realistic and ruthless.

So when the scales finally dropped from John's eyes, the result was unexpected: the truth set him free. The acknowledgement that he was a dead man removed much clutter from his mind. It became cold. Clear. Ultimately cunning.

For the first time in his life, John Quarry was a different animal: a survivor.

THREE

It wasn't going to be easy; Bud understood that very well. Though he'd gone in a different direction to what was expected, and was travelling on a route known to few, they'd still realize where he was headed. They'd also understand that if he did get to the mountains, they weren't likely to catch him.

It was just getting fully light when the Cruiser had left the ranch and, well out of sight, made its surprise turn; instead of going in the direction of the main road it headed south. They'd be watching at the intersection, of course, and when he didn't appear they'd soon get wise to his trick. But that would at least give him enough head start to get out of the immediate area.

The dirt road they were on, not much more than a rutted track, wound through the valley behind his ranch, climbing into the foothills, To the west, the tips of the Rockies already glowed pink. The ubiquitous stands of dwarf aspen were also picking up light at higher elevations. John, Bud's captive chauffeur, drove with sullen concentration. His son, quiet, now crouched on the side-facing rear seat immediately behind his father. Bud himself sat opposite.

"Keep on going to the top of this valley," Bud had commanded. "I'll let you know what to do then."

In his coat pocket was the pistol. At his feet, within easy reach, the hunting rifle. On the floor between the seats was the other gear he'd ordered: a sturdy rucksack, boots, heavy clothing, ammunition, a hunting knife, a stout rope, matches, utensils and a considerable amount of dried food. There were also bottles of water and cans of gas, but these he didn't need: he'd put them on the list to sow confusion as to his real plans, though he doubted anyone would be fooled for long.

Everything he'd requested had been provided. There was no map, but he didn't need one: even the Blood Indian Reserve, the land east of Waterton Park that was his interim destination, was familiar; he'd hiked and hunted all around there. Beyond the reserve were the mountains proper: to the south—Montana. Once there, with the Rockies as cover, getting out of the area was only a matter of stamina and common sense.

As they bumped along, Bud kept a monitoring eye on the road ahead and a wary one to the rear, and began packing. The jacket he put aside and the boots he put on. Everything else went into the rucksack: the clothes first, then the hardware and finally the food. He worked methodically but fast, wanting to get this part of the job over. Soon the way was going to get rougher, so directing operations would take more of his attention.

Briefly, he considered getting rid of his hostages and driving on alone. But he was far from home free, hours before he reached real safety. He needed to keep his insurance as long as possible. An alternative arrangement would be to tie up the man and drive himself. That might become necessary later, but for now things were best left as they were. Bud was so absorbed with these thoughts that, as he put the last things in the rucksack, he almost missed the most important item of all.

He was stowing the food, packages of dried fruit and beans,

when one of the items caught his attention. In fact, it was already stowed when it occurred to him that something had been a trifle odd. It was the second of two packs of dried fruit and—what? It had felt different—heavier—than the other. He took it out, trying to hold it steady in the jolting vehicle and examined it more closely. One end of the package looked as though it had been opened, then stuck down again.

Bud froze. His heart rate, which had settled down after their successful departure, speeded up again. He tore open the package. Inside was a compressed block of dried fruit but it was not solid; the block had been cut in half and put back together again. Pulling it apart, Bud discovered a hollowed-out interior. In the hollow was a black plastic box. On one side a tiny LED light blinked steadily. On the other was an embossed logo: GLOBAL TRACKING CORP.

He'd known the escape couldn't be that easy.

FOUR

John did as he was told, driving grimly onward. Nate had stopped crying and sat white-faced and silent. After things calmed down and they started travelling up the valley, their captor had divided his energies between giving directions, keeping surveillance and coolly packing his rucksack. For an older guy, Bud had extraordinary strength and resilience, John had to give him that. Also, the man had nothing to lose.

As they wound their way toward the top of the ridge, the land opened out into a rugged array of buttes and ridges, in some places bearing dense stands of dwarf aspen, in others grassy and relatively open. Soon John started getting glimpses of a winding river, emerging from a deeper valley miles ahead, which seemed to be their destination. As a backdrop to all towered the Rockies, majestic and grand but—as he understood what reaching them would entail—with a growing aura of menace. However, there was a long way to go yet. The immediate terrain looked fairly negotiable for the tough 4x4 and apparently they'd be continuing on this track for some time.

John needed all the time he could get, not that he had any sort of plan. But one thing was clear: as long as Bud and Nate were together, he couldn't do anything for fear of hurting his son. Somehow he had to get them separated. He'd not worked out how this could be done, but he did have one clue: Bud thought he was weak and a bit stupid, so perhaps this appearance could be used. But to do what? So far he had no clue.

John was pondering the problem when there came a sharp exclamation from behind. "Stop!" Bud cried, over the thump and rumble of the vehicle. "Hear me? Stop right now!"

John did so. The Cruiser shivered to halt. The sudden quiet was almost eerie. He twisted in his seat to look at Bud. Nate sat up and looked newly afraid. Both stared at their abductor. Bud's face bore an expression of mixed fury and understanding. In his hand was a small box with a tiny, winking light.

"What's that?" John breathed.

Gazing at the thing, Bud shook his head. Then he gave a low, rasping chuckle. "Jesus!" he whispered. "Jesus, of *course*!"

"What is it?"

"GPS locator."

"What?"

"Where have you been living, son? It's a goddamn *beacon*. Uses satellite tracking to tell the whole honkin' world exactly where you are."

John only barely stopped himself from laughing. "Really?"

"Damn, I knew it was too easy. I should have known. I use these things on my own trucks, for God's sake. The cunning bastards! Well—we'll see about … "

He dropped the beacon on the floor and lifted his boot, the intent obvious. John's heart fell. But at its apogee the foot stopped—paused—was gingerly lowered again.

In the silence that followed, Nate said his first words since Bud had hit John. "Toy!" the little boy whispered. "Toy?"

Bud bent and carefully retrieved the still-winking locator. He examined the gadget, turning it over in his hands. Now, surprisingly, he was smiling. "Yes," he said quietly. "That's exactly what it is, son: a toy—which more than one kid can play with. Keep going," and he pointed to the gleam of water in the distance. "A bit farther down you'll be leaving the road. I'll tell you when."

John did as he was bid. The GPS locator beacon, at first a cause for concern, now had bred in their captor a plan. John had no idea what that might be but it had certainly improved Bud's mood, and he was sorely aware of the need for a plan of his own.

Since this locator gadget had been with them from the start, obviously it had always been broadcasting exactly where they were. The fact that it had been concealed in Bud's things, rather than in the body of the vehicle where it was less likely to be discovered, had been a gamble: if Bud did manage to give them the slip, abandoned the 4x4 and reached the mountains, they'd be able to track him anyway. But the gamble had failed.

They were now driving down a rough incline that was almost a draw. Around a curve, at the bottom of a scrubby slope, was water; the river that John had kept seeing was now only a few hundred yards away. "There!" Bud commanded. "Go down there. Take it easy."

They left the road and bumped down the slope, coming at last to where the incline became too steep to negotiate. "This'll do. Stop here," Bud ordered. "Okay, give me the keys."

John did so. Logic indicated that it was not yet time for Nate and himself to be abandoned or harmed, but he felt apprehensive nonetheless. It didn't help that, after removing the clip from the rifle, Bud took Nate with him as he got out.

"What's happening?" John cried. "Where are you taking my son?"

"Calm down," the older man commanded, his expression unreadable. "The lad and I are going to take a look at the river. Come if you like."

This was all very strange. Bud, who'd just discovered that they were being tracked, was suddenly acting as though this was a picnic. John was quick to accept his invitation. After a short distance the incline became a steep bank, descending to the water in a tangle of rough grass and sage. The river itself was surprisingly substantial: cold, blue water, glacier-fed, bubbling down from the mountains at a good clip. John was reminded of another river, the Fraser, which had been a dark conspirator in his son's original disappearance. Newly alarmed, he scrambled to catch up.

"Bud, what are you doing?" John gasped. "Why are you bringing Nate here?"

They had reached the bank. Nate's feet were almost in the water. Bud turned and let go of the boy's hand. "Not bringing him anywhere, John. Just not leaving him with you. Can't have the two of you running off."

Set free, Nate scrambled to his father, grabbing hold of his leg. "Then why have we come here?"

From his pocket Bud produced something and held it up: the GPS beacon. This was now sealed inside a plastic bag borrowed from the supplies. Bud grinned, then pointed to a piece of driftwood lying by the bank. "Nate, bring that to me, will you, son?"

Nate looked up at his dad. Upon John's nod, he gathered up the piece of wood. Bud took it and knotted the end of the plastic bag around it. Secure inside this contraption, the GPS beacon continued to wink.

Bud winked too, solemnly, at Nate. "This is my toy now. My little ship. Want to see it sail?"

Not waiting for a response, Bud flung the thing far out into the river. As it was borne swiftly away, in precisely the opposite direction to their flight, John caught a last glimpse of the beacon—blinking to the heavens its false trail.

FIVE

"There's no doubt about it," Sergeant Oaks said. "The tricky bastard's not making for the US at all. He must have known we'd think he'd head for the mountains and decided to outfox us by circling around and heading north instead."

They all stared at the computer, at the blip on the screen that told the story. Instead of moving southwest, the winking light had suddenly slipped in the opposite direction and now, several miles from the ranch as shown on the web-based map, was creeping steadily away from the border.

Along with the others, Libby studied the screen. Constable Petty had explained that to avoid confusion, only one beacon had been used, hidden in Bud Wetherall's gear, the idea being that even after the Land Cruiser was abandoned they would still be able to locate him. The position of the tell-tale beacon showed that he was now in a narrow ravine with a river, where no vehicle could go, so he must have parted company with the 4x4—and presumably his hostages. How that parting had been effected, Libby did not dare think.

As soon as the new information was assessed, there was a flurry of activity. Sergeant Oaks got busy, organizing a stake-out of the terrain that the fugitive would be passing through. He and most of the others decamped in a hurry. Constable Petty was left to organize the retrieval of John and Nate. Although urgent, the pace of this was less frantic: either they'd be found unharmed in the abandoned Cruiser, or—the alternative needed no explanation.

Since Libby was familiar with the area, it fell to her to help Petty organize the search. On a regular map they pinpointed the spot where, according to the GPS, the Cruiser must have been abandoned. Though its route through the back country had been a rough track, where it had ended up was actually near a real road, which snaked into the hills via Waterton Park from the west. Highway 5 connected with this road inside the park and a squad car could reach the intersection in 20 minutes.

Libby and Petty started out immediately. An ambulance and assistance from the Waterton detachment would meet up with them on the way. Though worried, Libby was determined to be in on the rescue. To the others, her rationale was that her knowledge of the area would save time. Her private reason was that whatever the conclusion, she owed it to her friends to be there. With the Rockies up ahead glowing in the bright sunlight, Libby looked at her watch. Astonished, she saw that it was only mid-morning: it felt as if an eon had passed since the day began.

Arriving at the intersection, they found the reinforcements hadn't arrived. A call on the radio ascertained that they were only now on their way and with a wry look at Libby, Petty arranged a new rendezvous. They were already driving again as he gave final directions.

Moving fast, with only a short distance to go before they would be able to start looking for her abandoned Land Cruiser, Libby felt an uncomfortable mixture of emotions: relief that the wait was almost over plus a growing anxiety at what she might discover. Then, as they came over a rise, she caught a glimpse of water. It was not the Belly River, still some distance ahead, which ran through the valley where Bud had escaped and where they expected to find her Cruiser. This water was a little bit of a slough, without even a name, crouching beneath a feature Libby identified as Birdseye Butte. But looking at it, she suddenly had a strange feeling. Whether this was a real intuition or just fresh anxiety, she had no idea. But when it arrived the sensation rapidly grew intense. Something was very wrong.

SIX

John was as far as ever from a plan of escape. The GPS beacon, the most important measure to give them a lifeline, had been hijacked, converted into a decoy, all-too-cleverly turning the device against its masters. This did have one upside, however: it implied that their abductor meant to stick with the Cruiser and, by implication, themselves, for a while yet. As they prepared to resume their journey, a small incident provided the germ of an idea.

As soon as father and son were herded back to the 4x4, resuming their original places, Bud held out the keys. In order to take them, John had to remove his hand from his pocket from where, by reflex, he'd been about to produce his own keys, those to his MG. *Stupid!* he thought, settling into the driver's seat but then, after Nate and Bud had got into the back: *Maybe not.* As he continued to drive, John stealthily fished out his keys and placed them on the floor. He didn't know what use they might be but perhaps something would come.

When they'd climbed back onto higher ground, the Cruiser rejoined the dirt road and turned south. They were now running roughly parallel to the river, on scrubby ground that was almost flat. For a while they bumped along at a fair pace. To their right, beyond a series of ridges, the steeply rising Rocky Mountains were now an overwhelming presence. Soon they would run out of terrain that their vehicle could navigate, meaning the captives would be out of time.

As they came over a small ridge, Bud called a halt, directing John to pull in beside a nearby clump of aspen. Again taking the keys and Nate, he got out. "Stay here!" he ordered curtly, as if to a dog. "Back in a minute."

Taking the child's hand, he moved within the tree cover to the top of the rise and peered over. After some moments, he returned to the 4x4. "Okay, all clear," he said, hoisting himself and Nate aboard and tossing over the keys. "Get moving."

This time John fumbled with the keys and dropped them on the floor. Retrieving them, he caught sight of his own keys nearby—and suddenly had an idea. It was not a plan, yet, but a prologue: a small notion around which a plan might be built.

"What I was checking up ahead is a regular road," Bud was saying, "the Chief Mountain Parkway. It goes to the US border."

They came over the ridge and paused. Ahead was the road, smooth and inviting. "Really?" John said. "We're driving to the border?"

"Don't be stupid," Bud snapped. "When I go over the damn border, it certainly won't be here. All we're doing right now is *crossing* this road. Using it to get to a dirt track that goes into the hills not far to the west. Traffic here is usually light, and there's no sign of cops, but when you hit the road, turn right and drive like hell. I'll tell you when to turn off. Okay—go!"

John didn't go. He said, "But first, why don't we drop off Nate."

"*What?*"

"At the road, where people will find him. You don't need him now. He's too little to help the cops. Let him go. You've got me and I won't give any trouble, I promise."

Bud looked at John coldly. Without flourish or drama, he

produced his gun and pointed it at Nate's head. He said quietly, "John, neither of you will give trouble if I finish you right here. Maybe that's best. What do you think?"

John didn't answer. Scowling, he put the Cruiser in gear and drove. The plea for Nate had been spur of the moment but he hadn't really expected any other response. Reaching the road, he turned as directed and got onto the hardtop. After their rough passage, it felt as smooth as glass. Physical relief and mental dread now fought a battle: this comfortable road was bringing them all the more quickly to what must surely be the end of the line.

If they met another vehicle and were recognized, that could also be dangerous. But, as it turned out, he needn't have worried: no one appeared from either direction. They'd not been on the parkway more than three minutes, speeding west, when Bud clapped a hard hand on John's shoulder. "Slow down. Okay—here!"

Their captor was pointing to a tall rock by the side of the road on which something, now indecipherable, had once been painted. Nearby, a steep track ran south from the dusty ghost of an inter-section. John turned off and presently the track rounded a shallow ridge. As soon as they were out of sight of the parkway, Bud said again, "Slow down—*right down*—crawl. That's it. I don't want to leave a dust trail for anybody to see."

Not, as it turned out, that the precaution was necessary. It was at least another half-hour before the patrol car bearing Libby and Con-stable Petty passed by the same place—without slowing down.

SEVEN

"Over there is the Belly River, so my truck's got to be somewhere around here," Libby said.

Constable Petty had stopped the cruiser at the point where they could see the river: from there, the road went south to the Customs post at the border; the river valley, by a more circuitous route, wound upwards to the water's source in the mountains of Montana. But it was in the opposite direction that the searchers were interested. "This *is* where Wetherall left the cruiser?" Lyall asked again.

"Somewhere along this stretch," Libby replied. "According to the GPS reading, it has to be. They drove across country from the ranch and Bud took off as soon as he reached the Belly River, which is what we're looking at."

"Okay. But he wouldn't have left the vehicle where it could be seen." Petty pointed up a slope, bounded by a stand of aspens on the left and by the river on the right. "Maybe it's up in those trees."

"Yeah, you're probably right. Let's go."

But before she could move, Petty laid a hand on her arm. "Better let me take it from here, Lib."

"What do you mean?"

"Thanks for the help but this is a police matter."

She stared. "Oh, come on, Lyall. Bud's gone. There's no danger now."

Petty looked awkward. "I wasn't thinking about *that*."

"Then why …?" She stopped, realizing what he was getting at. "Look, Lyall, they're my friends. Whatever's happened, I have to go."

"Are you sure?"

"Sure!" She grinned bravely and slapped his shoulder. "But, hey, stop looking so serious! Those city folks are probably sitting in my truck with no idea where the hell they are—waiting for someone to come along. Let's go find them!" She pulled free and began walking, feeling nothing like as confident as her tone. She knew she had to do this, but her insides felt like ice.

By the time they topped the rise, the constable was beside her and simultaneously they realized the truth: the trees were too tightly packed to hide anything and the terrain was such that there was no place else where the Cruiser might be concealed. At least there were no bodies.

"Damn!" Lyall Petty said. "What now?"

Libby didn't answer. She was looking down at the river, the swift-flowing mountain torrent that had gouged out the ravine through which the kidnapper was making his escape. Since he couldn't have taken the Cruiser through there, and must have abandoned his hostages, where were they?

She scrambled down and stood at the edge of the river. It flowed by with a gurgling whisper, cold and swift. Water. *Water!* Again the sight of water gave her the feeling of something being wrong …

"Wondering about Bud Wetherall?" Lyall Petty asked. "Don't worry, at least we know where *he* is … " He broke off as he took in her expression. "What?"

Libby was still eying the water but as if something had leaped out of it and slapped her. Finally she said, "Lyall—that thing. How big is it?"

"What thing?"

"That beacon thing! That super-smart gizmo that's supposed to be keeping track of Bud."

Bewildered, Petty shrugged. "I dunno, Lib—pretty small. Small enough to hide in his stuff anyway."

"Small enough to *float*—on a log, or something?"

"Well, sure, I guess ... "

"Like a decoy? Laying a false trail?"

"But that's ... " Lyall broke off. He stared at the water. Then they stared at each other—then at the water again. Finally, Petty breathed a single word, "*Shee—it!*"

Then they were scrabbling up the bank like a couple of crazies.

Topping the rise, they saw that another patrol car had pulled in behind Petty's. There was no sign of the ambulance. While the constable hurried to get on the radio to relay their discovery—they were coldly certain now about what had happened—Libby remained above, searching desperately about.

Soon the second cruiser took off in the direction of the border. Constable Petty was on the radio for some time. When he was through, he called up to Libby. She didn't respond, so he went up the hill to join her. "There was an accident in the park," Petty said. "That's why there's no ambulance yet. And they could only spare one uniform so I sent him on to check at the border."

Libby was moving slowly back and forth, gazing down. Not looking up, she said, "He won't go there."

"I know it. But since we've no other leads, it's best to make sure."

"Did you tell the sergeant about the decoy?"

"Yeah—I got patched through."

"And?"

"They think that it's very possible."

"Possible? Lyall, it's what's *happened*."

"Yeah, I think so too. Anyway, till they actually find the beacon, the decision is to keep on with the surveillance down in the ravine and send more uniforms up here when they can."

Libby had continued examining the ground. At this point, she was beside the aspen grove at the top of the ridge, moving along parallel to the trees. As Petty finished his explanation, she quickly crouched down. "I think they may get here too late," she said quietly.

Petty moved in. "What do you mean?"

On her haunches, Libby pointed to a place near the trees where, amidst the dust and dry leaves, was the faint impression of tire marks. "That's my 4x4."

Petty crouched beside her. "Really? Are you sure?"

"Who else do you reckon's been driving round here lately?"

"But if he's not headed for the border, where? There aren't many places left to drive from here."

Libby rose and slowly turned to face the mountains. "There's one."

"What? Where?"

Libby pointed south to where, between two spurs of the looming Rockies, a dark cleft was visible. "Up there, the high end of the Blood Reserve, there's an old dirt road. It doesn't look like it from here, but it goes quite a ways in. Bud took me up a couple of times, hunting. That's the most likely route he'd take into the mountains."

"Right," Petty said. "How do I find it?"

"You don't!" Libby replied, moving off quickly. "Not unless I show you."

EIGHT

It was now or never. As soon as they left the parkway, heading directly toward the rearing crags, on what must surely be the final terrain the Cruiser could negotiate, John knew the time had come.

The faint dirt road headed up a steepening valley to a saddle half a mile away. What lay beyond was hazy: soaring hillsides, aspen and pine, barren rock above the treeline and in the far distance, a yawning gap in the looming mountain wall. This was Bud's destination, John felt certain. He was equally sure that if he didn't act now, before they ran out of road, it would be too late.

The next time Bud turned his ever-vigilant scrutiny to the road behind, John took his foot off the accelerator while at the same time yanking the hand choke full out. He got his hand back on the steering wheel before Bud looked around, and only then did he press the accelerator hard down again. Flooded with a vastly over-rich gas mixture, the engine coughed, wheezed and dropped sharply in power as they began to slow.

Bud grasped the back of the seat. "What in hell's happening?" he cried. "What are you doing?"

"I'm not doing anything!" John said defensively. "Something's wrong with the engine."

Making a thoroughly distracting flurry with his hands and upper body, trying to look afraid and disconcerted, he quietly let in the clutch and pumped hard on the accelerator, flooding the carburetor as he had done once before in his own car to fool Libby McGrew. When he let in the clutch this time, the engine gave a huge backfire, bucked and died completely, and they came to a halt. John then apparently became completely unhinged, while returning the choke to its correct position and deftly toe-flicking the accelerator to flood the engine more.

"I'm sorry, Bud," he cried, in what seemed to be growing confusion, "I don't know what happened. I don't know what's the matter … "

He turned the key of the starter, revving the engine over and over, but keeping his foot hard down on the gas. Now, even though the choke was back in, the carburetor was so thoroughly flooded that the task was hopeless.

"You stupid clown," Bud yelled, and Nate began to whimper. "What's the matter? What have you done?"

Now John was almost crying himself and as he put on this performance, he tried to remember whether he had talked about cars on that long-ago evening with Bud. He hoped not. "I haven't done anything, Bud. How could I? I was just driving—doing what you told me. I don't know anything about cars. Something's broken."

Bud calmed down. "Okay," he said grimly. "You better get out and take a look."

That advice appeared only to add fuel to John's increasing hysteria. "Me? I told you, I don't know anything about engines. Bud, please, I'm an actor, not a mechanic. I'm no good with my hands. I wouldn't know what's wrong if I saw it."

A pained look came on Bud's face, the contempt of the practical man for the effete. "Shit!"

"I'm sorry, Bud," John half sobbed. "But please—it's not my

fault. Don't take it out on me—on us. If something's wrong you'll have to fix it."

The other man's brow furrowed. He looked at John, then at Nate, then at the road behind. Though out of sight of the parkway, they were quite close to it. John's fervent hope was that Bud would want to get them out of here as soon as possible: surely—*surely*—he wouldn't want to ditch the Cruiser, and them, quite yet. *Oh, man*, he thought, *let this not be the worst mistake of my life.*

At last Bud nodded. "Yeah, I think you're right." Then came the gesture that had become routine, which John had counted upon. The man thrust out his hand. "Keys!"

"Oh, yes, of course. Here!" Apparently desperately anxious to please, to get this awful moment over, John snatched the keys from the ignition. He fumbled and they dropped.

"Just a minute!"

From the floor, shielded from the eyes of his captor, John picked up not the keys that had fallen, but those to his MG. "Here."

Bud grabbed the keys, jammed them into his left pocket. From the right he took out his pistol, the threat and the warning obvious. "Okay, I'll see what's wrong but you better hope it isn't anything much."

He swung open the back door and jumped out. Now came the big moment, the big test: would he take Nate with him? He didn't. He slammed the door shut and began walking around to the front of the truck.

At last John and his son were alone together.

NINE

"**A**re you sure it's this way?" Lyall Petty asked. They were driving along the Chief Mountain Parkway, back in the direction they'd recently come. The mountains towered ever closer; though bathed in the late-morning sun, to Libby they seemed increasingly ominous.

"Sure I'm sure," she said. "Be patient, Lyall, it's not far." They came around a bend and she laid a hand on his arm. "Okay, we're coming to it."

The car slowed, then stopped near where a large rock stood beside the road.

"This is it," Libby said. "The scratchings on that rock are supposed to be Blood tribe but I think it's old graffiti. Bud always used it as a marker. You can just see the road going off there."

Lyall wound down his window and peered doubtfully. "That's a road?"

"For all-terrain vehicles it is. Not for us. But it only goes in a couple of miles anyway. At the end there's an old cabin where we always parked. If Bud's going the way I think he is, he can't drive any farther than that."

Lyall stopped the engine. "And we can't drive any farther than here. Damn!"

Libby opened her door and got out. "Come on—let's get moving."

"Lib, I can't let you … " he began, but she cut him off.

"Yeah—yeah—you're not supposed to put civilians at risk. I know. But this is an emergency, Lyall. They need help, you don't know the way, we haven't got time to wait for backup and I'm going in anyway. Are you coming? Or do you maybe plan on wasting what little time we have trying to stop me?"

"Shit!"

"Yeah, I feel like that too." Libby gestured toward the mountains. "But up there's a guy and his son who're probably running out of time." She didn't add "if they're even still alive," but it was darkly implied. "So … ?"

Petty gave an exasperated grunt and heaved himself out of the cruiser. Shaking his head, he opened the trunk, removing a rifle and a clip of ammunition. He slammed the clip into the gun, then held it out to Libby.

She looked happily surprised. "You're giving me this?"

"Yeah—Christ knows what the sarge'd say but if you're determined to come, you can't be unarmed. You know how to use it, eh?"

"You know damn well I do. Thanks, Lyall. What about you?"

"I'll probably get my ass fired."

"You know what I mean."

"I've got my side arm. That'll be enough."

Libby took the rifle, checked the safety and slung it over her shoulder. She smiled quickly and her hand went out, to touch her old friend. Then she took a breath, adjusted the rifle and turned toward the mountains.

"Okay, Lyall," Libby said. "Let's do it."

TEN

John waited until Bud had moved around the Land Cruiser to the hood, while he stared with great anxiety through the windshield. He needed this part of the procedure to take place as slowly as possible. Time for the flooded carburetor to clear.

Bud looked up at him expectantly. John knew quite well what the man wanted, but he stared back dumbly. Finally Bud jabbed at the hood with his gun.

"Well—*open* the fucking thing!"

John mouthed apologies, apparently searching for and fumbling the hood release. While doing this he replaced the correct key in the ignition. Now, at last, he was free—potentially. With a flick of the key, he and Nate could be racing away up the valley with all their problems, literally, behind them.

If the engine started right off.

If he could get away quickly enough not to get slaughtered.

It was necessary to delay things as long as possible but if there were too much delay, Bud's practical eye might spot that there was nothing wrong. John had to time it just right. And there would only be one chance.

After a couple more fumbles at the hood release, John at last activated it. Meanwhile, Bud had been undoing the outside catch-es. If he moved near enough to the front to be caught, the way Will North had been, John never knew it. For when he raised his head again, Bud was already on the left side of the vehicle, lifting the hood.

Several minutes had passed since they had stopped. Bud looked at the engine.

Suddenly there was a noise from the back of the vehicle. John half turned to see Nate, who'd been glued to his seat in fear, hurling himself at him. The little boy's hands came around his shoulders from the back, reaching for comfort now that the source of his fear was farther off.

"Daddy," the little boy cried. "Why is Daddy-Bud being bad? Take me home, Daddy. Please, Daddy, please."

"Yeah, soon, kiddo, but get down now, please!"

He twisted around and thrust his son back and down, almost brutally, not taking his eyes off Bud, who was studying the engine. The push that John was compelled to give Nate was hard. He couldn't afford to have the little boy's head up, with what might be flying any second now. Betrayed by a second adult, Nate began to wail.

John shushed him, begged him to stay down, not daring to look back to check if he was. His foot was on the clutch and he depressed it. His right hand was on the gear lever and, with pounding heart, he pushed it slowly into first. The raised hood now blocked most of the front view from the windshield, but to the left, not four feet away through the glass, John could look at Bud as he stared down into the engine.

John's right hand eased up to the starter key, stopped—poised.

His right foot hovered over the accelerator.

It had to be more than five minutes since the engine stopped. If it wasn't ready now it wouldn't matter.

Bud shook his head, his lips pursed in concentration. He looked at the sky, and glanced up and down the valley. Finally he decided he would fiddle inside the engine. With a side glance through the window, he slipped the gun into his pocket.

Then John turned the key.

The starter motor turned and whined. From the tailpipe came a shattering backfire. The engine roared into life. John accelerated and at the same time let out the clutch. The 4x4 jumped forward, catching Bud's shoulder against the raised hood and knocking him sideways.

Then it stalled dead.

John's brain yawed in horror. His hand snaked down for the starter key, fumbled, found it, turned …

At the same time, Bud staggered sideways, clawing for his weapon.

The engine whined again—caught—died—caught …

Bud was trying to snatch revenge from his pocket but luckily, his reaching hand was the one that had taken the first impact. It was slower than it might have been. It found the gun and hauled it out, fumbling as he tried to get a proper grip.

The engine was roaring and John let out the clutch again, this time with good effect. The truck leaped.

The gun came up and fired.

Pointed too high, the first bullet snapped harmlessly over the roof of the cab. The second was better aimed. It smashed through the side window, passing an inch from John's cheek, kept going through the windshield and raised hood, which was now being pressed back by the Cruiser's increasing speed.

John changed from first to second gear without even knowing it. He couldn't see out front but navigated as best he could by the view from the side. He heard another gunshot and another and there were simultaneous clangs on the back of the 4x4. But they didn't seem to have any effect. John kept going. As his speed increased, it became more and more difficult to steer, but he couldn't slow down.

Nate in the back had made no sound since the start. John breathed a prayer that the child hadn't been smashed by the violent acceleration or hit by a bullet, but he couldn't spare time to look. He had to keep going, at least until he got out of range of the gun. Fear and excitement were growing, but excitement was strongest. As the sides of the valley whizzed by, and the shooting sounds grew fainter, a wonderful feeling began to build, waiting to blossom: escape!

They were making it! As that thought came, John realized that they must be almost at the top of the rise. In a moment they'd not only be out of range but out of sight. There came the sound of a final shot—far away—almost pathetic ...

The 4x4 jerked. From below, frighteningly close, came a much louder bang. The entire back end slewed sideways as the right rear tire exploded. The left wheel kept pushing, shoving the Cruiser around, bowling it inexorably across the saddle and onto the bank on the far side.

Then, as John clung to the wheel, gazing petrified though the windshield, blocked and blind, the Land Cruiser cleared the bank and went plunging into the draw beyond, a slope that grew steeper and more ragged by the second. Plunge deteriorated into free-fall and the world exploded in mind-bending chaos that became terror and then pain and finally, mercifully—the dark.

ELEVEN

John came to to find himself upended in the side of the cab. His consciousness returned swiftly and he understood that the tortured ending to the Cruiser's plunge had only just happened. There was a creak of wrecked and settling metal.

"Daddy—Daddy!"

Nate.

John snapped back into full awareness.

The vehicle was lying on its side in a shallow ravine, its nose half buried in a gravelly projection that had finally stopped its precipitous descent. John himself was lying bunched up on the passenger door.

"*DADDY!*"

John twisted himself around and saw Nate. His son was back in the far corner, on top of the crumpled rear-right window, which was now flat on the ground. Nate was covered in a mess of gear that had tumbled all around him: the rucksack and water containers and an assorted jumble of food. Right across the boy's shoulders lay the rifle, and it was this that Nate was struggling to push aside as John first saw him.

"Nate—it's okay—I'm coming!"

John heaved, got his legs turned and crawled along the side, which was now the floor, to his son. He pulled away the gun and some of the other junk, managing to free the little figure from its entanglement.

"It's okay, kiddo—okay now. Daddy's here."

"Daddy. Oh—Daddy."

Nate crawled and wriggled into his arms and began to cry lustily, which gave John a feeling of boundless relief. When little ones cried like that they might be scared, sad or furious, but they were not badly hurt.

In the mess, the impossibly contorted tangle they were in, he managed to hug his son, to rock him, soothe him, snuggle some reassurance back into the mad world. "It's okay, Nate," he whispered. "It's all right, kiddo. It's all right now."

And then, horribly, he remembered that it wasn't.

Of course they were not alone. Bud, whose last lucky shot had got the rear tire and caused this calamity, must have at least heard what had happened. He'd only been half a mile away when they'd crashed. Without doubt, he would be on his way, if only to pick up his gear. And when he found they were both still alive …

This realization hit John with sickly strength. Had he not been so keyed up it might have paralyzed him, losing precious seconds. He thrust his son aside, oblivious to the renewed howls, and scrambled for the rear door. With the Cruiser on its side, this had its hinge-edge parallel to the ground. If he could get it open, it would fall down like a flap and they could crawl out.

John grasped the handle and twisted. It wouldn't budge. He tried it again. Nothing. It was jammed. Their grinding, side-on passage down the ravine must have buckled something.

Ironically, however, the windows were still intact. To get out they would either have to break them, or climb up to the driver's door. That might be possible, but getting Nate and himself out that way in time seemed unlikely. So he decided to smash a back window.

Looking frantically for an implement to use as a club, he caught sight of the rifle. The butt would make a fine battering ram. John was now on his haunches in the confined space, his body in a crouch. Reaching for the gun, he examined the two rear windows, deciding which would be the best to smash. And he saw Bud Wetherall.

The back window of the Cruiser gave a clear view of the ravine down which it had plunged. At the top was a rocky knoll, and on this Bud was standing. John's eyes registered the man with the clarity of a picture. He was standing, chest heaving, gun at his side, looking down at the wrecked Cruiser. He was no more than 50 yards away. Then John saw Bud begin to move. With purposeful strides, picking his way carefully on the rocky ground but never taking his eyes off them, he started the descent.

This time John really was frozen. He didn't move a muscle until the man had moved several steps. Then adrenalin flooded his system, giving his next actions desperate swiftness. He picked up the gun and bashed the butt against the window. After two tries he knew that wasn't going to work. Bud was now only 30 yards away.

Then John realized with shock that the thing in his hands was a weapon and he turned it around frantically.

The enemy was 20 yards off, and lifting his own gun.

John raised the rifle, then realized that, of course, the ammunition clip had been removed. The weapon was useless; it was too late. Bud Wetherall saw all of this. He must have felt the irony of it too. Instead of firing, he nodded, apparently savouring the moment. With an icy smile he raised his gun.

For John, all rational thought ceased. Instinct took over. In the face of death, he deliberately turned his back, grabbed hold of Nate and fell with his body spread wide, crablike, covering his son.

He waited.

Waited …

Finally, still clutching Nate, John turned his head and looked back.

Bud stood there, gun raised, trigger finger tensed white.

Everything was very silent.

Then the pursuer leaned down, grasped the handle of the back hatch and, when it wouldn't move, gave it a kick that made it fall. He bent, peering through the opening, breathing hard. He chewed his lip, studying them, then shook his head.

"Not yet, my mad young friend," Bud Wetherall said. "I've got work for you."

TWELVE

As Libby and Constable Petty left the patrol car and began following the rough trail up the valley, they were well aware that time wasn't on their side. The tracks of Libby's Land Cruiser were clear enough, but there was no way of telling how recently they'd been made. The terrain was steep and rough, with little cover, their only advantage being that the quarry could have no idea they were coming.

On both sides the hills climbed steeply, the trees already sparse and scrubby. Half a mile ahead, a rise culminated in a saddle, beyond which the land appeared to open out again, dropping away sharply out of sight. Libby stopped, pointing to the top of the rise. "On the other side there's another small valley, the last before that pass you can see way up there. At the top end is the cabin I told you about. After that, it's hiking or nothing. Come on." But almost at once, she stopped again, peering at the tracks they'd been following. "Look at this—something happened here."

Petty joined her examination of the ground. With no warning, the tire tracks suddenly became deep and rough, the visual message unmistakable: at this point the Land Cruiser had accelerated savagely. Dust and stones had been gouged and thrown out for a distance of several yards, then regular tracks continued on again. After taking this in, they spotted something else: in the scree thrown by the spinning wheels were boot prints, the toes thrust deep, heading up the hill in the wake of the tire tracks.

"What happened here?" Petty breathed.

Libby pointed at the boot prints. "That's got to be Bud."

"The prints are on top of the tracks—he's running."

"Did they escape?"

Both stared at where the tracks disappeared over the ridge, half a mile ahead—then they were running. Minutes later they arrived, panting, at the top of the rise. From there the land descended into the valley Libby had described, a surprisingly lush depression clothed with brush, aspen and a sprinkling of sub-alpine firs. At the far end, where the bowl rose and narrowed into a cleft that plunged between two great mountains, they could see the tiny shape of a cabin.

Libby and Petty took this in, then continued to where they could see over a bank that plunged steeply off to one side. Lying at the bottom was Libby's Land Cruiser. Frantically the two scrambled down the steep incline. They made no attempt at stealth, knowing the occupants must either be gone or ... but Libby wouldn't let herself think about that. They got there at last. The Cruiser lay on its side, less damaged than might have been expected and quite empty of life. Most of the gear and stores that Bud had been given had vanished too.

"What do you think happened?" Libby breathed.

Lyall was examining what appeared to be a bullet hole in the back window. "Looks like John tried to make a run for it. Main thing is everyone seems to have been fit enough to leave the scene." He moved to the front of the wreck and felt the radiator. "Happened not all that long ago." He lifted his head to look across the valley. "You think that's where they're headed?"

"Has to be."

"I figure they've got maybe a half-hour start at most."

"But loaded down, and with Nate, they won't be able to go very fast."

"So if we move it, we might even be able to … "

He didn't finish. Libby, rifle slung over her shoulder, was already off at a trot. Hastily, Lyall checked his side arm and followed.

THIRTEEN

He was a pack horse, a mule, no more than that. John wasn't even sure why this temporary reprieve had been granted. He couldn't believe that Bud had put off the killing for any sentimental reason, nor did he really need help carrying the gear. Perhaps Bud simply wanted to keep his insurance till the last possible moment, when he reached the mountains proper and had no further worries about being apprehended.

Those mountains were now very near: a short trek, even on foot. Reaching them would surely be the end of the line. The end of the last truce. No doubt of that at all.

The track they had been following was easily negotiable by the Land Cruiser, had John not wrecked it in his escape attempt. They were descending into a small valley, the last stop before the real mountains began. Bud was up front, leading the way, the rifle hanging easily on his shoulder. John, loaded down with the rucksack, followed. Nate walked meekly beside Bud.

Since their recapture the little boy had not said a word. Shock, or some half-realization of what was going on, had turned him into a little zombie; mute, bug-eyed, uncomplaining, unnaturally obedient. With something beyond despair, John realized that what was happening was possibly deeply atavistic. Since Nate's real father had been unable to protect him, instinct drove the child to placate the strong man. The fact that this strong one was also ruthless and without pity was to a child unimaginable: he could not really comprehend the horror that lay ahead. John took a certain comfort in that.

But at the same time—absurdly—he hadn't given up hope. Plan after plan kept bubbling in his mind: find a handy rock and hurl it at Bud's head; wait till a distraction occurred then slip his pack and tackle Bud from behind; feign illness and then …

All ridiculous and futile. But he couldn't stop thinking about it. To do that would be to admit their doom and as long as Nate was alive, he couldn't do that.

But then, as they trudged along, getting ever closer to the end of the trail, something new came to him: not a plan but a naked understanding. Being out of options, he and Nate had nothing to lose. Therefore he had a duty to do something—anything—that might give Nate, at least, a chance of survival.

Bud, armed and in control of the child, had allowed John to follow, confident that the father would do nothing to jeopardize his son. But what if he were to do the unthinkable, escape, leaving Nate: what would Bud do? Possibly kill him immediately; that was the terrifying risk, the fear of which Bud was using to keep John in line.

But the man wasn't irrational. If John were to escape, Bud must know that hurting the child would lose him his only remaining bargaining chip. So, if nothing else, at least they'd be back in a position where bargains might be considered. Surely making a try for that situation was better than trotting like lambs to the slaughter.

John had come to this conclusion when they rounded a bend, entering the heart of the valley. To the right was a roughly circular area, filled with scrub and small trees. To the left, a patch of weedy meadow. At the top end, about quarter of a mile distant, was a cabin.

FOURTEEN

Ten minutes after leaving the wrecked Land Cruiser, Libby and Petty picked up the trail. They had moved down into the valley, often almost at a run, but it was not until they were nearing the bottom that they finally saw the unmistakable outline of footprints: two different sets of large prints, and a child's.

Lyall, who'd surprised Libby by having a remarkable degree of stamina and speed despite his bulk, gave a small grunt of triumph. "It's *them*! Damn, Lib, it's them."

"It sure is."

"How far is the cabin from here?"

"A mile, maybe."

"Then they may be there already."

"Let's just hope not."

Without another word they started off again. This time, since the trail was obvious, Lyall led the way with Libby close on his heels. Because they were now clearly going into danger, Lyall had considered pulling cop-rank and once more trying to insist he continue alone, but he knew Libby well enough to be aware how far that suggestion would get him. Anyway, she was a tough woman and a crack shot. Pretty soon, he might be only too glad of a backup.

They went fast, at a half-jog through the rough but open terrain. It was now necessary to strike a balance between speed and stealth: if the quarry could be taken by surprise before reaching cover, that would be ideal. But, in the short time remaining, this was very unlikely. Now the tension was growing, increasing with each step until it was almost a physical presence. So it was with a feeling of awful inevitability that, only minutes later, they heard the shots.

FIFTEEN

The instant John saw the cabin he knew that his last chance had come. As Bud paused to gaze up the valley at their destination, John acted. He slipped the pack from his shoulders, dumped it, then took off at a run for the trees. He had almost reached them before Bud realized what was happening. Then there was a cry, the abrupt double click of a rifle bolt, a deafening explosion.

In the act of diving for cover, John felt something pluck at his left arm. It slewed him around slightly while propelling him even more swiftly forward, so that when he fell behind the bushes to which he'd been heading, he came down on his side, slipping and rolling painfully.

Another shot rang out. There was a slap and whine, and dust spurted from the ground near where he lay. John scrambled, crawled, heading for heavier cover, made it to a clump of trees, got behind them and ran. He wasn't truly trying to get away, simply to hide long enough for Bud to realize his dilemma. If he harmed the child, there'd be no reason for the father to do anything but keep running. If he pursued the man, there was nothing to stop the boy escaping.

What John needed was for Bud to decide on the second scenario. As he waited, he became aware of a dull throb in his left arm:

it was dripping blood. But there was no time to be concerned about that, because suddenly Bud acted. John could hear him approaching fast through the trees, at a speed that must mean he was alone.

John began to run again, keeping hidden, but circling to a higher point where he'd be able to see the clearing and the cabin. He managed to get there and stuck his head up warily. Below, standing alone, was Nate. Ignoring the approach of the enemy, John stood right up and waved.

"Nate! Nate, run! Get out of there, kiddo—*run*!!" And then, to the one chasing him: "Here! I'm up here, you bastard. Come and get me!"

There was a crashing in the bushes. Nate, in the clearing, stared across at his father but did not move.

"Run, Nate! *Run away—RUN!*"

The crashing continued, but no longer coming nearer; it was going away, back toward the cabin. Then Bud himself reappeared, heading for the child. He reached and bent down, preparing to scoop the boy up. But at that moment something astonishing happened.

From farther off, at the entrance to the clearing, came a shout. John saw two figures coming at a run: the RCMP constable, Lyall Petty, and Libby McGrew.

Before John could recover from his own shock he saw Bud Wetherall twist around, slap the child sideways, drop to one knee and raise his rifle. There was a sharp crack and Lyall Petty appeared to be yanked backward by an unseen hand. He landed flat on his back, skidded in a slur of dust, lay still.

Bud began to adjust his aim, and now John yelled out. But Libby's recovery was quicker than his own. Before the second shot, she dropped to the ground. Then she was crawling for the safety of the trees. Bud took another ineffectual shot and changed his mind. Bending around he grabbed the child, lifting him easily with his left arm. Holding Nate as a shield, he backed off toward the cabin.

John leaped and slid down the hill, raced back through the trees. In intermittent glimpses, he could see that Bud, with Nate clutched firmly, had almost reached the cabin.

From nearby, came a groan. Lyall Petty, chest soaked in blood, was trying to sit up.

"Libby!" John yelled. "Where are you?"

"Here!" The voice came from his left, then her head appeared not more than 10 yards away. John gestured toward Lyall Petty. "Cover me."

Libby nodded, raised her rifle. But Bud was still too busy getting himself and his captive out of danger to be a threat right then. John raced to the fallen policeman, dragging him out of the open. The man was heavy, and his own wounded arm was beginning to feel on fire, but he managed to pull the constable behind the bushes that also sheltered Libby.

Libby put down her rifle and crouched beside Petty. John knelt on the other side. The front of the policeman's shirt was drenched crimson, but at least the wound seemed well away from the heart. As they leaned over him, Petty's eyes slid open. Seeing Libby he grinned. "Hi, Lib—you okay?"

Libby's eyes flickered to John. "Sure, Lyall. You're the one I'm worried about."

"Oh—forget it—just a flesh wound." Petty gritted his teeth. "Don't worry about me. Bastard still got your kid, John?"

"'Fraid so."

"Then that's the only thing that matters now. Our job is to protect our kids, eh?"

"I know it, man. I'll get him somehow."

Petty nodded with difficulty. "Yeah, you will. First time I saw you I thought—that's one stubborn fool!"

"Thanks, Lyall."

"You bet. Stubborn fool." Lyall gave a throaty chuckle. "Go get him, cowboy."

SIXTEEN

After they had made Constable Petty as comfortable as possible, John stood up. "I'd better get started."

Libby stared. "Started? *Where?*"

"To the cabin."

"John, you'll never make it. He's killed his wife and wounded a cop. He's got absolutely nothing to lose by shooting you too."

John nodded. "I know it but he might fancy a trade."

"Trade?"

"Me for Nate."

"Why should he bother?"

"You should have heard him earlier, back in the motorhome before we left. He was furious that I'd caused him so much trouble. He must be a damn sight madder now. I figure if I can give him a choice, he'll get a bigger buzz out of offing me than Nate. When a guy's got no place to go, a last bit of revenge might seem good."

Libby looked at John hard. She didn't express surprise or fear or approval—just nodded seriously. "You could be right. But what's to stop him killing both of you?"

"Nothing."

"Exactly!"

"But I've still got to try."

"Mmm—I guess you do." She strode across to John. She did not look at his face but with fixed concentration at his left arm. Evidently the wound was only superficial, for the bleeding had stopped. "How does that feel?"

"Okay. Pretty soon, it may not matter."

Savagely Libby hugged him, and then the arm did hurt. "Don't say that, John. But listen—whatever happens up there, whatever the outcome—try to do one thing for me."

"What?"

"Figure out some way to get Bud to show his head."

With his hands conspicuously raised, John walked slowly through the clearing. When he was 20 yards from the cabin Bud's voice called out, "Stop there."

John did so.

"What do you want, John?"

"To make an exchange."

"Yeah?"

"Me for Nate. What do you say?"

A pause, then Bud gave a laugh. The sound was unusually high, almost cracked. "What's to stop me shooting you right now?"

"Nothing. But none of what has happened is Nate's fault. He's only a little boy who doesn't know what's going on. He never did anything to you. You were even going to bring him up as your son, remember? Let him go—please! And you can do whatever you want with me."

Again the laugh. "Very noble, John. What if I want to kill you both?"

"Then you'll do it. But you'll never get away."

"Why not?"

"Come on! You've seen Libby down there. Once she goes back

and tells where you are, and also that you've wounded a constable, the Mounties will set up the biggest manhunt in history. The Yanks will get in on it too. You haven't got a chance."

Another pause. "So—an exchange, eh?"

"Me for Nate. Well?"

"Okay—walk back a ways."

"Back?"

"Pick up my rucksack. Bring it here. Then we'll talk."

Why did Bud want the rucksack? Because he was determined to run. Whether escape might still be possible John didn't know, but he had no reason to argue. He shrugged, made his way back through the clearing. When he picked up the rucksack, Libby called out from the bushes. "What's happening, John?"

"I'm getting his gear. He won't discuss any kind of exchange until I bring it."

Libby's voice was grim. He could clearly visualize the hard line of her jaw. "He must think he can make it. Maybe he can at that. Well—better give him what he wants."

As John turned to start up the clearing, Libby's voice came again.

"John?"

"Yeah?"

"Just so you know—I love you."

John made his way back to the cabin. It was built of logs, with a low doorway and an empty window frame over which had been hung a tattered canvas curtain. There was a single step up to the door. John stopped just below.

"Come up, John," Bud called. "Get in here."

Hefting the rucksack, heart pounding, mouth suddenly very dry, John obeyed. Inside, the cabin was so dim that he was momentarily blinded. The plank door, which had been pulled open, banged shut, As the rucksack was taken from him, John's eyes began to adjust.

The first thing he saw was Nate. His son was sitting, arms around knees, eyes huge, on the floor beneath the canvas-covered window. The trauma of earlier had progressed to deep shock. He was not looking at his father, did not even seem aware of the new presence. Seeing him, a wave of love hit John, so strong as to make him feel almost dizzy. He fought it back and turned to Bud.

Their captor was in the act of slinging the rucksack into a corner with his left hand. In his right was his Colt automatic. With it he motioned to the floor.

"Sit, John."

"First let my boy go. Then I'll do anything you want."

Slowly Bud shook his head. "No deals, I'm afraid."

"What? You said … "

"I said for you to bring my gear, then we'd talk. You brought it and we're talking. What I'm saying is, no deals."

"You're not going to let either of us go?"

"Not now."

"What do you mean—not now?"

Bud Wetherall made a sound of furious exasperation. "Damn you, John," he snarled. "Damn you to hell—this is your fault!"

"What?"

"I'd almost decided to let you go, you idiot! God knows why—maybe because you're so damn ridiculous. Anyway, I thought that if we made it here I'd have enough of a lead to leave you behind. I couldn't let you know that till we arrived, but that's how it was. Then you ran away, and Libby and that cop had to show—and now the Mountie's shot—and I've got no choice. So you can just blame yourself."

John was taken aback, but only momentarily. He didn't know whether he believed any of this, but it didn't matter. Whether it was true, or a cowardly justification, the cold fact was that they'd be just as dead. Able to think of nothing better, he said again, "You'll never get away with this."

Bud nodded matter-of-factly. "So you keep saying. But I'm going to have a damn good try. I'll certainly make it over the border."

John managed an unconvincing laugh. "You forget Libby. She's already on her way to give the alarm."

Bud's laugh was very real. "Don't act like I'm stupid, John. I know Libby very well. She's incapable of leaving with you two in here. She won't be going anywhere till she knows it's too late to help. And then," he shrugged, "I'll hunt her down before she can get back to the highway."

John had little doubt that Bud could do what he said. This was real. It was happening. Acknowledging this, he knew that there was one last thing he could try. It would be of no help to himself, but it was an outside chance of saving Nate. He had to do it. Letting his shoulders fall in an attitude of dejection only slightly more acute than he actually felt, John said quietly, "Okay. If you have to do this, I don't want to see my boy killed. Do it, to me, first, please. Then— you know! But make it quick. All right?"

Bud's face was stony. "Yes."

"Could I please hug him goodbye?"

"Sure—do it."

John walked to Nate, lifted him. The boy was as limp as a doll. John held him hard, his feet moving imperceptibly on the floor. He pretended, though it needed little acting, to break down, to sob and shake, as he hugged more and more violently—and edged ever closer to the window. Then, at the height of a particularly stormy sob, he extended his arms and threw Nate violently at the curtain.

The little body hit the ancient canvas, making it billow outward. A second later there was an explosion, and John felt something like a fist strike him below the right shoulder blade. He collapsed, but not before he saw Nate strike the windowsill, teeter—and fall out.

John was on the floor, shocked and numb but quite conscious. From there he could clearly see Bud, face contorted in anger and surprise. The smoking gun now swung from John toward the door. In two quick strides, Bud strode to the door and wrenched it open. Looking out to the left, at the place where Nate must have landed, Bud's expression changed to satisfaction. He raised his pistol.

John cried out. Instinctively, to better his aim, Bud stepped into the doorway.

There was the crack of a gunshot.

Strung between horror and shock, John was nonetheless surprised at the tiny sound made by Bud's pistol. He was even more astonished to see that the eye that had been squinting to sight the pistol had vanished, to be replaced by a jagged hole.

The gun dropped from Bud's hand. For a moment he stood quite still. Then, as delayed reflexes acknowledged the fact that life had departed, his human form turned to meat—which gravity deposited smartly on the cabin floor.

JOHN SAW ALL this happen as in a dream. There was a period of timeless dark, then something was moving him, talking to him and he remembered that the girl had locked him in the freezer and now she was … He opened his eyes to see Libby. She was crouched beside him, and he noted with mild surprise that she didn't have any top on. She was tearing her shirt into strips, with which she began to bind his chest.

Only then did John realize that Nate was there too, sitting in the background, watching. Considering that he'd been dragged across half the province, terrorized and tossed unceremoniously out of a window, he looked remarkably calm. John managed something that felt like it might pass for a smile. "Hey there, Nate."

"Hello, Daddy."

"Sorry I had to scare you like that before. You okay?"

"Yes, but Daddy—Bud's hurt his head."

"Too bad about that, eh?"

Libby smiled at Nate and finished tying off John's wound. He became aware of a new sound, the chomp-chomp of helicopter blades approaching. He looked at Libby in surprise. "Reinforcements? How long have I been out?"

"Not long, John." Libby held up a cell phone. "Bud's! Somehow I managed to get a signal."

"You're a marvel."

Libby grinned. "Takes one to know one, I reckon."

"Daddy?" Nate said.

"Yeah?"

"When we get home can I have another bear?"

"You bet ... " John started to say, but Libby gently put a finger over his lips. While wondering whether he had the energy to reach up and kiss her, he passed out again.

ABOUT THE AUTHOR

Ron Chudley is the author of two other TouchWood mysteries: *Old Bones* (2005) and *Dark Resurrection* (2006). He has written extensively for television (including *The Beachcombers*) and for the National Film Board of Canada, and has contributed dramas to CBC Radio's *Mystery, The Bush and the Salon* and *CBC Stage*. He lives with his wife, Karen, in Mill Bay, BC.

ALSO IN THE TOUCHWOOD MYSTERY SERIES

BY RON CHUDLEY

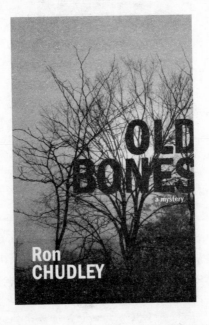

The discovery of an ancient auto wreck in a remote lake triggers an unexpected chain of events . . . an intriguing novel of mystery, memory, regret and redemption.

"A moody psychological novel with a series of finely drawn characters."
—— THE GLOBE AND MAIL

ISBN 13: 978-1-894898-33-1
ISBN 10: 1-894898-33-8
$12.95

ALSO IN THE TOUCHWOOD MYSTERY SERIES

BY RON CHUDLEY

Elizabeth and Tom's tranquil life is suddenly disrupted by a singular event: out of the flames and horror of 9/11 come riches beyond anyone's wildest dreams. But with the wealth comes danger and relentless pursuit by a grim figure whose motives may be a lot darker than justice.

"The characters are skilfully realized and the redemption is startling and tempting. A satisfying read from cover to cover." —HAMILTON SPECTATOR

"The dialogue is smart and fast, and he writes good descriptions . . . the basis of the story is the old 'be careful what you wish for.'" —THE GLOBE AND MAIL

ISBN 13: 978-1-894898-48-5
ISBN 10: 1-894898-48-6
$12.95

ALSO IN THE TOUCHWOOD MYSTERY SERIES

BY STANLEY EVANS

A billionaire's daughter has vanished, and Coast Salish cop Silas Seaweed is on the hunt . . . *Seaweed on the Street* is a fast-paced tale that introduces a new hero to lovers of mystery.

"Makes great use of West Coast aboriginal mythology and religion . . . Let's hope Silas Seaweed returns."
—THE GLOBE AND MAIL

ISBN 13: 978-1-894898-34-8; ISBN 10: 1-894898-34-6
$12.95

Silas Seaweed has his hands full with a mysterious disappearance, a murder, stolen art turning up in auction houses and a rumour that plans are afoot to loot a Salish archeological site . . . unravelling these strangely interconnected mysteries becomes a life-and-death quest.

"The writing is wonderful native story telling. Characters are richly drawn . . . I enjoyed this so much that I'm looking for the others in the series." —HAMILTON SPECTATOR

ISBN 13: 978-1-894898-51-5; ISBN 10: 1-894898-51-6
$12.95

A missing-person case turns into a murder investigation, and solving the case pulls Silas Seaweed into Salish mythology and ritual, culminating in a terrifying underwater vision quest—one from which he may never return.

ISBN 13: 978-1-894898-57-7; ISBN 10: 1-894898-57-5
$12.95